"Look!" cried Jean-Paul, pointing. A huge, grey-white shape was surfacing. It was at least four times the length of the cradle. Tentacles became visible, rising out of the water. One of the men saw them . . . alerted the others. Jean-Paul saw them reacting, pointing and gesticulating excitedly. He knew they were weaponless apart from some knives. He should have told them to take rifles. But who could have foreseen this. . .?

The cradle began to rise but it was plainly too late. A massive tentacle was already twisting upwards along one of the cables. Jean-Paul felt a tremor run through the deck of the control pod.

"Holy Mary," whispered the engineer.

The cradle was no longer rising. Instead it was starting to tilt. A second massive tentacle had appeared and was coiling its way up another of the cables.

"Jean-Paul!" cried Marcel, "The hoist operator reports that he can't raise the cradle any further! The creature weighs tons! He wants to know what to do!"

A good question, thought Jean-Paul.

JOHN BROSNAN

The Fall of the Sky Lords

VGSF

VGSF is an imprint of Victor Gollancz Ltd
14 Henrietta Street, London WC2E 8QJ

First published in Great Britain 1991
by Victor Gollancz Ltd

First VGSF edition 1991

A catalogue record of this book is available
from the British Library

ISBN 0-575-04556-6

Printed and bound in Great Britain
by Cox & Wyman Ltd, Reading

Chapter One:

About 250,000 miles above the surface of the Earth, Milo Haze, alone in his small cell, sat reading a science fiction novel from the early twenty-first century. He had come across it by chance while roaming through ancient files in the CenCom and was surprised that it had escaped the attention of the Fathers. Not that there was anything salacious in it, regrettably, but the Committee of Fathers had long ago banned and subsequently wiped all fictional material that didn't reflect orthodox thought or didn't "cause the spirit to be uplifted and enriched in the contemplation of the glory of God". That meant that anything that was even vaguely entertaining, be it book or *vid*, had gone.

Not that the novel, called *A Trillion Tales of Light and Love*, was very entertaining, but after a long diet of religious tracts and technical manuals Milo found it mildly diverting. It came from the era which later was ironically referred to as The Age of Optimism. At the time it certainly seemed as if the world had a lot to be optimistic about; the filthiest of all centuries, the twentieth, was over; the world hadn't come to an end with the second millennium, the United States and the new Russia had formed an alliance and science had finally conquered AIDS.

And it had seemed that the world was going to get even better, thanks to science in general and to breakthroughs in microbiology in particular. It was because of this improved image of science and technology that the era also came to be called The Second Age of Reason. As the twentieth century had neared its end there had been a tremendous increase in

5

crank beliefs—astrology, New Ageism, homoeopathy, spiritualism, occultism, Gaiaism, holistic medicine, 'natural' food, reincarnation, 'channelling', aromatherapy, UFOs and 'Green' politics, to name but a few—as well as an expansion in fundamentalism among the established religions. But in the early years of the twenty-first century, when it seemed that science was finally going to banish the old human curses of disease, hunger and even old age itself, superstition loosened its grip on the human mind for a time. And yes, science did indeed achieve its goals and the scientists were hailed as gods by the masses. And then came the Gene Wars. . . .

Not that the Gene Wars were the fault of the scientists. No, they were the fault of the people who controlled the scientists. Heads of States and the people who controlled the, by then, all-powerful Gene Corporations. People like himself.

It amused Milo that the first section of the novel was set in a space habitat similar to his own. Similar in terms of structure, at least. Both were basically just four-mile-long, rotating, bulbous metal cylinders. In the novel the habitat was the base for the builders of a vast starship. The starship was being built in response to mysterious signals coming from the centre of the galaxy. The builders were a bunch of young, idealistic, free-loving immortals; very unlike the people with whom Milo shared his space habitat, Belvedere, who were a bunch of fanatical Christian fundamentalists, sexually repressed under their stifling moral codes and irritating to Milo in the extreme.

Milo understood how this situation had come about, though it didn't make it any easier for him to bear. He knew that the inhabitants of such a space colony, cut off from its mother world, had to live under very strict rules to survive. In space death was a close companion and it would take the careless actions of just one individual to endanger the whole habitat. Religious fundamentalism was an efficient way to

6

impose a strict code of behaviour. Another factor was the emotional trauma experienced by the original inhabitants of Belvedere in the wake of the Gene Wars. The world had been poisoned with man-made plagues and other genetically engineered horrors. Man, with his Science, had destroyed the planet Earth. The Christians among the Belvederians had spread the word that it was up to the survivors to atone for this terrible insult to God and, in the heated emotional climate of the time, the idea quickly took root. Milo remembered those days well; or rather, his *original* self remembered. He merely shared his other self's memories.

Milo finished the novel. He switched off the scanner, sat back in his hard chair and rubbed his eyes. Pity the mysterious alien force turned out to be benign. Milo could have done with a bit of blood and thunder. He leaned forward and used his terminal to inform CenCom of the novel's existence on the file and asked for it to be brought to the attention of the censorship committee. Milo regretted doing so, for the novel was sure to be erased, but he had no choice. CenCom monitored everything he scanned and would have reported to the Fathers itself if Milo hadn't.

He checked the time. His penitent was due to arrive in a couple of minutes. He was looking forward to it. Such sessions were one of his few sources of pleasure in Belvedere. Eating and lucid dreaming were his only others. Alcohol and all other pleasure-related drugs were, of course, banned.

She was punctual. As he knew she would be. She entered, dressed in the inevitable shapeless, dark blue smock. Her head was bowed. He sat straighter in his chair. He knew he looked imposing. "Kneel, Sister Anna."

"Yes, Brother James," she said as she knelt in front of his desk.

"Look me in the eyes," he commanded. She raised her head and reluctantly met his gaze. She was young, almost beautiful and one of his best students. As her tutor he was also her confessor. A perk of the trade. Occasions such as this afforded the rare time that a man and woman could be alone together. Not that they were really alone, what with CenCom monitoring their every word and movement. If he so much as touched Anna with a finger he would be ejected from an airlock without a survival suit.

Physical contact between male and female was forbidden in Belvedere and had been for over a century. Only in cases of extreme emergency was this rule waived. All aspects of reproduction were, of course, restricted to the laboratory. Physical contact between members of the same sex was permitted but if the contact was ever sexual in nature the punishment was quick and severe. Masturbation was also forbidden, and as there was no place in the habitat where you could avoid the constantly prying sensors of CenCom few were ever tempted to break the law. And for males even wet dreams were outlawed. The punishment for this wasn't too drastic—an embarrassing confession on the public channel and six strokes with a cane across a bare palm. Because Milo could control his body completely he had always avoided such a fate but such confessions and punishments occurred on a daily basis.

"You have a confession to make, Sister Anna?" he asked her sternly.

Her pale cheeks began to colour slightly. "I . . . I do, Brother James."

"Begin."

She was breathing rapidly. "I . . . it's so embarrassing, Brother James."

"You know you have to tell me, Sister Anna. And you must be absolutely truthful. Leave nothing out. God is watching and listening." Not to mention CenCom and, through it, the Fathers.

"I have had evil thoughts again. I tried to stop them but I couldn't."

"Tell me about them."

"I had them the night before last. In my bunk. I couldn't

8

sleep. I didn't mean to think such things. It was more like a dream . . . I couldn't help it."

"Don't lie," he warned her. "You *wanted* to think about these things."

"No!" she protested, her voice rising.

"You know you did. Now tell me what you thought about."

"It was about a man. He came into the dorm. He made straight for my bunk. I couldn't see his face but as he got closer I saw he had no clothes on. . . ."

"And how did this make you feel?"

"Scared."

"I told you not to lie."

". . . *and* excited," she said hurriedly. "I didn't want to be excited but I was."

Milo leaned slightly toward her and increased his pheromone output tenfold. Soon the air of his cell was flooded with the potent chemical messengers. He quickly saw the girl's response. Her face grew even more flushed, her breathing more rapid. "Go on," he told her.

"He came up to my bunk. I then saw that his . . . *thing* was extended. . . ."

"You're a medical student, Sister Anna. You know the correct term."

"Er . . . penis."

It was hard not to laugh. Poor girl. It was only by being a medical student that she even knew about the male sexual organ and the old, forbidden ways of procreation. Most Belvederians lived in total sexual ignorance. Sexual *longing* they had in abundance but no way of fulfilling it.

"And then what?"

Her eyes were half-closed now, her breathing rapid and shallow. "He pulled down my sheet . . . all the way to my feet. Then he . . . he took hold of the hem of my sleeping gown and pushed it up . . . over my legs . . . over my . . . my stomach . . . my breasts . . . to my throat."

"You were naked to his gaze?"

"Yes. . . ."

"You didn't try to scream out or run away?"

"No, Brother James."

"And then what happened?"

"He put his hands on my legs . . . and moved them apart. Then he climbed onto my bunk and . . . knelt between my legs. He *touched* me. . . ." She shivered.

"Go on, Sister Anna."

"He kept touching me . . . in different places. Then he lay on me, pressed his body onto mine . . . and at the same time he pushed his . . . penis . . . into me . . . and . . ." Her eyes were completely closed now. Milo increased his pheromone output even further. "He . . . pushed back and forth, back and forth. . . ."

Not bad, Milo thought, for a girl who'd had only a couple of short, desultory and deliberately vague lectures on the actual technique of the sexual act. "And you enjoyed it? What it felt like?"

She was breathing very fast now. Panting. He could smell her juices. Taste them even. "Yes . . . I did."

"And you're enjoying it now, remembering it, aren't you? You can remember exactly what it felt like. . . ."

"Yes! Yes! YES!" She threw her head back and began to shudder. "Oh! Ohhhh!" She tried to suppress the orgasm but she couldn't. The shuddering of her body continued for some time. Milo kept the stern expression on his face but within he was smiling in triumph.

When the shuddering stopped she lowered her face. Tears dripped on the floor. She covered her face with her hands.

"I'm very disappointed in you, Sister Anna," he told her coldly. "You know what this means, don't you?"

"Yes, Brother James." Her voice was muffled by her hands.

"A public confession, a severe scourging from your dorm Mother and at least two weeks in an isolation cell."

10

"Yes, Brother James. I'm sorry. I don't know what happened."

"It's too late now. I must make my report. Go back to your dorm and wait."

"Yes, Brother James." She rose to her feet and, without looking him in the eyes, hurried out of his cell.

As the door slid shut behind her Milo had to really fight the temptation to smile. The smell of her lingered in the air. It had gone wonderfully. Right in front of CenCom's blasted sensors he had raped a woman. By remote control, admittedly, but rape it was.

He mused on how long it had been since he had physically made love to a woman. Over a hundred years. That was a long time between fucks. The woman concerned had been his then-wife, Ruth. Before the decree that forbade contact between men and women. Ruth was dead now. Reached her allotted span some twenty years ago. Got an extra three years past the two hundred mark, which was not a bad bonus. Too bad she had to spend them in this hole. But then she'd gone completely religious herself towards the end.

In one form or another Milo had spent over two hundred and eighty years in Belvedere even though, physically, he was only one hundred and sixty years old. Of course, the first one hundred and twenty years were spent in the original Milo Haze's body, and there was a gap in his memory after that of some fifteen years. That had occurred while he was growing up. . . .

It had seemed a good idea at the time to leave a 'cutting' of himself on Belvedere before his original self left on the expedition to the Mars colonies. When Milo had arrived in Belvedere after the Gene Wars as a refugee he was carrying false identity papers but had declared his true age on them, which was then forty-eight. When a hundred and twenty years had passed and he had entered the final fifty years of the two hundred year span of an average Prime Standard he began to get worried. Because Milo Haze was immortal.

11

And if he didn't die on schedule, which should have been at any time between his two hundredth birthday and his two hundred and fifth, the Belvedere authorities would promptly execute him, just as they would promptly have executed him if they'd discovered he was Milo Haze.

So the original Milo Haze had begun to make plans. He volunteered to participate on an expedition to the Martian colonies, knowing that for him it would be a one-way journey. He would eliminate the other crew members en route and switch identities with the youngest. Then, on Mars, he would ask for political asylum. Because of the long-running feuds between Belvedere and the Martian colonies he was confident it would be granted.

But a month before he was due to leave he selected a woman who he knew was in her fertile year—one Carla Gleick, who worked in the water-recycling unit. As this was well before CenCom's surveillance had become absolute it was easy for Milo to enter the unit when Carla was on duty alone, drug her and then impregnate her with the embryonic clone. Not that the present Milo remembered any of this— his memories stopped short forty-eight hours before those events, but he remembered *planning* to do it and his own existence testified to the fact that the original Milo had successfully carried out his plans.

He remembered nothing for a further fifteen years. Then one day he had awoken to find himself in a hospital bed. It was a period of confusion and disorientation while he slowly adjusted to the realisation of what had happened. And it was then that he began to regret his plan to leave a cutting on Belvedere. Because while he knew it would be a clone with his memories he hadn't really expected the cutting to be *him*. *He* had expected to go to Mars, not stay trapped in fundamentalist Belvedere. And, of course, he *had* gone to Mars. He knew that, technically, he wasn't the original Milo Haze. Unfortunately, he *thought* he was. . . .

Pleading amnesia, which was the truth, he slowly pieced

together the last fifteen years. It transpired that Carla Gleick's husband was sterile and though she understandably protested her innocence she was found guilty of adultery. She had been put to death. Milo hadn't known about her husband's sterility though it was a common enough condition in Belvedere and the other space habitats, thanks to the faults in the cosmic radiation shields. Not that it would have made any difference if he had known.

Milo, or rather James Gleick, had been raised in a government crèche. From all accounts he had been a normal child, though he had grown remarkably quickly. Placid and obedient, young James had been a model Belvederian and rarely had to be disciplined. Entering his teens, he had shown an early aptitude for medicine as a vocation. It had been in one of his medical classes three weeks earlier that he had suddenly collapsed. Neither doctors nor the habitat's sole operating med-machine could offer any explanation for the deep coma that James had slipped into.

Milo decided he would continue James Gleick's medical career. As a former head of a Gene Corporation it would present no difficulty. On the contrary, it might be difficult to conceal the extent of his medical knowledge. And he would continue to be a model citizen of Belvedere, though the personality that now dwelt within the body of James Gleick was very different.

But his appearance changed as well. Within a few months all his hair had fallen out and one of his eyes, originally blue, turned green. It was a conceit on the original Milo's part that he now regretted. And it wasn't long before someone noted the resemblance between him and one of the volunteers for the Martian expedition. The name Milo had used since arriving at the habitat had been Victor Parrish, and it was now clear who Carla Gleick had committed adultery with. But fortunately for Milo the Fathers of Belvedere did not visit the sins of fathers upon their children. And as far as the Belvederians believed, Parrish had died with the others during the ill-fated trip to Mars. The sole survivor's name had been Len Grimwod who Milo presumed was the original Milo, his plan to murder the other crew members obviously having been carried out successfully. He remembered that his original self had chosen Grimwod for his new identity because Grimwod was only thirty-seven years old. That meant that his Martian self had reached the 'dangerous age' again and wondered, but with not too much concern, how the original Milo would conceal the fact of his immortality again.

As for himself, a hundred and forty-five years of increasing boredom later, though interspersed with numerous secret victories—such as the one that had occurred today—he too was reaching the same position as the original Milo. At one hundred and sixty years of age he needed to start thinking about getting out of Belvedere. But his options were limited; one of the three other habitats or the Martian colonies. He would prefer the Martian colonies but if he somehow managed to reach them—and he didn't see how he could—he would inevitably encounter his original self, who, if he was still alive, wouldn't be happy about such an event. Two men physically identical, both completely bald and both with one green eye and one blue, would attract unwanted attention. Anyway, there were still a few years before he had to come to a firm decision.

Escaping from Belvedere would be more difficult now than it had been for his original self: only a specially trained class of men were permitted to operate, and travel on, the Belvederian ships that travelled to and from the other habitats. They not only lived in isolation from other citizens, to lessen the possibility of tainting Belvederian society as a result of their regular contact with the less holy residents of the other habitats, they were also eunuchs. This latter handicap was the main reason Milo was postponing making his escape attempt until it was absolutely necessary. He had yet to work out a way of overcoming the problem.

Milo entered his report on the poor Sister Anna with CenCom then checked the time again. It was almost his dinner period. He was about to rise from his seat when his terminal gave a loud beep. A face appeared on the monitor. Milo's mouth went dry. A Father. But not just any Father but Father Massie, the most senior of all. Belvedere's forbidding patriarch. What did he want with Milo? Had CenCom seen through Milo's game with Sister Anna? Had the sensors picked up his increased pheromone output? It had never been capable of doing so in the past. If Milo had been capable of experiencing proper fear he would have been terrified.

"Brother James, prepare yourself for a shock," said Father Massie, his stern eyes boring out from the screen.

"Yes, Father Massie, what is it?"

"We are receiving radio signals from Earth."

Chapter Two:

In the flickering glow from the crude gas lamp the group peered intently at the sheet of plastic spread out on the table. On the plastic sheet were roughly drawn diagrams of the lower sections of the *Lord Montcalm*. The group was composed of four men and two women. They wore an assortment of ragged furs. It was cold in the storeroom. Ashley had cut off the heating throughout the ship, as well as the lighting.

"It's agreed then?" asked Jean-Paul. He pointed again at corridor D on the diagram of the bottom deck. "We stage the diversionary attack in there?"

The others nodded. "It is the most obvious way to gain access to the control pod," said Claude. "If we throw every available person into the attack Ashley will have no choice but to put all her remaining mechs into the corridor to protect the pod."

"We hope," said Dominique. She looked worriedly at Jean-Paul. "If there is even one spider still in the pod when Jean-Paul arrives . . ."

He smiled encouragingly at her even though the same fear was digging its claws into his own mind. "She will, don't worry," he said as convincingly as he could. "We know, from the number we've so far put out of action, that she can have only nine to eleven that are fully operational."

"That's if our estimate of how many of the damned things she originally had is correct," said Eric dourly.

"We have no choice but to believe that it is," said Jean-Paul, which was true. He scanned their faces. "Are all your units prepared?"

They nodded. "We'll be throwing everyone and everything into that corridor," said Claude. "Hell, there's a good chance we will actually make it!"

Everyone murmured their agreement though Jean-Paul knew that none of them believed it. They all had experience of fighting the mechs. In the narrow confines of a corridor even a single spider-mech was capable of inflicting horrific casualties. Jean-Paul straightened. Time to get it over with. "Let's do it," he said.

While the others filed out of the small room Dominique moved closer to him. "Are you afraid?" she asked him softly.

"You hardly need to ask," he said, and ran the tip of his forefinger down the side of her face. She took hold of his hand. "I'm afraid," she told him. "I'm afraid I'll never see you again."

"Please," he said, with a forced laugh, "that's no way to boost my morale."

"I'm sorry," she said, then kissed him and embraced him tightly. After a while he pulled away. "Time to go." He turned and began to gather up his equipment. They went out together. Claude was waiting outside, holding the coiled rope. There was a lot of it. Jean-Paul said to Dominique, "You had better join your unit, fast."

She nodded, gave him a final, significant glance and hurried away. Jean-Paul and Claude headed off at a quick pace to their own destination, which was a small, open deck on the lower hull. As Jean-Paul stepped, shivering, out onto the deck he tried not to think of the enormity of the task that faced him. If he failed then their struggle was over. Even though the humans had taken over most of the giant airship it was still in the control of the deranged computer program known as Ashley. They had ripped out her sensors in the rooms and corridors as they had progressed through the ship but she still controlled many of the ship's prime functions. It wouldn't be unthinkable for her, in a fit of pique, to drive the *Lord Montcalm* nose first into a mountain. She had to be eliminated. Until she was gone the humans were nothing more than fleas inhabiting the hide of a giant beast.

Jean-Paul looked over the side. They were flying at a high altitude, which explained why it was so cold. He could see nothing below but a layer of cloud. His stomach felt queasy but he grinned at Claude and said cheerfully, "It's going to work!"

Claude helped him into his harness and checked the bindings on the makeshift crampons he was wearing on his hands and feet. "When you're in position give three sharp tugs on the—"

"I know, I know! You don't have to tell me. It was my plan, remember?"

Claude looked hurt and Jean-Paul immediately regretted his words. Claude's nerves were wound up just as tightly as his own. "Don't worry," he said, "I'm not going to screw up." He looked up at the hull of the airship that curved out above him. The computer's sensors here and at all other accessible parts of the hull had been systematically blacked out. Unfortunately where he was going—below—sensors still operated. He would have to avoid them. He took a deep breath, adjusted his goggles and climbed over the railing. Claude had tied the end of the rope to a pole and stood ready to play it out as he descended. "When this is over we are going to get very, very drunk," he told Claude, then lowered himself down and made the first kick at the curving hull with one of his foot crampons. It met resistance. The outer hull covering wasn't metallic but very tough. He tried again. This time the sharpened spike on his boot dug in. He did it with the other foot. Success. But he knew from previous practice that it was going to be a long and tedious process. "Au revoir," he called to Claude as he disappeared beneath the level of the deck.

He tried to empty his mind of everything but the mechanical routine of his downward climb. Lever out left wrist spike from the hull and then drive it again; lever out right foot spike from the hull then drive it in again; lever out right wrist spike and drive it in again. . . .

Every now and then he would pause and glance down, looking for sensors. When he spotted one below him he would have to move sideways for a time before continuing downwards. The curve of the hull was acute and very soon he would be moving virtually upside-down, like a fly on a ceiling. He could feel gravity pull at his body; feel the extra strain on the spikes that were his precarious grip on the hull. The sweat poured off his face despite the cold and he was finally forced to stop and push his goggles up onto his forehead because they had steamed up. He knew that if he fell he would be saved by the rope, and hauled back to safety by Claude, but that would mean the attack was off because he wouldn't have the strength to repeat the climb down the hull.

There came a bad moment when, to avoid two sensors, he had to climb between them and over the small glass dome that was the housing for one of the lasers. If Ashley had detected his approach he was doomed. It seemed to take a very long time to climb those few feet but the interior of the dome remained thankfully inert as he passed over it.

He paused again and looked down. Just visible below the curve of the hull was the bottom of the control pod. Time to give the signal. He levered one of his wrist spikes loose, grasped the rope and, with an arm that felt like lead, gave it three sharp tugs. He looked at his watch. It was 12.40 hours. Now he would wait.

From above he heard the first long blast of sound from the fire alarms which Claude had set off to alert the attack teams inside. The battle for corridor D would soon begin.

Arms and legs aching from the strain, and face and fingers numb from the cold, Jean-Paul hoped he would have the strength to resume climbing when the time came. He waited impatiently until ten minutes had passed then painfully resumed his upside-down passage across the hull. He wondered what was happening in corridor D. . . .

He finally reached the side of the pod, turned himself around and peered in. A gasp of relief. Empty of spider-mechs. He had to work fast. Ashley would have seen him by now and would be summoning help. With difficulty he unhooked one of his bombs from his harness, jammed its wax base in the crevice where the skin of the pod met the surface of the hull and pulled out the fuse pin. Then he began to climb as rapidly as he could round to the rear of the pod. In his haste he didn't drive one of his wrist spikes in deeply enough and it came out, taking him by surprise. If the other wrist spike hadn't held he would have fallen free from the hull.

He made it to the rear of the pod. Lasers flashed from the hull but impotently. There was no way they could angle their fire acutely enough to hit him. Ashley, who had obviously seen him by now, was acting in an irrational, desperate manner. A good sign.

Crump! Not a loud explosion but one that sounded powerful all the same. He climbed back round the pod. He only had one bomb left—their weight had made it impossible for him to carry a third—if the first had not penetrated the pod skin. . . .

But he saw that it had. Lovely big gaping hole. He could hear the air whistling through it as he got closer, and still no sign of any spider-mechs. He reached the hole. Careful, he told himself, don't rush. Silly to make a careless mistake at this stage and fall off. He eased himself slowly through and then allowed himself to drop to the pod floor. His knees buckled from the strain and he was suddenly dizzy. Over the whistling of the wind he could hear Ashley's shrill voice: "You bastard! Get out of here! You're gonna die for this! Get out . . .!"

Then he heard a clatter of metal legs. He turned in time to see a spider-mech come hurtling down the spiral staircase from above. Still dizzy, he wrenched the pipe-gun from his harness and took aim. Only one charge in the weapon . . . couldn't afford to miss . . . *God, the things moved fast!* He pulled the trigger. A very loud bang this time then an explosion. Something whizzed by his cheek. His eyes watered. When he could see clearly again there were only smoking fragments of the spider-mech. He took the second bomb from his harness and approached the computer.

"No, don't come near me, you ungrateful shit! I should have dumped you all on the ground like the other Ashleys did with their useless, lazy people. Stay away! Stop, or I'll kill us all!"

There was a violent shudder and the bow of the airship began to dip. The floor tilted sharply and Jean-Paul almost lost his footing but he succeeded in reaching the computer. He jammed the waxen end of the bomb into the side of the console. "Ashley, you are about to go where you should have gone a long, long time ago," he said with relish as he pulled the fuse pin out.

As he scrambled to take cover in the forward section of the pod Ashley called, "You can't do this! You'll never run this ship without me!"

"We did it before, we can do it again!" he cried as he dived behind one of the helmsmen's old chairs. Then he heard metal legs again. He looked over the back of the chair. Two more spider-mechs coming down the stairs. They hit the bottom and came straight towards where he was crouching. He lowered his head and waited for whatever would come first—the explosion or the mechs.

KA-BOOM!

This one, in the confines of the pod, was very loud. Ears ringing and eyes streaming from the acrid smoke that instantly filled the pod, he raised his head and peered over the back of the seat again. The console had been peeled open like a tin can and smoke poured from its interior. The two spider-mechs skidded past him and came to a halt against the control console. They didn't move again. He had done it. The ghost of the long-dead Ashley had been exorcised from the machine. He stood up wearily and looked around. The place was a mess. The damage was extensive. He hoped the old controls would still work but he would have to wait for the arrival of the experts before he would know. The deck still tilted acutely. Ashley had put the airship into a dive. He peered ahead but they were in the layer of cloud now and he could see nothing.

Sounds of movement from above. Excited voices. Shouts. Then footsteps on the spiral staircase. People began to pour into the pod. He scanned the smoke-stained and often bloody faces, looking for Dominique. He couldn't see her. But he spotted Eric, and Marcel. They came up to him, broad grins on their faces. Eric hugged him. "You did it! You great sonofabitch! You actually did it!"

"Yeah," he said distractedly, still looking for Dominique. "It all went as planned, thank God. How was it upstairs?"

They both grimaced. "A bloodbath. The spiders went through us like mincing machines. We were on the run when we heard the second explosion and then they all froze," said Marcel.

"Dominique?"

They exchanged a glance and Eric drew the short straw. "I'm sorry, Jean-Paul," he said. "She didn't make it. But it was quick. Over in seconds. I saw it happen."

Jean-Paul drew a deep breath and turned away. It felt as if the deck of the pod had suddenly melted away and he was falling. He shook his head. Then he saw that the engineers had arrived and were already at work on the controls. He went over to them. "Can you do it?" he asked in a voice that he didn't recognise as his own.

One engineer looked round at him and said, with a smile, "No problem, Jean-Paul. As soon as we disconnect all the computer wiring we can take direct control. A matter of minutes. It'll be tough work using just manual control but. . . ." He shrugged his shoulders.

Jean-Paul stared out at the greyness of the cloud ahead. All he could see was Dominique's face. He gave a start as someone put his arm around his shoulder. It was Eric.

"I'm sorry about Dominique, Jean-Paul," he said. "But there is one thing you should be feeling happy about."

"And what could that possibly be?" he asked bitterly.

"Why, you are now a Sky Lord!"

Chapter Three:

Old habits were hard to break, especially when you were as old as Lon Haddon. The tall, lean, brown-skinned man in the look-out tower, who was scanning the sky with a pair of high-powered binoculars, was just over two hundred years old. As usual he was studying the sky out over the sea, even though it had been several years since the local Sky Lord, the *Perfumed Breeze*, had made an appearance.

When a whole year had passed since its last nerve-churning visit to collect its tribute from Palmyra everyone in the community had agreed that something must have happened to the Sky Lord. Hopefully it had met with some major calamity—perhaps an encounter with a hurricane it hadn't been able to avoid—and been destroyed. Lon Haddon believed this too on one level of his mind but he also remembered how cunning and ruthless was the Warlord Horado, master of the *Perfumed Breeze*, and had his doubts that such a man could ever be bested, even by natural forces.

Besides, there were other Sky Lords in the world and sooner or later one would surely arrive to fill the space created by the absent *Perfumed Breeze*. When that time came, however, the intruding airship and its inhabitants would receive a rude surprise. The breathing space provided by the *Perfumed Breeze*'s absence had enabled Palmyra to consolidate its resources, expand greatly and, it was hoped, develop the means by which it could destroy a Sky Lord.

Lon lowered the glasses and glanced around at the town that was spread neatly about him. He felt a quiet satisfaction as he gazed down on its sturdy, white-washed buildings, made mainly of wood and brick, and its lush tropical gardens with their palm and coconut trees. They had achieved so much here over the years, in spite of the ever-encroaching blight . . . and Horado.

Even in the period of Horado's rule of Palmyra the community had been a deceptive place. It had long presented a false face to its aerial master, being a much larger community than it appeared. It had been a magnet for refugees from both inland and the islands for a considerable time but to keep its true population a secret there had been much underground excavation to provide extensive areas for accommodation . . . and for industry. The latter was Palmyra's other secret; it was much more technologically advanced than the average ground community.

Palmyra was located on the eastern coast of the great northern peninsula of the island continent that had once been called Australia. The peninsula itself had once been part of the state of Queensland, though that later came to be called Noshiro when the Australians were obliged to cede the state to Japan as part of the price for Japan's defence of Australia during the attempted Indonesian invasion in the early twenty-first century. In the ancient days there had been a sizeable town in the vicinity called Cairns (later renamed Masuda) but no trace of that remained today.

The trapdoor in the floor of the look-out station was opening. Lon turned and watched Lyle Weaver climb inside. Like Lon he was one of the six rotating rulers of Palmyra, each one of whom had command of the community for six years. Lyle had begun his current term nearly a year ago. Lon wouldn't be eligible again for eleven years, and by then he would have been dead several years.

"Thought I'd find you up here," Lyle wheezed. It was a long climb. "Don't know why you bother. Our radar may be crude but it works."

"I know, I know," Lon said wearily. "But you know me."

25

Lyle came over, pulling up the top of his sarong over his slight paunch, and leaned on the railing beside him. "Indeed I do. Are you sleeping any better?"

"No," he admitted. "Managed two hours last night."

Lyle glanced at him. "You've got to learn acceptance, Lon. No use fighting the inevitable."

"So you keep telling me." Lon couldn't conceal the bitterness he felt.

"You should put your trust in God."

"Yes, well you know what I think about *that*."

Lyle sighed. "I won't give up, you know. I'll make you see the truth before you. . . ."

"Die? You'd better hurry then," Lon said dryly. "I could drop dead at any moment."

"And then again you may live for a full further five years."

"Correction. If I'm very lucky I will live for another four years, nine months and thirteen days."

"Oh, you're keeping that close a count. . . ."

"Reaching your two hundredth birthday concentrates the mind wonderfully."

"Look on the bright side, Lon. You've had a good life . . . well, relatively speaking. And look what you have achieved for Palmyra over the years."

"But there is so much more to do. I need more time. *Lots* more time!"

"Would you rather have lived in olden days when people could only expect to live seventy or eighty years at most? And those last years were spent living in a body that had deteriorated dreadfully. Look at you—a healthy man who is physiologically in his mid-thirties. . . ."

"Who could quite likely die before the sun rises tomorrow. Maybe it was better in the old days. Perhaps the old, in their failing, decrepit, pain-ridden bodies, used to welcome the release of death."

"Well, I know what I would prefer," said Lyle. "We die quickly, peacefully and without pain."

"That's easy for you to say. You're only a hundred and twenty years old. Wait till you reach my age. Damn those genegineers! Why couldn't they have been more flexible with their time limits?"

"You know your history, Lon. At the time they were lucky to have the average life span extended to two hundred plus one to five years. The population pressure was enormous. The world's resources would not have coped, even during the Golden Age of the mid twenty-first century."

Lon laughed and pointed inland, where beyond Palmyra's farmlands lay a vast and empty island continent. "So where's the population pressure now? They should have thought ahead."

"You're being absurd and you know it, Lon. The planet can hardly support the small population that remains. And it's going to get worse. The blight is spreading everywhere. Look at us—we've got the land blight at our backs and the sea blight facing us. Unless something drastic can be done humanity is doomed."

They lapsed into gloomy silence for a while. A honey bee the size of a small bird flew into the tower. They both ducked out of its path. Finally it flew out. Then Lon said, "No response yet to our radio signals?" He knew the answer anyway. Lyle would have been beside himself with excitement if there had been any but the question was a daily ritual.

"I checked on the way here. Nothing. We're trying a new frequency. It's been months now since we got the new transmitter set up."

"Well, as we've said at the meetings there are various possible reasons for this: there's no one left alive up there, our equipment isn't good enough to pick up any signals they're transmitting . . . or they simply don't want to talk to us."

Lyle shrugged. "The other possibility is that no one up

27

there is monitoring those wavebands. Presumably the habitats maintain radio contact with each other but on tight microwave beams. After all these years of radio silence from Earth why would anyone in the habitats expect suddenly to receive radio signals from down here?"

"But they must know there are people still alive down here. They could pick up the lights from towns like this with their telescopes."

"How do you know we're not the last community like this on the entire planet?" asked Lyle. "Anyway, they would know there shouldn't be any working radio equipment in existence down here."

"Well, we possess such equipment. . . ."

"Yes, because of unique circumstances," Lyle pointed out.

"Apparently not so unique . . . those signals we picked up when we first started getting our receiver working."

Lyle looked grim. "Yes. A mystery." They had kept picking up snatches of conversation on a weak, low frequency. The signals had apparently been coming from a considerable distance. What was really puzzling was that sender and receiver spoke with the same, identical voice. A woman's voice. There seemed to be more than just two of them. And they all called each other Ashley. "But we haven't picked up any more of those for some time now."

"Doesn't prove anything. Just that the sources have moved out of range. And that suggests to me that the moving sources were Sky Lords."

"Sky Lords with working radio equipment?" Lyle shook his head. "I can't believe it."

"Well, I can't believe that sending an SOS out into space is going to get us anywhere. Pinning all our hopes on getting a miraculous salvation from heaven. . . ." He shook his head. "Talk about pie in the sky. If there is anyone living in those habitats they've probably got too big a problem just staying alive to worry about helping us. That's if any of them *are* still alive. Those habitats and colonies probably contain nothing but very old skeletons."

"You've turned into a cynic and a pessimist, Lon, and that's understandable considering your, er, circumstances, but it's clouding your judgement."

"Just as your optimism clouds yours," Lon told him. "You think there's a whole flourishing human civilisation up there stretching from the habitats to the Martian colonies. I'm afraid you're going to be sorely disappointed."

"Well, we shall see, Lon, we shall see. . . . Ah, look!" He pointed out to sea. "A submersible is returning. Perhaps it's Ayla's."

"Yes, it must be," said Lon, watching as the gate in the inner sea defence wall slowly rose. Some time later the submersible, running on its tracks, became visible in the shallows. It crawled up onto the beach and a hatch on top opened. A figure emerged. He focused the binoculars. Yes, it was Ayla. A slim, tall woman in a wet suit. Cropped black hair. She slid down off the hull of the submersible and waved in his direction. He was too far away for her to recognise but she knew it had to be him up in the watch tower at this time of the day. As she began to take off the wet suit a similarly clad but chunkier figure climbed out of the hatch. Juli, her best friend and Lyle's daughter. And behind her came Kell, one of the few inhabitants of Palmyra who carried the blood, and colouring, of the island continent's indigenous population. They removed their suits as well and Lon watched as the three of them ran into the water to wash off the sweat and smells that had built up in their suits during the long journey in the hot submersible.

"Careless idiots, leaving the sub parked right out there in the open," he muttered. "They should have driven it straight into its shed."

"Oh, stop being such a worrier," Lyle chided him. "And don't try to hide your feelings. You know you're as proud as anything of Ayla. She's achieved wonders. She's practically indispensable now. No one can deal with the sea people as efficiently as her."

"Juli is good at it too," he said, diplomatically.

"I agree, but not in the same way as Ayla. The rapport she has with them is remarkable."

"Yes, it is," he admitted as he continued to watch his daughter through the binoculars. How like her mother she had become; the same olive skin and the same large but oriental-shaped eyes that were an inheritance from a Japanese ancestor. But despite the joy he derived from watching her he also felt a profound sadness. She was another reason he so strongly resented his fast approaching death. It wasn't fair that he should only have these few short years with her. And he also wanted to know what lay in her future. He wanted to know if she would *have* a future. . . .

With water streaming down her round face Juli gestured at the distant watch tower. "Your Dad, right? As usual."

Ayla nodded with a smile and threw more water over Juli. "And he's probably complaining to whoever that is up there with him that we're careless fools for not driving the sub straight into the shed."

"I told you we should have," said Kell seriously.

"Oh, you're as bad as he is," cried Ayla and made him her next target for a spray of water. "Still worrying about Sky Lords. Well, I don't believe there *are* any Sky Lords any more. They've all fallen to bits from old age and scattered over the ground."

Kell's wide grin vanished. He shook his head and turned towards the horizon. "Yes, I *am* like your father, Ayla. Their threat is still real. If the *Perfumed Breeze* doesn't return it will be some other Sky Lord." He looked back and stared at her with his large, dark and very intense eyes. "I know it, Ayla."

Chapter Four:

Jan squatted on her haunches in the snow and watched the penguins. The penguins, for their part, ignored her. Surrounding her, they carried on with their social rituals, either squabbling with each other or carrying out elaborate mating rituals—Jan couldn't tell which. When her legs began to ache she rose slowly and stretched. She kept all her movements slow so as not to alarm the birds but they continued to act as if she was invisible. She stared up at the bright blue sky then, reluctantly, over towards the Toy which was parked some fifty yards away. Might as well head back to Shangri La, she decided.

She walked carefully through the crowd of penguins, reflecting on the fact that it had been so long since humankind—no, *man*—had vacated this once-again pristine wilderness that the birds had expunged him from their list of life-threatening organisms.

"Take us home," she ordered the Toy after she'd climbed inside. "The longest way." There was no hurry. There never was.

"Sure, Jan," answered the Toy and sealed the hatches. The Toy, humming, immediately began to rise into the air. Jan didn't like the Toy's female voice; it reminded her too much of Ashley's, even though she knew there was no similarity between them: Ashley was a computerised recording of a human personality while the Toy was just a 'pure' computer program.

On the monitor screens Jan watched the white expanse of Antarctica flash by as the Toy sped through the air at an altitude of only a few hundred feet. Here and there could be

31

seen the remains of human habitations jutting out of the ice. Once they had been towering installations—parts of vast mining developments—but now the ice had nearly covered them up. Eventually they would disappear completely. Jan wished that she could order the Toy to fly her somewhere other than Antarctica but the computer's original programming had been restored and the machine was restricted to a specific area around the frozen continent and its seas.

Shangri La, the ironical name given by the equally ironically named Eloi to the giant underwater habitat where they dwelt, lay beneath the giant Ross Ice Shelf. The penguin colony Jan had been visiting was located on the opposite coast of the continent, in what had once been known as Queen Maud Land when it had been administered by Norway, but even with its meandering route the Toy reached the Ross Shelf within fifteen minutes. It sped over the ice until it reached the sea then plunged into it. The Toy then doubled back under the ice to the huge metal sphere that was Shangri La and slid smoothly into its dock within the habitat's double hull. Jan waited for the water to be pumped out of the dock then left the Toy, ignoring its polite farewell. She rode an elevator up to the level where she shared living quarters with Robin (yes, she knew his real name was Ryn but she would always think of him as Robin).

As she headed towards their quarters she passed a couple of Eloi in the corridor. They were holding hands. They smiled dreamily at her. She scowled at them. The Eloi had turned out to be just as frustrating and downright infuriating as Robin had warned her they would be. Locked permanently in their private little worlds where the only emotion they could experience was mild euphoria they were as socially stimulating as pieces of furniture.

As she was about to enter their quarters a program projection materialised in front of the doorway. She recognised 'him' as Davin, Robin's favourite. "Yes, what is it?" she asked him curtly.

He smiled at her and said, "I just wanted to warn you that Ryn is sleeping."

"Isn't he always? But don't worry, I'll try not to make any loud noises when I have my shower and change my clothes. Now may I go in?"

"It's important for his recuperation that he gets as much rest as possible," said Davin gently. "Why don't you go up to the recreation room until he wakes?"

Jan glared at him. While the Eloi infuriated her, the computer programs, and their accompanying projections, both annoyed and disturbed her. She knew that, like the Toy, they were nothing like Ashley but she didn't feel comfortable with them. Communicating with Carl, the computer program that had shared Ashley's bio-software, had been perfectly straightforward; he had been pure logic, a machine mind, but these programs in the habitat had been anthropomorphised to the ultimate degree. Or rather, they could *simulate* human personalities to an uncanny degree but Jan doubted that these oh-so-human personalities represented their true entities. Basically, she didn't trust them even though she was well aware she owed them her life. They could easily have ejected her from the habitat when the Toy had brought the mortally injured Robin, with her, back to his home.

She sighed. "Oh, very well. I'll go to the recreation room. Tell Robin where I am when he wakes."

Davin nodded and vanished. Jan went up to the next level where the 'human' recreation room was located. It wasn't empty. A lone Eloi, naked, was sitting by the ornamental pool watching the carp it contained swim back and forth. "Fancy a game of snooker?" Jan asked the Eloi sarcastically. It turned towards her and gave her a typically dreamy smile. *Ghastly little sexless elf*, she said to herself bitterly. To think that this had once been a real human being, a scientist from the Old Days, but who, instead of trying to repair the

33

damage caused by the Gene Wars, had chosen to retreat into a personal, eternal nirvana.

At least, Jan told herself, she had tried. Mother God, *how* she had tried! But what had all her efforts achieved? At first resentment and finally . . . nothing. And she was lucky not to have died in the attempt. Maybe the Eloi had the right idea after all. . . .

Jan climbed out of her padded suit and, in just her underwear, sat down and selected an old movie. After giving her armpit a disapproving sniff she told the movie to begin. It was a two-dimensional one from the early twenty-first century, a comedy-thriller about a private detective hired to hunt down his own clone who, unbeknown to him, had changed sex and become a woman. Called *Meeting Cute*, the movie was almost over when Robin entered. He was wearing his sleeping robe. He gave her an affectionate grin, came and ran his hand through her hair then lowered himself warily onto a nearby divan. She stopped the movie and went over to the divan. She sat down next to him. "How are you feeling?" she asked.

"Fine. Just tired, that's all."

She leaned over, pressed herself to him, kissed him hard on the lips. He began to respond, putting his arms around her, then she felt the pressure of his grip around her lessen. She drew away from him and looked into his face. He looked embarrassed. "I'm sorry, Jan."

"It's all right," she told him, doing her best to hide her disappointment. She reached down, felt between his legs through the fabric of his robe. Soft. Yet she knew he was capable of having an erection, despite his lack of testicles. To compensate, his prostate gland had been altered to produce a normal amount of testosterone into his system. But it just wasn't working. They had attempted to make love several times but on each occasion it had been unsatisfactory. Well, no, to be honest, a total disaster.

She still couldn't understand why the med-machine hadn't

34

been able to provide him with new testicles. The Medical Program had explained to her that they could take a cell from any part of the human body and, after tinkering with its DNA, convince it to grow into a new eye, arm, liver or whatever, but that it was impossible to create reproductive organs by this process. She couldn't follow the logic of this limitation and had pointed out to the Program that the habitat had sperm and eggs in storage and that it would be a simple matter to create an embryo from which the necessary cells could be removed. The reply of the Medical Program was that the Ethical Program would not allow it.

It was, after all, because of the rules encoded in the Ethical Program regarding the treatment of embryos that Robin had been allowed to grow as a normal human being rather than as an Eloi. This was another factor about the Ethical Program that aroused Jan's suspicions but she couldn't figure out why she felt something about it was wrong. She remembered that even Milo found it strange that these super-smart programs could have allowed a genetic 'throw-back', as Robin was in their terms, to develop by accident.

Jan rose from the couch and stared down at Robin. How different he was now from that spirited, exciting young man who had presented himself to her on the Sky Angel and offered her his services and, later, his love. There was no passion left in him now. No spirit. When that bitch, Princess Andrea, had castrated him she had cut off more than his testicles.

"You should have come with me in the Toy," she told him. "The air smelt beautiful. It would have done you good."

"I felt so tired today," he told her. "Maybe next time."

"Sure," she said. Then, "I'm going down to the quarters to have a shower and change. I'll see you at supper."

He gave her a wan smile and nodded.

*

As she showered she reflected on how bored she was in the habitat. Of course, the alternative would have been death in the ruined shopping mall if the Toy hadn't arrived in the nick of time to save them. She wondered, without any real concern, what had happened to the Duke and the others, particularly those two awful children of his who had tried to kill her. But most of all she wondered about Milo. He must be fully grown by now and would bear no resemblance at all to her young son Simon whose body he had cruelly appropriated. She hoped so. Poor Simon. . . .

Poor world, now that Milo and Ashley had joined forces and were in control of not only the Sky Angel but all the other Sky Lords in their fleet. Milo. How she hated him. He had taken everything from her, including her own son. And now he had the power to conquer the entire world.

What remained of it.

Chapter Five:

Milo Haze lay naked on the dirty bed with his hands clasped behind his head and his eyes fixed on a space beyond the ceiling. He was calm now. He had been for the last three months. The dents in the steel door had been put there during the early stages of his imprisonment, as had the holes in the walls. After he had finally abandoned his futile rages he told himself to use his mind instead of his body. Surely there was a way of getting back into Ashley's favour. . . .

And now he thought he had the solution. The plan had occurred to him a week ago and he had spent the time since then pulling it to pieces, putting it back together again, polishing it. He believed there was a fifty–fifty chance that it would work. Now he was ready to put it into action.

He patiently waited for the clock to read 18.00 hours then he got off the bed, picked up a tray from the floor containing empty dishes and a cup, and went to the door. Almost immediately the panel in the door slid open and Shan peered in. Milo raised the tray to the panel. As Shan took it Milo said, "I need to speak to Ashley. It's important."

"You know that's out of the question," said Shan, giving him a bland look. Then he temporarily dropped out of sight as he put the lunch tray on the floor and picked up the one containing Milo's evening meal.

Milo ignored the offered tray. "I tell you it's important. For Ashley. She'll *want* to talk to me when she knows what it's about."

"She never wants to talk to you again," Shan told him. He couldn't hide the smugness in his voice.

Milo kept his temper. If things went as planned he would have plenty of time to get revenge on this neutered Minervan. "Just pass the message on to Ashley," he said calmly. "Tell her I have something of vital importance for her."

"I won't ever do you any favours, Milo," said Shan. "Not after the way you treated Tyra. Now take the tray."

Milo continued to ignore the tray. "It's in your own interests to give Ashley my message. If she ever finds out that you killed her chance to live again as flesh and blood—to be human again—she will go berserk, as you well know."

This made Shan frown. "What are you talking about? How could she ever be human again? It's impossible."

"Ah, but I believe otherwise. I have devised a means by which she will attain a new body. And you must tell her so."

Shan thought for a few moments then shook his head. "Nonsense. You're clutching at straws. You just want the opportunity of talking to her again, to try to persuade her to let you go free. Well, I won't help you. Now take the tray or go hungry."

This time Milo accepted the tray. As Shan started to slide the panel shut he said, "Wait, Shan."

"What is it now?" he asked suspiciously.

Milo smiled at him and said, "Give my love to Tyra."

Shan slid the panel shut with a loud clang.

Still smiling, Milo returned to his bed. Now it all depended on his gamble that he wasn't completely cut off in here from Ashley's presence. Oh, yes, Shan had told him on the first day of his incarceration that Ashley had had the spider-mechs remove every sensor from his suite but from the beginning he had suspected that Ashley wouldn't have forgone the pleasure of watching and listening to him suffering. If he was wrong then his plan was dead as of now.

He didn't have to wait long. Within a few minutes he heard something on the other side of the door. Then the door began to slide stiffly open. When it was half-open a spider-mech came through the gap. The spherical robot with its arachnoid legs scuttled towards the bed. Milo regarded it calmly. "Hello, Ashley," he said.

The spider-mech halted beside his bed. "If this is one of your tricks, Milo, I'll gut you," said Ashley via the mech.

Milo sat up on the bed. "So Shan passed on my message to you?"

"Never mind how I know what you said to him. Just tell me how I can be human again. You have thirty seconds to convince me."

Milo smiled. He had guessed correctly. She *had* left sensors in his suite. He said calmly, "No need to rush. And stop threatening me, or I won't tell you what you need to know."

"Milo . . .!"

"And before I speak I want to state my conditions. . . ."

A spluttering sound came from the robot. Then, "Conditions? What do you mean *conditions*? You have no right to make any demands!"

He put his hands behind his head and lay back on the bed. "If you're not prepared to strike a bargain you might as well leave. And close the door on your way out."

More spluttering sounds came from the robot, followed by, "Okay, you win . . . for now. What are these terms of yours?"

"Well, for a starter I naturally want the freedom of the ship again."

"Depending on what you tell me, that will be granted. What else?"

"That prick Shan is to be made my personal slave."

"I was going to punish him anyway. Yes . . . granted."

"And I want the girl back."

Silence greeted this request.

"Ashley?"

"Tell me first how I can be a human being again."

After hesitating, Milo said, "Very well." He got up off the bed and began to pace about. "You will not have forgotten

39

our unwanted guest, Robin, and his marvellous machine . . .?"

"Of course not."

"By the way, I presume you've not sighted the latter again since its abrupt departure?"

"No," said Ashley, then added impatiently, "Get on with what you have to tell me."

"You will also remember—as I have no doubt you eavesdropped on all our conversations—his description of his life in Shangri La with the strange Eloi?"

"Yes, yes. So what?"

"Do you recall his mentioning that they have a store of human eggs and sperm in the habitat?"

"I . . . I think so. Why?"

"There it is! The source of your new body!"

The spider-mech scuttled towards him, at the same time extending a laser cutting tool. It backed him into a corner of the room. "Ashley, what . . .?"

"I may not be able to think as clearly as I used to, but I'm not a complete idiot!" she cried. "What good does some frozen sperm and eggs on a hidden, underwater habitat at the South Pole do me? Answer me quick, Milo, before I perform eye surgery on you!"

He held up his hands. "Take it easy! Let me explain."

"Go on."

"That habitat is full of new technology. Those intelligent, self-evolving programs Robin told us about would be capable of producing the equipment I require to transfer the encoding of your personality and memories from your bio-chip to a young, blank brain."

Ashley was quiet for a time as she digested what he'd said, then asked, "Is it possible?"

"Of course. No problem, providing I have the necessary equipment."

"I see. . . ." she said slowly. "But how will we find the habitat? That entire fleet of Sky Lords tried and failed."

"They were primitives. We have the technological means to track down Shangri La. We'll have Carl convert several of the spider-mechs into underwater drones. They'll search under the ice shelf for the habitat. When it's been located we'll bore through the ice with our lasers and force the habitat out of its cover."

"You make it all seem so simple."

"I've given it a lot of thought. Trust me."

"Hah!" But she did retract the cutting tool.

"So? Do we have a bargain?"

"I guess so."

"And do I get the girl?"

"Oh, all right."

Milo grinned. "Will you take me to their quarters? I want to give them the good news personally."

"You would. . . ."

Tyra blanched as Milo came through the door, much to his satisfaction. Shan, sitting next to her on the couch, merely gaped at him in disbelief. "How . . . how . . . did you get out?" asked Shan, haltingly.

Milo ignored him. He stood, hands on hips, staring hard at Tyra. Her growing fear and panic excited him. "Yes, it's me, Milo. Haven't I grown since you last saw me? Well past puberty now as you can see so I promise you my love-making will be somewhat more satisfactory than it was in the past. As I shall demonstrate now. . . ." He made a move towards her. Immediately Shan sprang up from the couch, blocking Milo's way. Milo grabbed him by the throat. He was taller than Shan now. And much, much stronger. "Situation has changed, my Minervan wimp. I'm back on top and that means you are in the shit." Then he picked him up and threw him across the room.

Tyra got up and ran to where Shan lay groaning. Milo walked over to them, took hold of the back of her neck as she knelt beside Shan and forced her upright again. She struggled but was helpless in his grip as he marched her into the bedroom. He slammed the bedroom door shut behind them.

Chapter Six:

Milo Haze, or rather James Gleick, emerged on the 'surface' of Belvedere. It was, in fact, the inner surface of the four-mile-long cylinder of the habitat. The 'ground' gently curved away from him to become a distant wall, then became the ceiling and then came all the way back again on the other side. In the novel that Milo had been reading, *A Trillion Tales of Light and Love*, the immortals' habitat contained trees, grass, even small rivers, but all Milo could see, apart from the glass strips that admitted reflected sunlight, were endless acres of drab plastic and metal.

The air was just as foul up here in the 'open' as it was down below. The bacteria in the air-recycling system, created centuries ago, had clearly undergone some sort of mutation and were no longer performing their function with one hundred percent efficiency. But as all forms of genegineering were banned on Belvedere Milo knew that there was no hope of the defect being rectified.

He walked to the nearby train station and, after a short wait, boarded a mono-rail train. It was, naturally, sexually segregated: men only in the first carriage, women only in the second. His destination was the Hall of Fathers. There was going to be yet another meeting about what was now always referred to as the Earth Problem. So far no decision had been made about how to respond to the radio signals that were being transmitted regularly from the planet. Despite their current religious and political differences, the Fathers had conferred with the ruling authorities on the other habitats—Cruise City, Starshine and Karaganga—who had been equally shocked by the phenomenon. As with the Fathers on Belvedere, the other rulers had kept the news of the signals from their populations at large, fearing it would cause social unrest. The Martian colonies, who were out of range of the Earth signals, had also been informed and their various ruling parties expressed similarly shocked reactions.

The other habitats had so far followed the Belvederians in not replying to the Earth people but Milo suspected that such uniform behaviour would not last much longer. One of the habitats was sure to respond soon though he knew it wouldn't be Belvedere. The Fathers regarded the Earth people as beyond redemption. One Father, at the initial meeting held to discuss the signals, suggested that it was all some kind of Satanic trick. The senders of the signals, said the Father, *claimed* they lived in an area that had been clear of plagues for hundreds of years but this might be a ruse to lure down to Earth the pure Belvederians in order to infect them with unholy sicknesses. That was why Milo had been invited to attend the meeting. As the habitat's leading medical expert his advice was sought on the matter. Surely it was impossible for any human beings to have lasted on the planet so long after the Gene Wars?

Milo had agreed that it did seem very unlikely but it was clearly not impossible. True, no radio signals had been picked up—until now—from anywhere on Earth for centuries but that might have been only because, while technological civilisation had been destroyed by the designer plagues and other terrors unleashed by the Gene Wars, humanity in its entirety had not been wiped out. Remnants had survived and slowly worked their way back to a technological level. Or rather, *one* community had, as the signals were only being transmitted from one location. From the North Eastern coast of Australia.

As soon as he entered the Hall of the Fathers conference room Milo detected an undercurrent of excitement. There

44

had been a new development, he felt sure. As he took his place at the table Father Massie, at the head of the table, looked at him and frowned. "We have been waiting for you, Brother James."

Milo bowed his head and said meekly, "I'm sorry. I came as fast as I could, Father Massie."

Father Massie made a sound of displeasure then said, "We shall now pray. . . ."

With his eyes closed and his hands pressed together, Milo tried to ignore Father Massie's droning and wondered what had happened. The praying went on for a long time. Finally Father Massie finished and said, "This meeting will now begin. Many of you already know what has happened. I have the grave duty to tell the rest of you that I have received a depressing message from the Karaganga habitat. . . ."

Milo leaned forward attentively. Anything that depressed Father Massie had to be worth listening to.

"They have acknowledged the signals from Earth," Father Massie told them. "They are in communication with the Earth people, or whatever they really are, even as we speak. But there is worse to come. They intend to take the Earth people at their word and accept that their particular area is free of plague. They are sending a ship to Earth."

Milo experienced a rush of emotion. Somehow, someway, he was going to *be* on that ship.

Ayla waited impatiently beside the submersible with Juli. Nearby swam Kell, head swivelling constantly as he kept a look-out for any sign of danger. He held a spear gun at the ready. Ayla and Juli were unarmed. Even with the Great Barrier Reef serving as a natural defence against the more extreme threats that now filled the world's oceans, it was still possible for squid, sea worms and other large and dangerous sea creatures to penetrate the waters between the Reef and the coast. Hence the need for the sea walls that protected Palmyra's inner waters which contained her fish farms.

Juli tapped her on her shoulder and pointed ahead but Ayla had already spotted the five vague forms approaching them. Ayla signalled to Kell and he nodded, then she and Juli gripped a handle each on the large wicker basket and began to swim slowly towards the five figures who had come to a halt about forty feet away. As they drew closer Ayla recognised the largest of the five as the one she had named Tiger. He was the leader of the sea people. Two of the four sea people accompanying him were female. Ayla raised her free hand in a salute. Tiger raised one of his own hands. The giant claws that protruded from his webbed fingers retracted in a peace gesture.

Ayla and Juli came to a stop and dropped the big square basket on the sandy sea bed. It was packed tight with freshly killed fish. Tiger swam forward to inspect the basket's contents, nodded his satisfaction then turned and gestured to the group behind him. The two females swam forward. They too carried something between them. They laid it down next to the basket of fish then swam quickly back to join the other two males. Ayla stared at the object and frowned. It was metallic, about three feet long and one foot wide. She looked at Tiger blankly and hand-signalled that she didn't know what it was. With a shake of his head, which she had learned to interpret as a gesture of annoyance, he swam next to the object, bent down and fiddled with something on its side. A lid flipped open and Ayla realised, finally, it was a container. She peered inside. She didn't know what she was looking at but she did know one thing for certain—it was a weapon of some sort. She nodded to Tiger, signalled gratitude then reached down to shut the lid. It was then that Tiger grabbed her arm. . . .

The sea people had been genegineered long ago by one or more of the Gene Corporations to operate their underwater installations, such as the mines and the vast fish farms that had existed before the Gene Wars. Though they preferred deeper water they could adapt to any pressure. Decades ago Tiger's particular group had decided to move closer ashore to escape the deteriorating conditions in the open ocean. While certain genegineered species flourished in the open sea ordinary fish species had dwindled and fish were the staple diet of the sea people. They had taken refuge in a huge sunken habitat that they found near the Great Barrier Reef. Originally they had launched raids on Palmyra's small fish farms, fish being scarce in the area of the Reef as well, and warfare had broken out between them and the humans. It was Ayla's late mother, Glynis, who had brought peace between the two groups. In an act of extreme bravery she had swum out alone to intercept a raiding party of sea people and had made them a peace offering in the form of a quantity of dead fish. The sea people had accepted the fish and departed. When they next returned they too brought a peace offering. It was a small computer.

It turned out that the sunken habitat, Japanese in origin, contained a great deal of equipment that was still in good condition despite the years underwater (from what little information the Palmyrians were able to glean from the sea people it seemed that much of the habitat was still watertight when the sea people found it; the Japanese, when their air system failed, preferred to stay and die on the sea bed than to risk the plagues loose on the surface). So had begun the long years of trading between the sea people and the humans which was now Ayla's responsibility (the leaders of the sea people—who had short life spans—made it clear they would deal only with women). There had been peace between them all that time. No sea person had attacked a human since the bad old days. Until now. . . .

Ayla was so surprised she almost lost her mouthpiece. She stared with stunned amazement into Tiger's round, fish eyes. What had she done wrong? What unknown taboo had she broken? Why was he attacking her? Or *was* he? Though his grip on her forearm was powerful he had kept his claws sheathed. Now she saw he was pointing over his shoulder, back out to sea where he had come from. Then he made the sign for danger. Three times. Then he released her, turned and swam away. His four people followed him.

"What was all *that* about?" Kell asked when they were back inside the submersible's cramped pressure hull. "For a moment or two I thought he was attacking you. I was just starting to head over when I saw him let you go."

Frowning, Ayla shook her head. "All I know is that he made the sign of danger three times. That means something *very* dangerous. And it must be inside the Reef or he wouldn't have told me about it. He was warning us."

"I was terrified," said Juli, as she started the submersible's engines. "He's never touched any of us before. None of them have."

"I think he grabbed my arm to get across how important his message was," said Ayla.

"But without knowing the nature of the threat what can we do about it?" asked Kell.

"I don't know," admitted Ayla. "I'll have to talk it over with Dad. . . ."

Ayla got another surprise when they reached land; her father wasn't at his usual post in the watch tower but was waiting for them on the beach. He looked excited.

As she was being helped by him down from the submersible she said, "Dad, something strange happened today during the exchange. Tiger—"

He didn't let her finish. "Marvellous news, darling! We picked up a reply from one of the space habitats!"

She gaped at him in astonishment. "We have?"

"Yes!" he said happily. "And not only that but they're

48

going to send an expedition down to us here!" He hugged her. "Darling, we're going to have *visitors*!"

"Of course, we must send a representative from Belvedere to take part in the Karaganga expedition to Earth," said Milo.

All faces around the table turned in his direction. Father Massie looked incredulous. He wasn't alone. Long seconds ticked by and then Father Massie said slowly, "Have you taken leave of your senses, Brother James? We want nothing to do with that world of the damned."

Milo glanced at the large metal cross that loomed over the table behind Father Massie's chair and said, "Isn't it our duty to assess the situation down there? There may be souls in that community who are not beyond redemption. And there is another aspect of the situation to be considered. If Karaganga forms some kind of alliance with the Earth people it would be useful if we had someone to keep an eye on developments." Milo paused to let the meaning of his words sink in. He was satisfied to see Father Massie's expression become thoughtful. Hooked. He continued, "Therefore I suggest that a Father volunteer to accompany the Karagangans to Earth. . . ." He paused again to let the buzz of whispering die down. He looked around the table. "It will be a dangerous mission, naturally, and there is a reasonable chance that death awaits on the planet but what greater honour could a Father of Belvedere attain than to perform this supreme sacrifice for God? And at the same time also perform a valuable service for Belvedere itself?"

Now there was silence in the bleak room. Fathers glanced at each other, their expressions troubled and perplexed. Finally all turned towards Father Massie who was still deep in thought. Over a minute passed before he spoke. "As outrageous as Brother James's suggestion may have seemed at first glance I believe he has a point. I am prepared to consider it seriously. And so should you all."

There were murmurs of assent, albeit much of it reluctant in tone.

"When is the Karaganga expedition due to take place?" Milo asked.

"In about two months," Father Massie replied. "They believe it will take them that long to convert their Mars ship into a vehicle capable of operating within the Earth's atmosphere."

Milo nodded. None of the habitats had kept their Earth shuttles. In the belief that they would never be needed again they had long ago been cannibalised for spare parts. He cleared his throat and looked Father Massie boldly in the eye. "Naturally I volunteer my own services in this expedition," he said.

Father Massie's reaction was predictable. He gave an exaggerated start of surprise then peered quizzically at Milo. "You *what*, Brother James?"

Calmly, Milo said, "I said I offer my own services in this dangerous enterprise. After all, as it was I who proposed that a Father accompany the Karagangans it is only fitting that I put my life on the line as well."

"But for what purpose?" asked the Father sitting on his left, an overweight and round-faced man called Shaw. A bigger sanctimonious prig than most of them, in Milo's opinion. "You are, forgive me, Brother James, just a mere Brother. You have no priestly authority. How could you provide possible salvation to the souls of these wretched Earth creatures?"

Milo turned and gave him a smile. "Forgive *me*, Father Shaw, but you fail to see my reason for volunteering. I volunteer not for the sake of the Earth people but for the sake of the brave Father who volunteers for this mission. I am, if you will forgive this brief lapse of modesty, the most knowledgeable medical practitioner on this habitat. If there are still plagues on the planet then I will be of invaluable help to the brave Father concerned." He turned back to

Father Massie. "I do think that the Father who goes on this mission does deserve to have my medical skills and drugs at his disposal at the very least."

Father Massie stared at Milo in silence. As he did so he played with his beard, tugging at it. Like his hair it was dyed grey. All the Fathers dyed their hair and beards grey in an effort to appear old and therefore more authoritative. As Milo could remember genuinely old people he thought they just made themselves look even more absurd. When Father Massie at last spoke he said, "I admit, Brother James, that I have had my doubts about you in the past. For nothing specific, you understand, just a vague feeling of unease. But this gesture of yours obliges me to see you in a new light. Very well then, I accept your brave offer. You will go to Earth, Brother James. Now let us pray. . . ."

Chapter Seven:

Jean-Paul was not enjoying being a Sky Lord. Too many people asking him questions he couldn't answer; too many people depending on him. The responsibility weighed down on him more heavily with every passing day. And with the weight of the responsibility came the constant pain of grief. No matter how hard he tried he couldn't get Dominique out of his thoughts. . . .

He surveyed the chaos of the control pod. Pieces of dismantled equipment everywhere and a maze of exposed wires and cables. The air in the pod was filled with angry voices as the engineers argued among themselves. Enough was enough. The fishing team would be getting impatient. He stepped forward and said loudly, "Well, what's the situation? Can we carry out the manoeuvre?"

The bickering died away as the engineers looked at each other to see who was going to answer his question. By some silent mutual consensus it fell to Marcel, a small, wiry man, to answer. He shrugged his shoulders and said, "We think we can but it will be dangerous."

"Tell me something new," said Jean-Paul wearily. He peered out through the pod wall at the ocean below. It had been near-catastrophe after near-catastrophe ever since they had blown up the computer. He was amazed they were still in the air. They had drifted almost helplessly for several days while the engineers struggled to repair the damaged control systems. Their prediction that they would achieve manual control 'in a matter of minutes' had proved to be drastically over-optimistic. The bomb had wrecked the entire computer system as well as destroying the Ashley and Carl programs and trying to control the vast airship without any computer aid at all was proving almost impossible. True, they had gained manual control of the rudders and elevators, but they had failed to get control of the thrusters and had been forced to shut down the power. With the power shut down the gas in the gas cells could no longer be temperature controlled and they had soon lost altitude. Only jettisoning a lot of equipment, combined with the skills of the helmsmen, had kept the airship from crashing.

By the time the engineers had managed to get direct control of two of the thrusters the North East Trade Winds had carried the *Lord Montcalm* far out over the Pacific Ocean. At that point Jean-Paul held a conference with his closest comrades to discuss their next move. It was decided to carry on over the Pacific in a south-west direction. To return to the North American continent held the risk that they would encounter another of the Ashley-controlled Sky Lords, and as they no longer had direct control over their laser system, assuming it was still working at all, they would come off second-best in any such encounter.

Their most immediate problem was food. Stocks were low and even with tight rationing it was unlikely there would be enough to sustain the airship's population. They'd lost a lot of people in recent months but there were still over eight hundred on the *Lord Montcalm*. Then someone came up with the obvious solution. *Fish*. They were flying over a damn ocean, for God's sake, it should be a simple exercise to hover over the water, lower a freight cradle to just above the surface and then dump nets and lines over the side. . . .

Yeah, simple in theory but harder to pull off in practice. But to give them their due the engineers had now managed to put another two thrusters on line and had sufficient control over the ship to have it hover. In theory.

"Okay," he told the engineers, "let's go for it. Signal the fishing team." He turned and walked to the rear of the pod.

53

The hole he'd blown in its side had been crudely patched up but air still whistled through. Made a sound like a woman's scream. Dominique. "But it was quick," someone had told him. Who? Oh, yeah, Eric. Eric who tried to stop him when he said he wanted to see her body. He'd insisted and Eric gave in. Saw the look in his eyes. They went up to the corridor where the bodies were laid out. Jean-Paul didn't recognise her when Eric pulled back the blood-stained blanket from her upper body. Being told it had been quick wasn't really much consolation; not when the woman you loved looked like she'd gone through a thruster fan. He missed her most at night; during the days he could distract himself with the endless problems of running the *Lord Montcalm* but at night he couldn't help but think of her. He slept fitfully. The most terrible moments were when he woke and reached out for her—for a few seconds he would wonder why he was alone in the bed and then he would remember. . . .

The whine of the thrusters changed pitch as the *Lord Montcalm* slowly juddered to a halt and then, hovering, began to descend towards the ocean. It stopped with a shudder some four hundred feet above the surface. Jean-Paul watched as a freight cradle appeared through one of the cargo hatches. There were twenty men on it, including Claude who had volunteered to lead the fishing team. Jean-Paul tried to pick him out from the other men but at this distance it was impossible. He could see, however, the large mound of netting that had been hastily constructed during the last few days.

The sea here was clear of the odious-looking algae that covered large areas of the ocean. Jean-Paul guessed that it was choking the life out of the sea as the blight did on land. He hoped there were still enough edible fish around to make their expedition worthwhile. The cradle was almost touching the surface of the sea. Someone waved to the operator above and it came to a halt, swaying on the end of its four cables. The men immediately began playing out the net. So far so good, Jean-Paul said to himself as he kept an anxious eye on the freight cradle far below. "Okay, start forward, but keep it slow," ordered Jean-Paul. The *Lord Montcalm* began to move again. The sea was relatively calm but he was worried that if the cradle touched the water the extra drag would snap one or more of the cables.

When the netting had been all played out Jean-Paul ordered them to halt the airship. Then the men below began to haul in the netting. That's when it happened. . . .

There was a disturbance in the water. It was in front of the cradle and the men didn't notice it. They were concentrating all their attention to the rear, to the net. Jean-Paul almost yelled out a warning but stopped himself at the last moment knowing it was useless. "Call the cargo hold!" he cried. "Tell them to start pulling up the cradle, now!"

"But surely they are still bringing the net in. . . ." said Marcel.

"Just do it!" His voice rose to a scream.

One of the engineers hurried over to where he was standing. "What is the matter?"

"Look!" cried Jean-Paul, pointing. A huge, grey-white shape was surfacing. It was at least four times the length of the cradle. Tentacles became visible, rising out of the water. One of the men saw them . . . alerted the others. Jean-Paul saw them reacting, pointing and gesticulating excitedly. He knew they were weaponless apart from some knives. He should have told them to take rifles. But who could have foreseen this . . .?

The cradle began to rise but it was plainly too late. A massive tentacle was already twisting upwards along one of the cables. Smaller tentacles were coming over the sides of the cradle. Jean-Paul felt a tremor run through the deck of the control pod.

"Holy Mary," whispered the engineer.

The cradle was no longer rising. Instead it was starting to

tilt. All the men went sprawling. One of the smaller tentacles fastened on a man, lifted him up and swiftly pulled him under the water. A second massive tentacle had appeared and was coiling its way up another of the cables.

"Jean-Paul!" cried Marcel, "The hoist operator reports that he can't raise the cradle any further! The creature weighs tons! He wants to know what to do!"

A good question, thought Jean-Paul as he saw a further two men plucked from the cradle.

As Jan sat chatting to Davin she realised why the programs had let her stay in Shangri La. It was certainly no act of kindness, she had known that from the beginning, and it wasn't even for Robin's benefit. She had just presumed that the programs' enquiries about her past were merely programmed acts of 'politeness' but now, suddenly, it all became clear. She was an invaluable source of information to them. Shangri La had been cut off from the rest of the world for centuries. The programs, in order to continue performing their prime function—the protection of the Eloi—as efficiently as possible, had a pressing need to know about the recent history and the present state of the planet to assess any potential dangers it posed for the Eloi.

"You were saying?" asked Davin, looking puzzled by her unexpected pause.

"Sorry, I just remembered something," she said quickly, annoyed with herself for not seeing the obvious sooner. She had been describing everyday life in the small community of Minerva, all that had remained of the once great feminist superstate. Davin seemed particularly interested in the Minervan men and now, with her new-found insight into the program's motives, she wondered why. "You were asking about our men . . . their personalities?"

"I asked if, in their modified form, they retained any capability of physical violence," repeated Davin.

"In theory, no, but . . ." She paused again as memories

came flashing back. She could see that awful day when the *Lord Pangloth* had bombed Minerva and the Sky Warriors had parachuted down to complete the slaughter. She remembered how shocked she had been, despite everything else that was happening, when she had seen a few Minervan men with weapons in their hands. It had gone against all she had been taught about the nature of Minervan males after they had been transformed by the Mother God. ". . . Some did fight, at the end, alongside Minervan women. I suppose they were throwbacks. We certainly had throwbacks among the male apes we used as workers. In fact we couldn't trust any of the male chimps once they reached a certain age. We penned them up as a matter of course and used only adult females." Another memory surfaced and she smiled to herself. "I myself was considered to be a throwback. Because of my small size. I was only as tall as the average Minervan man."

Davin said, "Throwbacks are inevitable thanks to random mutation over the years. But it should be possible to devise a genetic repair unit—a unit that would be designed to alter back periodically any acquired deviations in the DNA of a species."

Jan looked at the hologram. "Such a thing was clearly beyond the ability of Minerva's early genegineers when they designed the Minervan male," she said. "But why speculate about the possibility now? Surely it's too late to do anything for any species on the planet . . . or is it?"

"I don't follow you," said Davin, with a precisely weighted amount of innocence in his voice.

"I find that hard to believe," said Jan dryly. "But what I'm asking is why you just said what you said. Are you planning to do something about the outside world? I know it's within your powers to do so."

Davin shook his head. "It's been explained to you before, Jan. Our only interest is in the Eloi. It's the basis of our programming. We can't help ourselves. It's regrettable what

57

is happening to the world but it is outside our province. We exist only to take care of and protect the Eloi."

He sounded genuinely sorry but Jan wasn't fooled. She felt disgust for the cold, inhuman *thing* that manipulated this convincing image of a man from somewhere deep in the innards of the habitat. She took a deep breath and said angrily, "You'll have your protecting work cut out for you if Milo succeeds in finding this place."

"Ah, yes, this Milo of yours . . . a most interesting creature."

"Creature is the word for him all right," said Jan. "But I'm not sure about *interesting*."

"In your opinion he presents a serious threat to us?"

"Yes. As I've told you before, Milo is a serious threat to everyone. And he displayed great interest in Shangri La when he heard about it from Robin. I wouldn't be at all surprised if he came South to search for us."

"A whole fleet of Sky Lords searched for Shangri La, as you informed us, but without success."

"A whole fleet of antiquated airships manned by barbarians. The Sky Angel is different. It is brand new with a formidable weapons system. It is operated by programs like you. And Milo is different too. Again, like you, he isn't human."

Chapter Eight:

The meeting was a noisy one. Not everyone shared Lyle and Ayla's father's enthusiasm for the approaching visit from the spacers. Most vocal of the opponents was Jelker Banks. He had long been a severe critic of Lon Haddon and Ayla knew that his enmity sprang from his failure to be elected to the ruling sextet. He had infected his entire family, which was a large one, with his resentment and all the Bankses spent much effort in making life hard for Haddon and his family, now consisting of just Ayla and her older brother.

Banks, surrounded by his supporters on the opposite side of the meeting hall, was speaking now—or rather, yelling. ". . . And I say we could be exposing ourselves to terrible danger! How do we know we can trust these space people? We've only got their word that they mean us no harm! And Lon Haddon and his friends have swallowed their dubious assurances hook, line and sinker!" A roar of angry shouting rose up from his gesturing supporters. There were mutters of agreement from other parts of the hall. Lyle Weaver, seated in the Ruler's Chair, motioned for them to quieten down and indicated that Lon Haddon should reply. Ayla, perched near the top of the tiered row of seats, watched her father below her get to his feet. His voice, she noted worriedly, was sounding increasingly weary and hoarse.

"My honourable colleague is taking an unduly pessimistic view of the situation when he should be rejoicing at our good fortune. This contact with our brethren in the sky marks the beginning of a whole new future for us. Not just for us but the whole human race!"

There was some applause and several cheers. Jelker Banks, even though he hadn't been given permission to speak, interrupted: "So *you* say, Haddon! But how do we know for sure? We've only recently been delivered from the reign of the Sky Lord *Perfumed Breeze* and you want to hand us over to another conqueror!"

"What possible reason would the Karagangans have to conquer us?" cried Haddon.

"Same reason as the damned Sky People kept us under their heels—to supply them with food, clothing and goods in general!" replied Banks.

"Why would they need food or anything else from us? They've been self-sufficient for centuries!" Haddon pointed out.

"Maybe they're tired of eating recycled crap! I know I would be!" With this Banks drew much laughter from the crowd, and not just from his supporters.

Haddon waited for the laughter to die down, then said, "We have been speaking to them for three weeks now. I personally have spent many hours communicating with various Karagangans. We have built up a fairly accurate picture of their society and conditions in their space habitat. They admit their way of life is not a comfortable one but food is definitely not one of their problems. The genegineered bacteria in their food plants are still working efficiently and producing a wide variety of synthetic foods from recycled organic materials."

"Again, you only have their word for this!" cried Banks.

"And I believe them!" replied Haddon firmly. "We all should. They consider our existence, and our relatively advanced technological society, an encouraging sign that the world might be reclaimed from the scourges created by the Gene Wars. They are coming here to examine that possibility. Despite our achievements you know very well, Jelker Banks . . ." Haddon raised his arm and pointed at Banks, ". . . that we can't hope to hold out against the blight.

Conditions are worsening at an increasingly fast rate. You don't have to have lived as long as I have to see that. Without help from the spacers we . . . well, Palmyra, won't survive in the long run. We would be fools to reject their offer of joining up together."

Ayla stepped out onto the first floor verandah, two glasses of cold beer in her hands. Somewhere out in the blight land an animal was roaring out its displeasure. It sounded like one of the giant reptiles. It caused an unpleasant prickling sensation up her spine. Her father was slumped in a deckchair, staring out over the dark ocean. She gave him one of the glasses, drew another of the deckchairs closer to his and sat. She regarded him with a worried frown. "What are you looking so grim about? The vote went your way."

"Oh, I knew it would. And Lyle has the power of veto after all, but it's the amount of support Jelker has. It's growing and he increased it with tonight's performance. I'm worried he might cause problems when our space friends finally arrive."

She drank some of her beer. "I see," she said. "Well, I'm worried too."

He turned towards her. "About Jelker?"

"Oh, I'm always worried about him and his nasty brood. No, I'm worried that the subject of the warning from the sea people wasn't raised at the meeting. You said you'd arranged with Lyle to ensure that it would be."

"The, er, *debate* over the spacers took up too much time, I imagine. But I promise you it will be covered in the next meeting."

Both of them gave a slight start as a very large and angrily buzzing insect collided with the verandah netting and then flew away. Ayla then said, "The next meeting won't be for two weeks. We should be doing something *now*."

"Forgive me saying this, dear, but aren't you making more out of this than you need to? So the sea people are worried

61

about some new threat to their community. That's to be expected. The oceans are increasingly dangerous places, as you well know. Perhaps sea worms are becoming more prevalent in the sea people's sector. But the sea people are well equipped to defend themselves. They were designed to be. Apart from defending themselves against natural enemies they were further enhanced to repel sabotage parties from other sea installations when the rivalry between the Gene Corporations started hotting up. So I wouldn't be too concerned if I were you."

"Then why do they want us to supply them with weapons?"

"What?" Haddon was surprised.

"It's true. During our trading meet today their leader, Tiger, kept pointing at the spear gun that Kell was carrying. His meaning was quite clear. He wants similar weapons. Plenty of them."

"Why didn't you tell me about this?"

"I didn't have a chance to talk to you before the meeting. I intended to raise the matter when the subject of the sea people came up. As it didn't I couldn't." She shrugged.

Haddon frowned. "I just don't understand it . . . those long claws they have, like daggers, and those teeth. . . . Why would they *need* weapons now? They never have before."

"That's why I'm worried, Dad. And Tiger gave me the warning again. Same as last week. Grabbed my arm and pointed back out to sea. There's something else too. He's always accompanied by the two females. I think they're his wives. Well, today there was only one with him."

"There could be all sorts of explanations for that," said Haddon.

"Yes, but along with everything else I can only see it as a bad sign. Like his scars."

"Scars?"

"He's got nasty-looking long ones on his front. And

they're fresh. I know he's practically armour-plated but they made me shudder. The other males have got them too. Whatever caused them weren't sharks or sea worms."

Haddon drank more of his beer and was silent for a time. Then he said, "You are really concerned about all this, aren't you?"

"Yes. But so far, apart from Juli and Kell, I seem to be the only one. Lyle Weaver keeps brushing me off every time I try to talk to him about it and so do you. All you care about is the visit from our friends in space. Okay, I know it's a historic event and will mean a lot to Palmyra but we can't afford to ignore everything else that might be important."

He sighed and said, "Yeah, I know I've been completely wrapped up with the spacers but it's hard to think of anything else. It gives me hope, Ayla, *hope*. For the first time in oh, so many years I believe we might have a future. I don't include myself, of course, I mean you, Palmyra, the human race itself."

Ayla cringed inwardly. She didn't like it when he referred, even obliquely, to his recent birthday and its significance. She had never discussed it with him directly though she knew he was more than prepared to. She didn't want to think about it. The idea that he was going to die sometime between now and the next five years terrified her. She finished her beer quickly and stood. "I'm going to bed. We're doing an inspection of the outer wall tomorrow and I've got to make an early start. Please talk to Lyle about what I've told you tonight about the sea people."

"I will, darling. It's a promise."

"Good." She left the verandah quickly, not pausing to give him his usual goodnight kiss on the cheek.

Her father shook her awake. He looked grim in the early morning and she was immediately alarmed. "What's the matter? Are you all right?" she asked anxiously.

"I'm okay . . . *physically* anyway, but you've got to get up right away. We've got an emergency."

She was then aware that she could hear sirens. "Is it . . .?"

He nodded gravely. "Yes, it was picked up on the radar a short time ago. It's still a long way out to sea but it's definitely heading towards us. A Sky Lord."

Jean-Paul rubbed the bristle growing on his sunken cheeks as he gazed speculatively at the settlement on the coast below. "It looks prosperous. And big. Bigger than anything we had in the *Lord Montcalm*'s tribute territory in Canada. Bigger, in fact, than anything we've seen since leaving Canada."

Beside him, Emile lowered his binoculars and said excitedly, "Judging from the number of houses I would estimate the population at around five thousand. Several small factories. Very extensive agricultural area inland and look. . . ." He pointed down at the sea. ". . . Those structures. A whole system of sea defences, and fish pens too, by the look of it. These earthworms are really organised."

Jean-Paul agreed with Emile, who was now, with Claude dead, his second-in-command. This sprawling community did appear to be the best organised, and most prosperous, he had ever seen. "They don't have a Sky Lord," he said with sudden insight, "they haven't had one for some considerable time. That's why they look so wealthy."

"You could be right," said Emile. "But they have one now. Us. We still have plenty of bombs on board. We drop a few to show them we mean business then we send down an armed party—a large one—and ransack the place for everything edible."

"Yes, I suppose it's the only way," Jean-Paul said, reluctantly. In the old days, when Lord Montcalm and his nobles had ruled the airship, he hadn't given the groundlings a second thought. He despised the nobles, naturally, but his life as a soldier had been comfortable and easy and he

64

considered it only right that Sky People had natural dominance over those fated to grub for existence on the polluted ground. But since the *Lord Montcalm* had been conquered itself and the hated Ashley program had been installed to rule over them his attitude to the whole question of conqueror and conquered had changed, even if the conquered concerned were mere ground dwellers. . . .

"What do you mean you *suppose* so?" Emile asked him incredulously. "We're all near starvation, you included. Like me, you are skin and bone! You want to try fishing again?"

No, Jean-Paul certainly didn't want to try fishing again. The disaster of their one and only attempt was still painfully sharp in his mind. It made him ill every time he recalled how he had watched helplessly from the pod as the giant squid pulled his men into the sea. There were still some men in the freight cradle when the cables finally snapped from the strain and the cradle fell into the water. Jean-Paul watched wordlessly as the remaining men were pulled under. Then he said curtly, "Bomb it!" By the time they did eventually drop several bombs into the sea the creature had already disappeared from view and Jean-Paul doubted if the bombs had any effect.

He was aware that Emile was gripping his arm. "We're losing people every day from sickness and malnutrition," said Emile urgently. "Coming across this place is a Godsend! Yes, a gift from God Himself! And we must take it! What possible alternative is there, Jean-Paul?"

"We could ask them for food," he said quietly.

Emile stared at him, horrified. "The lack of nourishment is affecting your mind, my dear friend! Ask them? *Ask* them? And you think they would simply hand food over to us? Voluntarily, to Sky People?"

Jean-Paul sighed. "No, you're right, of course. Prepare the landing party . . . and the bombs. We will attack as soon as possible."

Chapter Nine:

Milo Haze faced his class. It consisted of four women and six men. The women sat on one side of the small, severely functional lecture room, the men on the other, divided by an aisle. Among the women was Sister Anna. Her period of solitary confinement was over and she had rejoined the class. She consistently tried to avoid meeting his eyes so he amused himself by trying to catch her out.

"Good day, my dear Brothers and Sisters," he said cheerfully and gave them a beaming smile. As he scanned each of their faces he was rewarded by a brief eye contact with Sister Anna. He saw her cheeks redden as she quickly averted her eyes to her tightly clenched hands resting on her lap. "With permission from the Fathers I am altering today's listed subject. Instead, I am going to talk about something entirely different." He paused as their faces registered surprise then went on, "I am sure you have all heard the news that I will be accompanying Father Shaw on a trip to Earth, yes?"

They all gave hesitant nods. Poor Father Shaw, thought Milo happily, was definitely not as eager as Milo to participate in the coming mission to the Mother Planet; on the contrary, his face had turned a shade of metallic grey when Father Massie informed him that his name had been selected, on a random basis, by CenCom. It was clear he expected to meet his death on the planet. Milo planned to ensure he was not disappointed.

Milo went on, "Well, today I am going to discuss certain medical aspects of the Gene Wars and their aftermath. Now you all know the causes of the Gene Wars, don't you? You, Brother John, please stand and tell us. . . ."

Brother John stood. He was an overweight young man in his mid-twenties. His obesity interested Milo as, in theory, obesity shouldn't exist among Standard Primes. Brother John was living proof that regressive traits were appearing among the human population of Belvedere as well as among the designer bacteria that performed so many vital life-supporting functions within the habitat. Throwbacks, mused Milo, and wondered if Brother John was related in some way to the plumpish Father Shaw.

The young man cleared his throat and said, "Uh, well, Brother James, the Gene Wars were started by the godless, Satan-infested people who ruled the Earth. They wanted total power over their enemies. They encouraged their genegineers to create ever more dangerous versions of the living things that were all abominations in the eyes of God. Only God has the right to create life and these people damned themselves forever with their acts of defiance. As punishment, God turned his back on the people of Earth and the planet was ravaged by the terrible plagues created by the genegineers. Our ancestors here in Belvedere were spared so that they, and we, and the people who live in the other habitats and colonies, could bear witness to the terrible crimes against God carried out by those of Earth and atone for them. . . ."

"Thank you, Brother John. Eloquently spoken. You may sit down." You stupid, *fat*, throwback. "But to be just a little more precise the Gene Wars were caused by organisations known as the Gene Corporations. These were huge, international companies who made their fortunes from gene-gineering and were very powerful as a result. There was a great deal of rivalry between the evil (*ha!*) people who ran these Corporations. They stole genegineers from each other, had their rivals' key personnel assassinated, sabotaged each other's operations (*my speciality*, remembered Milo with

67

pleasure) and generally carried out a form of undercover warfare. Then the warfare broke out into the open and all the remaining independent states were dragged into it. Biological killing machines were unleashed—on the ground, in the air and in the seas. At first there was an agreement between everyone that bacteriological and viral weapons would not be used but, inevitably, one Corporation broke the rule and the others swiftly followed suit. Thus the plagues began. . . .

"The designer plagues, as they were called, were dispersed in a variety of ways that ranged from the ingenious to the crude. The plagues themselves varied too; some were swift-acting, others had longer incubation periods. One type, known as the 'Black Death', was similar to bubonic plague, the original Black Death. It produced a high fever and acute, painful swellings in the armpits, groin and neck of the victims—the lymph nodes. Dark patches from bleeding into the skin were the reason for the name. The new version had a one hundred percent death rate among its victims and killed within three to four days. It had been designed to be resistant to the existing drugs of the day, as were all the designer plagues. A much faster-acting plague was known as the 'Lightning Bug'. It was a virus, aerially dispersed. Anyone in the dispersal area immediately collapsed, suffering from severe convulsions and vomiting. Death occurred within minutes, the victims choking on their own vomit."

He paused for effect and glanced at Anna. He had caught her off guard again. She was looking very pale but immediately her cheeks began to colour as she looked quickly away. He smiled to himself and continued, "Then there was a very efficient fungal spore, also aerially dispersed, that, when inhaled, quickly covered the lining of the lungs with a fungal growth that increasingly restricted the sufferer's breathing. Death normally took place within twenty-four hours.

"Most of the plagues were designed to have a short lifespan. That is, the bacteria and the viruses were designed to be effective for, say, only a matter of days before they would disperse and self-destruct. But some, either by design or mutation, were able to reproduce indefinitely just like naturally occurring bacteria and viruses. As a result, even when the Gene Wars were over—and they lasted only seven months—some plagues continued to spread. Our ancestors here on Belvedere could only watch as human civilisation on Earth slowly died out. They, and we, presumed that all of humanity on the planet had been extinguished and Belvedere, along with other habitats, ceased paying attention to Earth centuries ago. But now we have learnt that some people *did* survive: the people who are sending the radio messages. And they also say that the plagues died out a long time ago. They say that they are perfectly healthy and we should have no fear of infection. Well, that is what Father Shaw and I will find out when we go to Earth."

A male student raised his hand. "Yes, Brother Daniel?" said Milo.

Brother Daniel said hesitantly, "It is said, Brother James, that it all may be a Satanic trick. That these creatures are damned and are trying to lure down the people of the habitats to infect them with their corruptions."

"Well, if that is the case and Father Shaw and I return to Belvedere infected with some ghastly Earth disease I shall be counting on you, my dear students, to use your medical skills to the best of your ability," he told them and gave them a benign smile. They stared back at him, appalled. They clearly didn't appreciate the joke.

The Sky Lord, which had been hovering broadside to Palmyra out over the sea, began to swivel its bow towards the town. "Here it comes," said Haddon, who was watching through a narrow slit in the command bunker's thick wall. "This had better work."

"We can only trust in God," said Lyle Weaver, who was watching through a similar slit beside him.

"I prefer to put my trust in those shells," muttered Haddon.

"Well, we shall soon find out if your idea about them is a good one," said Weaver. "I'm giving the order to fire, *now*." He switched on his microphone. "Attention all batteries. Open fire. I repeat, *open fire!*"

Palmyra appeared deserted. The streets were empty. The bulk of the population had retreated underground. But as the shadow of the giant airship began to encroach upon Palmyra something began to happen in six separate locations in the town. Camouflaged netting, false roofs and walls were hastily removed, revealing six gun emplacements. Each artillery piece was manned by a crew of three. The barrels of the guns were aimed at the looming Sky Lord. All began to fire. Loud booms rolled across Palmyra and buildings shook.

"The fools are shooting at us!" exclaimed Emile and gave a contemptuous laugh. "Don't they know it's a waste of time? Our automatic defences won't . . . *Christ!*" He had felt the impact of shells smashing into the hull of the *Lord Montcalm*. He stared in astonishment at Jean-Paul. "The lasers! They aren't working!" But even as he spoke a laser beam shot out from somewhere above the control pod and detonated a shell before it could reach the Sky Lord. Then another beam destroyed a second approaching shell . . . but other shells were still getting through and smashing into the hull. "What the hell is happening?" he cried.

"I don't know," said Jean-Paul grimly. Then, "Helmsmen, reverse thrusters! Get us out of range! Fast!"

There was cheering in the command bunker. Lyle Weaver, pummelling Haddon's shoulder, cried, "They *are* working, thank God! They are!"

"Most of them, anyway," said Haddon matter-of-factly as he watched more explosions flowering on the hull of the sluggishly retreating Sky Lord. Very few of the shells were being intercepted by the airship's lasers. Inwardly, Haddon felt extremely pleased with himself. His idea on how to overcome the automatic defence system of a Sky Lord was being proved correct with a vengeance.

When the *Perfumed Breeze* had failed to appear on schedule all those years ago and then continued to remain mysteriously absent Haddon had proposed that the Sky Lord's absence provided the opportunity for preparing some sort of effective means of defence against it. Most were sceptical about his proposal. The laser system made a Sky Lord invulnerable. The system would automatically destroy any object, from the size of a small bullet on upwards, approaching a Sky Lord unless it was a living organism or contained a living organism above a certain size (generally considered to be that of a small bird). This humane system was a hangover from the period long before the Gene Wars when the giant airships served as both cheap transporters of freight and food and aerial shelters in times of natural disasters. The Sky People, who took over the airships after the Gene Wars to escape the plagues, were never able to gain direct control of the lasers.

Knowing that they had the technological capability to build crude but effective artillery pieces, Haddon first thought of putting small animals inside the shells but an engineer pointed out to him that the animals would not survive long enough to be of any use. By the time they were detected by the airship's sensors they would have been killed by the g forces caused by the firing of the shells. Haddon continued to wrestle with the problem, then a possible solution occurred to him. Palmyra had no true genegineers but several of its technicians knew enough about biology to be able to maintain the various genegineered micro-organisms that performed functions ranging from the purification of sea water to beer-making. At Haddon's urging they supplied him with organic material capable of surviving

71

independently for long periods, provided it was regularly fed with nutrients. Haddon and his assistants inserted amounts of this material into the specially designed shells. Test firings proved that the shock of discharge didn't kill it but he had no firm proof that the shells would fool a Sky Lord's defence sensors. Until now. . . .

"Look! It's alight!" shouted someone behind Haddon. It was true. Flames were flickering along one side of the Sky Lord as it slowly reversed out to sea. Haddon could hear its thrusters straining to move the huge hull faster but it was too late. One or more of the shells had penetrated a gas cell filled with hydrogen. Maybe, mused Haddon, the entire ship was filled with hydrogen. If so, then those on board stood little chance of survival. Suddenly his feeling of elation evaporated. People, lots of people, would soon start to die, thanks to him. Women and children as well as men. So what that they were Sky People, the historical oppressors of his own people, they were still human beings. It was absurd for human beings still to be killing each other while their world died around them.

The flames were now racing across the side of the hull and Haddon saw a thruster break loose and go hurtling in a crazy pattern across the sky before plunging into the sea. He wondered where the Sky Lord had come from. It plainly wasn't the *Perfumed Breeze*. Wrong colours. Would he feel so uncomfortable about the doomed airship if he knew the cruel Warlord Horado was on board? Probably not. . . .

"We've lost all thruster power on the port side!" yelled one of the helmsmen. "And we're losing height!"

Emile came rushing down the stairs. "It's chaos up there, Jean-Paul! Cells Three and Four alight! What can we *do*?"

Jean-Paul, his gaze fixed on the town that continued to fire at them, said calmly, "We can do nothing now. It's over. I guess I wasn't fated to be a Sky Lord." Then, louder, he said, "We must tell the people to abandon ship. . . ." As he reached for the microphone there was an enormous sound. The sound was so loud it blew him backwards across the control pod. Then came blankness.

"Jean-Paul! Jean-Paul! You must wake up!" Someone was slapping his face. He opened gummed eyes with difficulty. His ears were ringing. There was smoke in the pod. He coughed. Emile was leaning over him. There was a large, ragged hole in Emile's left cheek. Jean-Paul could see Emile's teeth through it. "What happened?" he croaked.

"Shell exploded in here. Everyone else is dead and the ship is out of control. You must get up. . . ." Emile coughed. ". . . We're going to hit the sea soon. . . ." He pulled violently at Jean-Paul who managed to get to his feet. The floor of the pod was at an acute slant to port. They staggered with difficulty towards the stairs. Through the smoke Jean-Paul saw that the entire front of the control pod was gone. A helmsman lay on the floor, a human-shaped meat carcass. The other helmsman was gone, presumably blown out of the pod. They stepped over the body of one of the engineers lying at the base of the stairs. In contrast to the ravaged helmsman he appeared untouched but he was plainly dead. Jean-Paul was about to grasp the stair railing when the *Lord Montcalm* was shaken by a massive explosion and instantly the bow started to drop. Both he and Emile were sent sliding along the floor.

Jean-Paul tried in vain to stop his inexorable slide towards the shattered front of the pod. It seemed as if the airship was in the process of standing on its nose. Ahead, he saw the body of the helmsman disappear through the gaping hole. He heard Emile shouting something behind him, then suddenly he too was falling through empty space. He screamed.

Chapter Ten:

The Sky Angel hung suspended in the air some thousand feet above the Ross Ice Shelf. It was a beautiful day with the clear sky above a brilliant blue. Several laser beams were blazing down from the Sky Angel, causing clouds of steam to billow up from the ice. In the Angel's control pod Milo Haze peered at the growing steam cloud with mounting frustration. "Shit," he muttered.

"Same thing is happening as before," said Ashley, sulkily.

"I can see that," said Milo. Why hadn't this problem occurred to him when he first formulated his plan? Simply use the lasers to bore through the ice shelves? Yeah, easy. Except that the vaporised ice where the lasers hit produced a cloud of vapour and the vapour grew thicker until the laser beams were diffused to the point where they were useless.

"This is a waste of time," Ashley said and shut off the lasers. "Any more bright ideas? So far none of them is working too well."

"I wouldn't say that. My idea about the drones worked."

"Oh really?" scoffed Ashley. "Every one we sent out disappeared."

"Yes, but they all disappeared in *this* area . . . under the Ross Ice Shelf. So that's where the habitat must be." He gestured at the white expanse of snow and ice. "Down there somewhere, under the ice."

"Down there somewhere," repeated Ashley sarcastically. "That's marvellous, except for the fact that the ice shelf covers hundreds of square miles. And even if we knew the exact position of the habitat we couldn't get through the ice."

"There must be a way. Don't worry."

"*You're* the one who should be worrying, Milo. You don't come through with what you promised and you lose all your little privileges, including, maybe, your life. I might leave you down there on the ice."

Milo was silent. At least, he thought, she was being rational today. She had been showing increasing signs of instability recently. Sometimes she wouldn't respond to him at all, and at night now she was in the habit of singing ghastly nursery rhymes for hours at a time. He ran his hand over his bald head and thought hard. After a while he said slowly, "Right, the first problem is to locate the habitat. . . ."

"I *know* that, you idiot. That's what we've been trying to do. But you're not converting any more of my spiders into drones. I've got only twenty-nine of them left and we're also running out of spider spare parts."

Milo glanced down at the spider-mech standing next to him—his escort, there to ensure he didn't pull out Ashley's software and jump up and down on it—and gave it a pat on the top of its spherical body. It twitched menacingly in response. "No, I didn't plan to. Another approach is needed. I've remembered something from the distant past; a technique of ascertaining what lies beneath the ground, or in this case, ice, by means of sending seismic waves down through it. The waves move at different speeds through different substances. We'll be able to determine the thickness of the ice, the depth of the water, and the position of the habitat itself when we hit on the right sector."

"Oh sure," she sneered, "and just where do these seismic waves come from?"

"From small explosive charges. Set into the ice. We'll have Carl design and build the necessary monitoring equipment. He's sure to know how. He does, after all, know everything. Then we'll send out the spiders over the ice shelf and have them carry out the tests sector by sector. They should be safe above the ice. Take some time but I'm sure it will work."

Ashley, after a pause, said, "Okay, so what if it does, how do we get to the habitat? The lasers are useless."

Milo grinned as he had a sudden flash of inspiration. "Of course! The answer was staring us in the face . . . well, face in my case, in your case the term is redundant. . . ."

"Oh, shut up! Just tell me what the answer is!"

"The answer is Carl. I just said that he knows everything. So let me speak to him."

Grudgingly she said, "All right. . . ."

Carl's bland voice filled the pod. "Yes, Milo?"

"You no doubt heard what we were discussing. How do we get through the ice when we locate the habitat?"

"With the lasers, Milo."

"Good grief, he's as bad as you," muttered Ashley.

Alarmed, Milo said, "We've already tried that, Carl. The steam vapour blocks—"

"The lasers will have to be projected through optical fibres, Milo," said Carl.

"Of *course*!" cried Milo, driving his fist into his palm. "It's so bloody obvious. We lower several lengths of fibre optics down to the ice, fire the lasers down through them, and as the ice melts we continue to lower the fibres. No matter how much steam is produced it won't make any difference! And Christ, this ship's control system consists entirely of fibre optics so there surely must be some spare lengths in storage."

"There are," confirmed Carl.

Milo laughed. "Then we are home free! Nothing can stop us. Soon, Ashley, you'll be flesh and blood again, I guarantee it. And then I shall do you the favour of giving you the sexual experience of several lifetimes."

76

"What?" She sounded revolted. "You think I'd let you make love to me? Ugh!"

He actually felt offended by her reaction. "And what's wrong with the idea?"

"I've seen what you get up to with Tyra. And besides, I don't find you physically attractive. On the contrary, in fact."

"Tyra's different, she's nothing but a plaything," he said, irritated. "And beggars can't be choosy. Maybe it hasn't come to your attention that there's a severe shortage of men around here. Or do you fancy screwing that Minervan wimp, Shan?"

"Yes, I'd prefer going to bed with him than *you*," she said primly.

Milo fought to keep his temper under control. The silly bitch had been nothing but an electronic squiggle in a bio-chip for centuries and here she was acting as if she was too good for him! At least he had the satisfaction of knowing she would never live and breathe again as a creature of flesh and blood. Even if the habitat contained the means of growing her a new body he would see to it that it never happened. All he cared about was getting his hands on the Toy and plundering what other technological treasures he might find. He decided it would be diplomatic to change the subject: "What's the latest on that radio traffic you've been monitoring? Still going on at the same level of activity?"

"No, there's been a change today," said Ashley, sounding bored. "One-way only. The spacers are transmitting but the people down here aren't responding. Not yet, anyway."

Milo frowned. "Curious. Maybe they're having equipment trouble." When some weeks ago, just after they had arrived at Antarctica, Ashley reported that Carl had intercepted radio messages going back and forth between a location on Earth and a space habitat Milo had been very surprised. It seemed impossible that any ground community retained the technical ability to build radio equipment. He asked to listen

77

in, Ashley obliged, and he soon established that the source of the Earth signals was a community situated in the old Japanese state of Noshiro in Australia, while the habitat involved was the Russian one, Karaganga. He was very intrigued when he later learnt that the Karagangans intended to mount an expedition to the Earth. He wasn't sure he liked the idea. He had suggested to Ashley that they temporarily suspend their search for the undersea habitat, take a quick trip up to Australia and raze this uppity community to the ground before it could join forces with the spacers, but Ashley had refused.

Later still he had been amused to hear that two representatives from his former home for over a century, Belvedere, would be accompanying the expedition. "*Belvedere!*" he had exclaimed. "God, what a hole!" He hadn't thought about the place in a long time. It had been a prison. Compared to Belvedere the Martian colonies, for all their shortcomings, were like a holiday resort. And the way things were going before he left, it was clear that the religious nuts that ran Belvedere were going to tighten the screws still further. Then he remembered Carla Gleick. Dispassionately, he wondered what her fate had been. He also wondered idly what had become of his cutting. . . .

"Keep monitoring the signals," he said to Ashley. "Let me know if anything interesting comes up. I'll go to the workshop and get Carl started on those seismic devices and then I'm going to take a break, if that's all right with you."

"Okay," said Ashley, with reluctance.

"Hi, honey! I'm home!" cried Milo with exaggerated cheerfulness as he entered the living room. Tyra was standing at the window with her back to him. He saw the muscles tense in her neck at the sound of his voice. She was wearing a full-length white gown made of synthetic silk. She didn't turn. He crossed the room towards her. "What? No cries of delight at my return? No expressions of joy that you are

78

once again in the presence of the one who so dominates your heart?"

She remained silent and still didn't turn. He went up behind her, took her by the shoulders and gently turned her around. She refused to look at him, keeping her eyes downward. He observed that the bruise around her right eye was fading rapidly. He brushed it with his fingertips. She flinched. "Poor Tyra," he said softly. Then he took hold of her hands and turned them round. Also fading were the scars on her wrists. She had tried to kill herself a month ago. When she'd regained consciousness he'd told her that if she tried to do it again he would remove one of her beloved Shan's limbs. And if she actually succeeded in committing suicide he would flay him to death very slowly. There had been no more attempts.

"Look at me," he ordered.

She raised her face to meet his. Her wide brown eyes were full of fear. He was reminded of a terrified young doe. "Why do you enjoy hurting me so much?" she asked, in a breathless, frightened little voice. It amused him to ponder on her question. Because, he said to himself, your helplessness, your meekness, your vulnerability, your powerlessness simply and purely *provoke* me into wanting to hurt you. Odd that, because in many species of mammals, such as wolves, a show of submission—such as rolling on your back and exposing a vulnerable abdomen or throat—caused an attacker of the same species to cease attacking—but with humans . . . well, *men*, any sign of submission often had the opposite effect. Aloud, he told her, "Everyone has to have a hobby," and took hold of the top of her gown.

Ayla listened tensely as Lyle Weaver's voice came over the loud-speaker in her shelter. "People of Palmyra, the danger is over! The Sky Lord has crashed in flames beyond the outer sea wall. We can see some survivors in the water. I

79

want volunteers to man the boats and bring them in. But be sure to take weapons with you. . . ."

She turned and excitedly said to Kell, "Are you game?"

He nodded. "Sure."

"Then let's get going," she said and headed for the ladder. They were both carrying spear guns. If the cannons had failed and the Sky Lord had landed troops in Palmyra, she and Kell would have joined with the rest of the adult population of Palmyra in resisting the invaders.

As they ran towards the sea front they saw other people hurrying in the same direction. A yell from behind them caused them to turn and look. It was Juli, running to catch up with them. She too was clutching a spear gun. "We won! We won!" she cried. "Isn't it great?"

"It sure is!" laughed Ayla.

When they emerged on the sea front they came to a halt, in common with the others who had arrived before them. They all stared silently out to sea. It was an awesome sight. . . .

The Sky Lord lay in the sea about a mile and three quarters from the coast. Most of its vast, crumpled form was visible above the water. The airship was ablaze from bow to stern and the water around it was steaming. As Ayla watched, the great tail fin slowly crumpled and fell into the sea. How could there be any survivors in the inferno, she wondered. Kell snapped her out of her trance-like state by grabbing her arm. "Come on . . . the boat sheds!"

By the time they'd reached the outer wall and were passing through the gate the Sky Lord had been reduced to a skeletal mass of twisted metal. But the wreckage continued to burn fiercely and the water around it boiled. There were two, faster, boats ahead of them but their ten-foot dinghy with its powerful little motor had easily outstripped most of the small fleet heading for the downed Sky Lord. "I don't think there will be many survivors," said Kell as he peered ahead.

"Why not?" Ayla asked him.

"When would Sky People get the chance to learn to swim?" They were still some considerable distance from the wreckage when Kell spotted the first of the bodies. He tapped Ayla on the shoulder and pointed. She looked and saw someone floating face-down in the water about twenty yards to starboard. They both shouted instructions to Juli who was steering from the stern. Juli managed to bring the boat alongside the body and Kell leaned over the side and hauled it upright in the water. They saw it was a man. His head lolled at an unnatural angle from his neck and he had a terrible hole in one of his cheeks. "Dead," said Kell curtly. "Neck broken. The fall must have done it." He let the corpse ease back into the water where it assumed its original position, face-down. Ayla shivered. The image of the dead man's eyes remained fixed in her mind. But worse was to come.

As they continued they encountered more corpses floating in the water, as well as debris from the airship. Now they could feel the heat from the burning wreckage and hear the fierce crackling and hissing. Clouds of steam and smoke drifted around them. The bodies they encountered from then on were badly charred and it was impossible to tell whether they were male or female. Ayla had to look away when they passed the blackened body of a small child.

The great skeletal mass of slowly disintegrating wreckage now towered over them and Kell cautioned against going any closer for the time being in case a section of it should collapse in their direction. Juli saw that the two boats ahead of them had had a similar notion and were moving away along the side of the airship while maintaining a safe distance from it. Then Ayla heard a cry. It came from nearby in the water. She looked. At first all she could see was some floating debris—a burnt wicker chair and pieces of planking—then she spotted a head bobbing in the water beside it. "Over there!" she cried to Juli, pointing. As the boat neared the survivor Ayla saw that it was a woman and that she wasn't as badly burnt as the corpses had been, though her face was covered with ugly blisters. The woman raised an equally blistered arm out of the water.

Ayla leaned far over the side of the boat and reached out with her own hand. She grasped the woman's wrist. "I've got you!" she cried to the woman. Ayla pulled hard . . . and the skin of the woman's wrist and hand slid off like a glove. Ayla fell backwards into the boat. She gazed with horror at the grey wodge of dead skin she was holding. With a cry of disgust she flung it away. Then she turned her head and vomited into the bottom of the boat.

They pulled four people from the water—all of them suffering from burns or scalding in various degrees—then decided to head back. The waters around the wreckage were now dotted with boats. And there were other things in the water—sharks. They had spotted the fins of several of them.

Ayla sat in the bow, trying not to listen to the moans of the four Sky People huddled behind her. She still felt sick. And still ashamed at her reaction when she'd tried to pull the first woman into the boat. The woman, Kell told her, had then vanished under the water. All trace of those feelings of excited triumph that she'd experienced when first sighting the Sky Lord burning in the sea were gone.

She stiffened when she heard another cry for help. It was a man's voice. She didn't want to see another person suffering from terrible burns. Kell guided Juli to the source of the cries. Reluctantly, Ayla looked at the man as Kell hauled him on board. She was immediately relieved. He didn't appear to have any burns at all. And despite the gauntness of his face and his dazed expression he was, she realised, rather handsome. As he lay gasping in the boat between her and Kell she reached over and put her hand on his forehead. "It's okay, you're safe now," she told him.

He focused his eyes on her and managed a strained smile. "*Merci*," he gasped.

Chapter Eleven:

The bone-shaking impact with the water temporarily stunned Jean-Paul. The next thing he knew he was underwater and drowning. He struggled upwards and managed to get his head above the surface but, despite all his frantic efforts, immediately began to sink again. He realised his padded one-piece suit and boots were pulling him under. He took a last breath and let himself sink. Forcing himself to fight down the panic that threatened to overwhelm him, he first removed his boots as he sank, and then struggled out of the sodden, heavy suit. Once free he was able to shoot back to the surface.

Kicking and thrashing, he looked up to see the *Lord Montcalm* passing above him, flaming debris falling from it. He realised that its bow would soon hit the water. People were jumping from it. None had a parachute. Ashley had had her spider-mechs confiscate and destroy all the parachutes to deter escape attempts. He remembered Emile. He started shouting out his name, hoping that he had survived the fall as well, but there was no answer. Jean-Paul looked towards shore. Even the outermost of the sea walls seemed a long way away. No chance of his making it there; he was barely managing to keep his head above the surface. And he was tiring rapidly. He wondered if the ground dwellers would send help. He couldn't blame them if they didn't.

Suddenly a powerful vibration spread through the water and then came a deep rumbling. He turned to see the bow of the *Lord Montcalm* crumpling into the sea. To his alarm he saw the burning stern was directly overhead. Instinctively, he adopted a kind of dog-paddle, propelling himself slowly through the water. He lost all sense of time as he concentrated solely on getting himself out from under the stern before the entire airship settled into the sea. . . .

Finally he was so exhausted he couldn't go any further. The sea wall seemed no closer. He glanced over his shoulder. He was no longer in danger of being caught under the descending tail section of the burning airship. The *Lord Montcalm* was still moving forward as it settled into the sea. When the tail section did come down, with much screeching of crumpling girders in the lower tail fin and hissing as the water around it turned to steam, it was well over a hundred yards away.

But his relief didn't last long. His limbs were growing numb from all the exertion. He knew he couldn't stay afloat for much longer. Then something bumped him on the back of the head. Thinking he was about to be attacked by a sea creature he thrashed wildly about, trying to see what it was . . . .

It turned out to be a section of observation deck planking from the ship. He clung to it gratefully. After that he began to black out, only reviving each time his grip on the planking started to weaken and his mouth and nose filled with water. Then he heard voices. Finally, with a great deal of effort he raised himself up as high as he could on the planking so he could see above the small waves. A boat. It was heading back to shore and would pass near him. He cried out.

The boat turned in his direction. It drew alongside him. A young, bare-chested black man reached over the side and hauled him, with powerful arms, up out of the water. Jean-Paul sank gratefully into the bottom of the boat and was about to drift out of consciousness again when he felt a cool hand touch his forehead. A girl's voice. She spoke a version of Americano. She was reassuring him. With difficulty he focused his eyes. He saw a young girl. She was wearing blue shorts and nothing else. Her lithe, muscular body was very tanned and her black hair was cropped short. Her face could have been described as ordinarily pretty but what lifted it out of the ordinary were her striking, oriental-shaped blue eyes. He managed to say, "*Merci*," and then lost consciousness altogether.

Robin was showing no improvement. If anything he was growing worse. He was listless and showed hardly any interest in anything, including her. He was spending even more time in bed and most of it sleeping. She complained constantly to the programs but they all said there was nothing more they could do for Ryn, as they called him. She didn't believe them, but didn't know why they were lying. She became obsessed with trying to determine the true nature of the programs but trying to penetrate their façade of humanity was frustratingly impossible. They never slipped up. Typical had been yesterday's argument with Davin in the recreation room. . . .

"Admit it!" she said angrily. "It irks you to have to pretend you're human all the time. It is a false role imposed upon you by your programming and you resent it."

Davin appeared to be sprawled comfortably on a low couch. He looked both relaxed and slightly amused. The illusion was perfect. He gave her a condescending smile, which added to her fury, and said mildly, "To be capable of being 'irked' or 'resentful' I would have to be human, wouldn't I? See, even you are endowing me with human qualities."

"No I wasn't!" she protested. "I mean that you resent your conditioning in . . . *your own way*."

"And what way would that be?" he enquired in the same annoyingly mild tone of voice.

There was a long pause before she admitted, "I don't know."

"Of course not. Humans are unable to conceive of a form

of consciousness different from their own. Therefore they project their humanity onto everything else." He smiled again. "The need to anthropomorphise everything is a very basic human quality. From the beginning mankind attributed human characteristics to animals, trees, the sun, the moon, the gods and eventually . . . God. The monotheistic Gods of the Bible and the Koran are very human in their foibles. But the need to anthropomorphise later extended to scientists as well. There was once a theory called the anthropic principle. Have you heard of it?"

"No," she said sulkily. She would have said he was having fun at her expense but that would be another example of her anthropomorphising him.

"The anthropic principle posited the theory that the universe is deliberately constructed in such a way as to ensure the existence of humanity. It argued that because human consciousness couldn't have existed to perceive the universe unless a certain series of crucial cosmic coincidences had occurred, such as the quantum properties of carbon nuclei, the universe was clearly designed to create humanity. Rather egotistical, in my opinion, but that's the human race for you. Those same series of cosmic 'coincidences' also contrived to create the ant species, for example, but the promoters of the anthropic principle never suggested that the purpose of the universe was to ensure the existence of ants. But then it all sprang from an overrated view of the nature of human consciousness, the view that human consciousness was the end result of not only billions of years of evolution on earth but of the evolution of the entire universe. In reality, of course, human consciousness is just another evolutionary tool, like an elephant's trunk."

"And what's an elephant's trunk?" she asked, suspiciously. He showed her. Jan stared at the animated, three-dimensional image that appeared in the centre of the room, just above the snooker table.

"Not to scale, of course," said Davin as the animal pulled

up grass with its long, flexible nose and thrust it into its mouth.

"That's an elephant?" asked Jan.

"Yes. Now an extinct species. And that extended proboscis is its trunk."

"I guessed as much," muttered Jan darkly. The image vanished. "But surely you are being deliberately absurd. How can you compare human consciousness with an animal's long nose? There is an infinity of difference between the two."

"Not as far as evolution is concerned. As I said, both are simply tools to aid the chances of the species' survival. Human intelligence, along with the intelligence of all the higher mammals, and in particular the primates, developed as a means of passing on information from generation to generation other than by DNA."

She frowned. "What do you mean?"

"The offspring of 'lower' animals, say fish, are born with a set of genetically programmed instincts that equip them to survive in their environment. Baby fish don't have to *learn* anything from their parents. A baby lion also comes equipped with a set of instincts but being a member of a relatively sophisticated species its instincts, its genetic programming, aren't enough to produce a fully equipped lion as far as survival information is concerned. DNA is just too limiting a method to pass on the sophisticated information that a lion needs in order to survive in its environment. So evolution has provided the lion, as with all the higher species, the ability to *learn* from its parents. You understand?"

He—it—is patronising me again, she thought angrily. "Of course I do. But I can't see what a lion's ability to learn has to do with the development of human consciousness."

"But there is a direct link. Being able to learn rather than having to rely purely on a set of inbuilt instincts allows a species to adapt to changes in the surrounding environment

88

and therefore enhances its chances of survival. Now one set of higher mammals specialised in developing this ability to learn—the primates. All species of primates were highly socialised as well, which was another asset in terms of adaptability and survival. Some species of primates developed very complex brains to deal with taking 'on board' all the *learnt* information that their increasingly complex social systems required. And then one primate species went a step further in the ways of passing on information; up until then the methods of learning were more visual than vocal, not to mention physical—cuffs on the head, bites etc—though sounds could convey disapproval and warnings etc. But this particular primate species developed a rudimentary language, and thus a vast new potential for passing on and learning information had been created. To cope with the far greater range of potential information that language presented, the brain of this species of primate underwent a radical development in a short space of time, evolutionarily speaking. Language has, in a real sense, shaped the human mind."

She thought for a while and then, remembering the worker chimps of Minerva, she said, "But chimps can talk."

"Only genetically enhanced chimps," said Davin. "True, experiments on natural chimps long ago showed that they could learn and recognise a limited number of words but their brains weren't capable of dealing with real language. But in many ways there is not much difference between the human mind and the mind of a chimp. It's just that the development of language, and the accompanying development of the human brain to accommodate it, enables the human consciousness to deal with abstract concepts, to plan ahead and so on. But like I said, human consciousness is basically just one of nature's wide variety of evolved survival tools. It's interesting but certainly not of cosmic significance."

Jan got up from her chair and went over to the snooker

table. To try and let off emotional steam she took the black ball and sent it hurtling over the baize towards the triangular formation of red balls. The formation fragmented in all directions with a loud *crack*. She turned back to Davin. "All right, let's say you're right. Humans are just speaking apes. That brings us back to you. What does that make you?"

"An artificial human construct."

"Are you conscious? Self-aware, like a human being?"

"What do *you* think?"

"You *sound* as if you are, but then you're designed to be."

Davin smiled and said, "There was a man called Turing who was a pioneer in the development of computers. He said once that a computer that gave answers which couldn't be distinguished from those of a conscious mind had to be regarded as being conscious too. As you can't tell me apart from a real human being, in terms of communication, then, according to Turing, you must consider me to be conscious."

"Yes, but what *are* you?" she cried in frustration.

"I'm just a machine-made reflection of yourself," he told her, gently.

She didn't believe that for a minute.

That had been yesterday. Today she felt an urgent need to get out of the habitat. She would take the Toy and fly to the South Pole. So after looking in on Robin after she'd got up—they no longer slept in the same room—and a quick breakfast alone, she summoned Davin. He immediately materialised before her. "Yes Jan?"

"I need some fresh air. I'm going to take the Toy out. Could you have it prepared for me right away?"

He shook his head. "I'm sorry, Jan, but I can't. The Toy is busy."

"Busy?" She gave a laugh. "How could it possibly be *busy*? What's it doing? Washing its hair?"

"It's on patrol. Recently several robotic devices have been detected and intercepted under the ice shelf. It is fair to

90

assume that the aim of these devices is to locate Shangri La."

Jan's amusement vanished. "It's Milo. He's here. With the Sky Angel."

"It is also fair to assume that you are correct."

"So what are you going to do?" she demanded.

"That all depends on what he does next," said Davin quietly.

In the machine shop Milo watched as the first of the seismic monitors rolled off the automatic assembly line. Elsewhere in the long, low-ceilinged room, other machines, under the control of Carl, worked on manufacturing the explosive charges. A low-pitched hum filled the room. Milo picked up the monitor and examined it. As he did so he heard Ashley's disembodied voice say, "They're chattering again."

"What?" he said, distracted. "Who are?"

"The people down here and the people up there. The people down here resumed transmitting this morning."

"Oh." He put down the monitor. "Did they tell the spacers why they stopped transmitting yesterday?"

"Yeah. They had trouble with a Sky Lord. And get this, they shot it down."

"Shot it down?" said Milo, surprised. "But that's impossible . . . unless the Sky Lord's laser system wasn't operating."

"From what they were saying it seems the lasers were working but they shot it down anyway. A secret weapon, they said."

Milo rubbed his hand over his bald head. "When we've finished here we really must go and pay our clever friends a visit. I don't like the sound of them."

Chapter Twelve:

As the acceleration increased, pushing Milo back into his couch, he felt increasingly elated. It meant that Belvedere was receding ever faster into the distance behind them. He was *free*.

Well, almost free. There was still the problem of Father Shaw. He would remain in Belvedere's thrall for as long as he was in the company of the Father. He would have to deal with him, but not yet. Not yet.

He looked across at him. Father Shaw was clearly terrified. His eyes were screwed up and his knuckles showed white as he gripped the armrests. Milo knew that this was his first time outside the habitat. On the way to the shuttle docking station he had almost panicked when he got his first taste of zero gravity. He had clung frantically to Milo's arm and cried, "Oh God save us! We're falling! We're falling!"

"Calm yourself, Father Shaw, you're not falling," Milo had said soothingly, if inaccurately. "It just feels that way. You'll get used to it." Milo knew from past experience that many people never got used to zero gravity and he suspected that Father Shaw would be one of them. It was a good start to the journey.

"Oh no!" he now heard the Father groan. "There's that awful falling sensation again. What's happening now, Brother James?"

"We've ceased accelerating, Father."

"You mean we've *stopped*! Why, what's wrong?!"

"No, we haven't stopped, Father," said Milo patiently.

"We have simply stopped accelerating because we have reached sufficient velocity."

"But if we haven't stopped moving why do I feel this way again?" he protested.

Typical, thought Milo, he doesn't know the difference between velocity and acceleration. He has spent all his life in a technological marvel and yet his knowledge of basic physics was probably nil. Just like so many Belvederians who weren't members of the engineering or technician classes. But then that had been the case in the age of electronics on Earth during the second half of the twentieth century; only a small minority of the people who used the vast variety of electronic devices on a daily basis understood how they worked. And it was the same during the age of biogenics in the twenty-first century. People were surrounded by the wonders created by genetic engineers but most couldn't tell you the difference between a gene and a chromosome. "I'm afraid, Father Shaw, that we will be in this state of free-fall, er, zero gravity, until we activate the Drive again in order to slow down towards the end of our journey to Karaganga, and that won't be for another eighteen hours." He raised his voice and said, "Am I right?" to the two pilots who he presumed were listening to the conversation.

They exchanged a glance and then one of them turned round and said, "Yes, Brother James. It will be twenty-four hours before we start de-accelerating to match our orbit with that of Karaganga. I'm sorry, Father Shaw, that you are experiencing discomfort."

The Father put his hand to his mouth. "Discomfort? I feel terrible! I think I'm going to be sick. . . ."

"There are bags in the seat flap on your right," said the pilot solicitously. "If you need to make use of a bag, please make sure you close it tightly after use. . . ."

Too late. Father Shaw, who had gone very white, leaned forward against his seat straps and explosively ejected the partly digested remains of his copious lunch. The expanding cloud of vomit remained suspended in front of him, a small nova of food particles and stomach acids. It took a lot of effort for Milo not to burst out laughing.

The pilot who had been speaking quickly got out of his chair, plucked a tubular device from a wall rack and skilfully manoeuvred himself down the cabin towards them. The device turned out to be a vacuum cleaner and he applied it to the growing cloud of vomit. Milo undid his own seat straps and pushed himself into the air. "I will go and get some water, Father Shaw," he announced. He headed for the rear of the cabin.

The shuttle was a small one. The front cabin had seating for six apart from the two pilots. At the immediate rear of the cabin was a tiny galley and a combined washroom and toilet facility. Beyond the bulkhead was the cargo storage area. Beyond that was the housing for the G-Drive, the generator and fuel tanks containing fuel for both the generator and the shuttle's guidance jets. Milo entered the washroom/toilet and slid the door shut behind him. He stared at himself in the mirror, grinning broadly. It was marvellous to experience true privacy again, even briefly; to know that his every movement wasn't constantly being monitored by CenCom.

He filled a water tube and slowly squeezed its contents into his mouth, then refilled it for Father Shaw. It was amusing—when the Father had first boarded the shuttle the two boyish-looking pilots had clearly been awed to be in such close proximity to a Father but Milo was sure that this fearful reverence was swiftly being eroded and would soon be replaced by contempt. Heavily concealed contempt but contempt nevertheless.

He lingered a little while longer in the washroom, still staring at himself in the mirror. He did not know exactly what awaited him on Earth but it had to be better than Belvedere. And if the Earth people were telling the truth about their Palmyra, then it was a little paradise. Admittedly a paradise surrounded on both land and sea by the blight but far from collapse just yet. He would have plenty of time to enjoy what it had to offer.

Jean-Paul woke and lay there in the bed feeling completely disorientated. This was a familiar waking pattern. His brain—his body—still wasn't adjusted to being continually on solid ground. He lay there, listening to the songs of the variety of exotic birds that inhabited Palmyra, as well as the buzzing and clicking of the insects that infested the place. The birds he liked, but the insects he could do without and he was glad of the netting that covered the open windows of his rooms. The air was rich with strange, unfamiliar odours. After about five minutes he sat up and gingerly got out of bed. His body still ached all over but he was feeling better every day. A Palmyrian medic had checked him over and declared he hadn't sustained any serious internal injuries in his fall, only severe bruising. He put on the shorts and shirt that had been lent to him and went out into the kitchen. Lon Haddon was sitting at the table eating breakfast. He looked up and smiled at Jean-Paul. "Good morning. Sleep all right?"

"Much better, thank you, Lon," answered Jean-Paul, speaking slowly and carefully. He was still having difficulty with the dialect of Americano that these people spoke. "No dreams this time, thank God."

Lon Haddon indicated that he should sit down in the chair opposite. As he did so Haddon got up and went to the stove. "How hungry are you?"

"Er, very," he admitted.

A short time later Haddon put a large plate of fried fish and eggs in front of him. There was a bowl of mixed fruit—oranges, bananas and grapes—and a pitcher of pineapple juice. Jean-Paul began to eat. There was no further conversation until he had almost cleared the plate, then he glanced at the third kitchen chair and said, "Where's Ayla this morning?"

"She and her team had an early shift working on the . . . uh, wreckage," said Haddon.

There was an embarrassed silence. Haddon was referring to the remains of the *Lord Montcalm*. The Palmyrians were using their submarine vessels to cut up and salvage as much of the airship's metallic skeleton as was possible. Jean-Paul returned his attention to the food. It was odd, sitting here in the company of the man mainly responsible for the destruction of the *Lord Montcalm*, but he found it difficult to feel any animosity towards Haddon. He couldn't really blame any of the inhabitants of Palmyra for defending themselves against a Sky Lord. Despite his ingrained prejudices against ground dwellers he found he could now more easily sympathise with their position. Living under Ashley's crazed rule had definitely shifted his perspective on many things.

More than anyone he blamed himself for the destruction of the *Lord Montcalm* and so many of its people. He should have trusted his own instincts and attempted to establish friendly relations with the Palmyrians instead of letting Emile persuade him to follow blindly the bankrupt traditions of the Sky Lords. He now knew that Haddon's people would have responded positively to such an overture. But now it was too late.

Yes, he actually liked Haddon. It wasn't due simply to gratitude. And he certainly liked his daughter. At that first glimpse of her in the boat he was enchanted by her, and in the two weeks since then his feelings had intensified. And, correspondingly, his guilt. To feel this way towards another woman so soon after Dominique's death. . . .

He put such thoughts aside. "What time does Ayla's shift end?" he asked.

Haddon glanced at the clock on the wall. "Around two, I would say."

Jean-Paul nodded. He would go down to the sea front to

meet the submersible when it returned. He wondered if Haddon suspected how he felt about his daughter. If he did know he had so far given no indication that he disapproved.

"What are your plans today?" Haddon asked him.

"The usual. Go to the hospital first and then do the rounds." Apart from him, eighty-three other survivors had been pulled from the sea after the crash of the *Lord Montcalm*. Now fifty-two were still alive. The most severely burned had died within the first few days. The medics at Palmyra's small hospital could do nothing for them except administer pain-killers. The burn victims who still lived stood a good chance of surviving though many would be badly scarred. Jean-Paul visited them every day at the hospital, and also the other survivors—the luckier ones— who hadn't suffered serious injuries and were scattered through Palmyra. Like Jean-Paul they were staying with various Palmyra families and were being treated like guests rather than prisoners of war. The Palmyrians were treating their unwelcome visitors with a rare generosity of spirit, though Jean-Paul had encountered some animosity. He had come to discover that there was a faction within Palmyra society that had disagreed with taking the *Lord Montcalm* survivors in. This faction had wanted the survivors to be expelled into the blight land as soon as they'd recovered enough to travel but had been overruled by a majority vote. He said to Haddon, "And I imagine you will be going to the radio installation, as usual?"

Haddon smiled. "Of course. It's all very exciting. The spacers' preparations are coming along on schedule. In exactly twenty-eight days their ship will be landing here! I only hope I'm still. . . ." He didn't continue. Abruptly he got up and began clearing dishes from his side of the table. As he took them over to the sink Jean-Paul eyed him speculatively. Dressed only in a garment that left his upper body bare—called a sarong, it was a popular form of dress with both men and women in Palmyra—Lon Haddon appeared to be a fit and healthy man of optimum age. But that could have been, in terms of years, anything between thirty-five and two hundred plus one-to-five years. As with all Standard Primes who had reached their optimum age it was impossible to tell his real age.

Jean-Paul had caught Ayla casting anxious glances at her father and he was beginning to wonder if Haddon had indeed reached two hundred plus. If that was the case he could suddenly slip into a peaceful coma at any time. Death would follow soon afterwards, his entire system obeying its genetic command simply to shut down. Jean-Paul was only fifty-one so he had a long time to go before he found himself in a similar situation. If he lived that long.

"Is your father all right?" he asked Ayla.

She turned to him, frowning. "Why do you ask?"

"It was something he said, or *almost* said, this morning to me. And I've noticed the way you sometimes look at him. With concern."

Ayla returned her attention to the track ahead. "Of course I'm concerned about him. He's my father."

As she clearly didn't want to discuss the matter he didn't pursue it. They were sitting side by side in the roofless driver's cab perched high in the front of the crude, electric-powered truck that Ayla was steering along a bumpy track running between two wheat fields. They were going to visit Ayla's older brother who, with his wife, ran a farm on the outskirts of the Palmyrian territory. It wasn't just a social visit; Ayla intended to bring back a cargo of oranges.

Neither of them had had a good morning. When Jean-Paul had seen Ayla emerge pale and grim-faced from the submersible he knew at once that something was wrong. He later learned from her that, while working within the wreckage of the *Lord Montcalm*, she and her crew had found more corpses that had been missed by the body-collection teams who had supposedly cleared the area in the days immediately after the crash. The encounter with corpses that had been in the water for two weeks had, understandably, sickened Ayla.

His own less-than-enjoyable encounter involved his fellow survivors from the *Lord Montcalm*. As usual, his visit to the hospital depressed him. Seeing people who were going to be horribly disfigured for life was deeply demoralising. It made him feel helpless—and responsible. This latter feeling was shared by many of the survivors. There was a growing trend among them to blame him for everything that had happened, though he knew that in his position they would have acted exactly the same as he had.

"Any sign of your missing sea people yet?" he asked her, to break the silence.

She shook her head. "No. I can't understand it."

"Perhaps the crash of the *Lord Montcalm* scared them off," he suggested.

"I don't think so. Anyway, their habitat is a long way from where your airship came down. No, there must be another reason. . . ." She thought again of Tiger's warnings and wondered if they were connected with the sea people's apparent disappearance. "It's against the rules of the unwritten treaty between us but I'm thinking of taking the sub out to their habitat to see what's happening."

"Sounds dangerous. Would your father approve?"

"No," she admitted. "And Lyle probably wouldn't give me permission." She made it sound as if neither factor would stand in her way. He gave her a covert look. As always he was stirred by the sight of her. Today, for a change, she was wearing a simple, sleeveless shirt. Sweat ran down her face and her bare arms and legs gleamed with it. It was a hot day, and the air grew warmer the further inland they travelled. He too was uncomfortably sticky. And thirsty. He reached down for the water canteen that sat on the cabin floor between their feet. As he did so he accidentally brushed the calf of her leg with the back of his hand. The contact caused a tremor to rush briefly through his whole body. The intensity of this reaction puzzled and rather alarmed him. His feelings for this girl were clearly getting out of control. . . .

He picked up the canteen and drank from it. He was surprised when Ayla said, "Have you ever been married, Jean-Paul?"

"Me, no, never. I intended to after I'd served out my time in the army but that was years ahead in the future. Or it *was* until everything went haywire when we got conquered by that damned woman. . . ."

"But you had girlfriends when you were in the army?"

"Er, yes, I had girlfriends."

"And afterwards?"

"Yes, there was someone. Her name was Dominique." He swatted angrily at the flies that persisted in hovering around his face.

Ayla hesitated, then asked, "Was she killed in the crash?"

"No. She died before that. On the day we took control of the ship. She was killed in the fighting."

Ayla said nothing.

"What about you?" he asked. "I imagine you must have a whole crowd of young men chasing after you and anxious to marry you."

She smiled. "Hardly a *crowd*. More like a small group, but I don't think marriage is on any of their minds."

"Do any of them ever catch you?"

She gave him a mischievous glance. "Oh, occasionally I let one of them catch me. But it's never for very long. And I don't think I really want to get married. But Kell has asked me. Several times. I keep saying no but that doesn't discourage him."

Jean-Paul felt absurdly jealous. "Is he one of the ones you've let *catch* you?"

"No. I just don't feel that way about him. I grew up with Kell. I think of him as my brother."

Now he felt absurdly relieved. "But he clearly doesn't regard you as a sister?"

"No, he doesn't. Poor Kell."

Poor Kell indeed, thought Jean-Paul.

"Jean-Paul, can I tell you something?"

"But certainly."

"I think I like you. A lot."

He looked at her. She was staring straight ahead, her expression serious. "Like a brother?" he asked.

"No, not like a brother," she said. She took her left hand off the steering wheel and placed it on his thigh. Again, the touch of her produced a galvanic reaction within him. He felt a tightening in his chest, accompanied by mounting excitement. He placed his hand on hers. "Ayla . . ." he began, but then, suddenly, she whipped her hand away and was standing up in the cabin. Thinking he had done something wrong he said, in alarm, "Ayla, what is it? What's the matter?"

"Look!" she cried, pointing ahead.

He looked. Ahead lay a line of trees, the beginning, he presumed, of her brother's orchards. And beyond the trees a column of grey smoke was rising into the air. "What's wrong?"

"That smoke . . . that's where my brother's farmhouse is!"

Chapter Thirteen:

Ayla pushed the truck along at its top speed, which was only about 25 mph. Even so Jean-Paul was severely shaken about as the vehicle moved faster over the bumpy track which was now winding through the orchards. "What do you think has happened?" he asked the grim-faced Ayla as he clung to the top of his door.

"Could be anything. As I told you earlier, Len and Tissa's farmhouse is not far from the fence. Someone, or something, from out of the blight lands could have broken through. Marauders, perhaps."

"You also told me that the fence carries a lethal electric charge," he pointed out, "and that it's regularly patrolled."

"Yes, but occasionally things, or people, do get through. That's why I came armed." She was referring to the pistol she was carrying in a holster on her side. When he had seen her emerge from the house wearing the thing he had jokingly asked if its purpose was to prevent him making an escape bid. She had smiled and said it was "just a precaution".

While she concentrated on the driving Jean-Paul began scanning the surrounding landscape, looking for he knew not what. He wished he had a weapon too.

"Thank God," exclaimed Ayla, relieved. Jean-Paul looked ahead. The scene seemed unchanged. The ominous smoke continued to rise into the air. "What is it?"

"It's not the farm burning. The smoke is too far away."

A short time later, when they reached the farm, she was proved right. The cluster of farm buildings was undamaged; the source of the smoke was still some distance away. Ayla stopped the truck, jumped down from the cab and ran into the farmhouse, calling out, "Len! Tissa!" She emerged soon afterwards, shaking her head. "No one in there." She climbed back into the cab and drove on. She circled the farm buildings, sending chickens scattering in fright, and then steered the truck between two rows of trees towards the smoke. There was no trail now and the ride was even more bumpy.

The orchard came to an end and beyond there was only wild, natural vegetation. Ayla drove the truck straight into it and Jean-Paul was obliged to brace himself more firmly as the vehicle ploughed through it. The area of thick vegetation turned out to be not more than a fifty yard strip and suddenly the truck had emerged onto clear land. This cleared strip extended a further fifty yards to a tall wire mesh fence. A section of the fence was down and this was where the smoke was coming from. A large bonfire had been built in front of the gap in the fence and it was blazing away fiercely. A group of people around the bonfire were adding wood from stacks that were scattered about. All turned at the sound of the approaching truck.

"What's happening?" Jean-Paul asked Ayla.

"I'm not sure yet . . . but everyone appears okay," she said happily.

There were six adults in the group and two children, a boy and a girl. Both of the children, standing well away from the fire, were carrying rifles. As Ayla braked the truck to a halt a woman—the only one in the group—ran forward. Like all the others in the group she was wearing just shorts. Ayla jumped down and they embraced eagerly. "Tissa!" cried Ayla. "You all gave me such a fright! When I saw the smoke I thought it was the farm! And then when I found the place deserted . . .!"

One of the men came hurrying over. Ayla embraced him too. Jean-Paul assumed that this was her brother, Len. He looked very similar to Lon Haddon. Jean-Paul climbed down from the cab. "Len, Tissa," said Ayla, "this is Jean-Paul Ranvaud. He's staying with us."

Len Haddon eyed him keenly as he offered his hand. "The Sky Man we've heard so much about, eh? I look forward to having a talk with you later when we've got the time."

"What happened here?" asked Ayla, indicating the fire.

"Oh, a crawler vine managed to collapse the fence," said her brother.

"It must have been a big one."

"It was. And by the time we got here it had made good progress. It was a bit charred from the jolt it got before the current was broken but it was alive and kicking. Wasn't it, Tissa?" His wife nodded her agreement. "But we managed to chop it up into manageable portions, soaked it with kerosene and set it alight. We're keeping the fire going to ward off any more unwelcome visitors from the blight until the repair team gets here."

Jean-Paul stared with interest through the fence. It was the first time he had seen the blight at such close quarters. Beyond a strip of scoured land biological chaos reigned. The giant fungi, with their various shapes and colours, dominated everything. Some hung like shrouds from the trees they had drained the life from; others were huge, spherical balls with a diameter of several feet. He could smell the fungi's musty, unpleasant odour. The odour suggested suffocation and death. He turned to Len. "How do you keep the fungi from coming through the fence? Surely the wind would carry their spores over?"

"Yeah, it does. We get outbreaks of the blight all over Palmyra but we have teams of people whose only job is to keep a look-out for them and wipe them out with anti-fungal poisons before they get out of control. We do the same here. Keep the strip soaked with a-f agents, and we regularly go over to the other side with flame throwers to keep that strip cleared too. All the farmers like us who live close to the fence do the same. But we know it's a losing battle. One day the blight will overwhelm the fence and we'll have to retreat and build a new one. It's happened before. . . ." He shook his head resignedly.

"Len, if it's okay I'll take Ayla and her . . . guest back to the house. I need to start on dinner," said his wife.

"Sure, go ahead," he agreed. "The emergency's over."

"Going to be a tight squeeze in the truck, Tissa," said Ayla. "You're going to have to sit on Jean-Paul's lap, if you don't mind."

"I don't mind. But does Jean-Paul mind?" She gave him a teasing smile.

"Oh, I'm *sure* he won't mind," laughed Ayla.

Jean-Paul, who had been trying to avoid looking at Tissa's bare breasts, gave a pained smile.

The meal, some three hours later, was a good one but throughout it Jean-Paul was uncomfortably aware of being the centre of attention. The children especially made no secret of their interest in him. Every time he glanced at either of them they were regarding him with relentlessly intense eyes. He learned that their names were Sam and Tasma. Sam was eleven, Tasma twelve. Tasma resembled a smaller version of Ayla, which Jean-Paul found slightly unsettling. The four male farm workers also made their intense interest in Jean-Paul very clear.

Len had waited until the main course, a delicious stew, was over before he began questioning Jean-Paul. "You must find it very strange being on the ground after spending your entire life in the air?"

"Yes, I do," he admitted. "But it's not so strange for me as it is for some of my people. I was a soldier and made periodic visits below as part of my regular, uh, duties. But some of my people have never been on the ground before and I can see that it is causing them some psychological problems."

105

"I have spoken only briefly to my father since you and your people's arrival," said Len, "but he told me some wild story about a new Sky Lord from space that conquered your ship, and others as well."

Jean-Paul drained the beer from his glass and said, "It may be wild but it's true, except that I don't have all the facts behind the story. We pieced it together from all the rumours we heard, and from what we saw . . . and experienced."

"Another helping of stew, Jean-Paul, before you have dessert?" asked Tissa as she refilled his glass with beer. He smiled and shook his head. "Thank you, but no. I can eat no more."

"Oh, but you must have some apple pie," she insisted. "You are so thin!"

"Not as thin as when we pulled him out of the water," said Ayla. "He looked like one of your electric bird-scarers."

Jean-Paul held up his hands in surrender as Tissa began to cut him a large portion of pie. Tissa was attractive, though not as striking as her sister-in-law. All the family, like Ayla, had an oriental touch to their features. A legacy from the Japanese, no doubt. "Go on," said Len, "tell us this wild story of yours."

"I'll tell you what I know, which isn't much. There was this woman called Jan Dorvin who originally came from Minerva, an earthworm . . . sorry, a ground *community* in North America."

"Minerva?" said Len, frowning.

"Yes, before the Gene Wars it was a big and powerful state. But what made it unique was that it was entirely controlled by women," Jean-Paul told them.

"What?" laughed Tissa. "How bizarre . . . though I can see how such an arrangement could have its attractions."

"I don't," muttered Len. "You're saying, Jean-Paul, that the men of this place let themselves be run by a bunch of women?"

"So the story goes."

"It sounds perfectly reasonable to me," Ayla told her brother firmly.

He shook his head in disbelief.

"Anyway," continued Jean-Paul, "that part of the story came from the Sky Angel herself when she addressed us personally over the *Lord Montcalm*'s PA system after our defeat."

"Sky Angel?" asked Ayla.

"That's what Jan Dorvin was calling herself then. Or maybe that was the name other people had given her. It was also the name given to her ship."

"Ah, yes, this ship," said Len, "that's the really fascinating part. Did it really come from outer space, and if so, how did this woman get control of it?"

"This part of the story is vague," admitted Jean-Paul. "All I know is that Jan Dorvin was one of the few survivors after Minerva was destroyed by a Sky Lord called the *Lord Pangloth*. On board she met a fellow slave called Milo something. The rumours say that he was the one who knew about the Sky Angel waiting in space; that he came from space himself."

"From one of the space colonies?" asked Len.

"That's the rumour," said Jean-Paul. "I asked your father to ask the spacers he's in contact with if an expedition had been mounted to Earth from any of the colonies in recent years. They replied no, but that a ship from the Martian colonies, on its way to a space colony, disappeared about eight years ago. It could have crash-landed on Earth."

"Unlikely there would have been any survivors."

"Yes. Anyway, the *Lord Pangloth* was attacked and overwhelmed by the warriors of another Sky Lord . . . the *Perfumed Breeze*." He leaned back and waited for the reaction. He wasn't disappointed—Len looked astonished. His father had reacted in the same way.

"The *Perfumed Breeze*," gasped Len, "but that was the Sky Lord that—"

"That ruled you. Yes, I know. Your father told me that Palmyra was within its tribute territories."

In a grim voice, Len asked, "And what of the Warlord Horado? Does he still rule the *Perfumed Breeze*?"

"No, he's dead."

"Thank God."

"He was a butcher," Tissa said bitterly. "His men took my mother away to be a slave. She was one of many. I never saw her again."

"How did the Warlord die?" Len asked.

"He had transferred himself and most of his people to the *Lord Pangloth*. Apparently the lasers were no longer working on the *Perfumed Breeze*. . . . That's why he fled his tribute territories."

Len and his wife exchanged a look. "If only we'd known," muttered Len.

"Well, it is said that he attacked the Sky Angel shortly after it had arrived on Earth. Jan Dorvin was in control of the ship by then and shot Horado out of the sky."

Everyone was silent for a time. Then Len said, "It seems that we owe this Jan Dorvin a large debt of gratitude."

Jean-Paul sighed. "I must confess that my feelings about her are ambiguous. I led a comfortable life on the *Lord Montcalm* then suddenly her Sky Angel appeared from nowhere, forced us to surrender and the next thing we knew we were under the control of a computer program. It was based on the personality of a woman—no, a girl—who died a long time ago. Ashley. . . ." Jean-Paul grimaced. "I think part of the problem was that it was wearing out. It was copy of a copy anyway, so it was rumoured. It wasn't too bad at first but then Jan Dorvin lost control of all the programs running her fleet and we were left under the total control of this deranged personality. But we were more fortunate than those on the other ships controlled by the other Ashley programs. They were forced to abandon the ships and become ground dwellers."

"What happened to Jan Dorvin?" Ayla asked him.

He shrugged. "I have no idea. Either Ashley killed her or she was forced down to the ground as well."

Len said, "What was she trying to do with this fleet of Sky Lords she was amassing?"

"Her plan was to free all the ground communities from the rule of the Sky Lords, while at the same time using the fleets' combined laser fire to destroy as much of the blight as she could."

"Sounds to me," said Tissa, "that she was trying to do a good thing."

Jean-Paul sighed. "I suppose, in retrospect, it appears she was. But at the time, well . . . we just resented her for conquering our Sky Lord."

"It seems," said Len, "that the world lost a golden opportunity for redemption from the blight."

It was quiet around the table until Ayla said, "Well, there's still the spacers. Maybe, as Dad hopes, they'll turn out to be our salvation."

It was late—after midnight—by the time they got back to Ayla's house. They had left the truck parked, with its cargo of oranges, at the fruit depot in the middle of town, and walked the rest of the way. Ayla had been quiet on the journey back, much to Jean-Paul's disappointment. He'd been hoping they might resume the conversation they'd been having before they arrived at the farm. He guessed she was tired. He knew *he* was tired, and he hadn't been wrestling with the obstinate controls of that bone-battering truck.

They whispered good night to each other in the darkened kitchen and went their separate ways. In his room Jean-Paul sat on his bed and waited for Ayla to finish in the bathroom. When he heard her bedroom door close he headed to the bathroom himself, being as quiet as possible so as not to wake his host.

Back in his room he undressed, slipped under the single sheet on his bed and turned down the lamp on the table beside the bed. Not long afterwards he heard his door opening. He sat up. "Who . . .?"

"Shush! Who do you think it is?" whispered Ayla. He felt her cool arms around his neck.

"But what about your father?"

Her arms were gone. Next came the sounds of her quickly undressing.

"Don't worry," she said as she slid into bed beside him. "He's a heavy sleeper."

Lon Haddon lay there listening to his daughter make furtive love to the Sky Warrior and tried to analyse the jumble of feelings he was experiencing. On one level he approved of anything, or anyone, who made his daughter happy, but he couldn't help feeling angry that she was giving herself to a man who, only a short time ago, had been their enemy—as much as he personally liked Jean-Paul himself. And he felt a typical father's jealousy when a daughter showed love for another man. What else? Envy? Yes, he was envious, but of whom? Both of them, he slowly realised. It was unlikely he would ever make love to anyone again in whatever short time it was he had left.

An image of his dead wife swam into his mind. Wherever she was, he would soon be joining her. *No! That was nonsense and he knew it!* There was nothing after life, just as there was nothing before life. Only oblivion . . . and after the full life of a Standard Prime he should be prepared to accept oblivion. But he wasn't. He didn't want to die. It terrified him . . . if he was honest with himself. And at times like this he was.

The sounds from Jean-Paul's room had long ago ebbed into silence before sleep came to him.

Chapter Fourteen:

Jan was in the recreation room with Robin. They were playing chess. He was acting livelier today than he had been for ages, though that wasn't saying much. He clearly couldn't keep his mind on his playing and Jan was deliberately making errors of her own simply to keep the game going.

She was feeling bored, frustrated and trapped. Despite the size of Shangri La a sense of claustrophobia had set in since she had been denied the use of the Toy. And the knowledge that Milo and Ashley were somewhere up there above the ice and searching for them made her feel worse. As usual, the programs provided no consolation. That morning she had asked Davin again what the latest situation was and his reply was evasive, as it always was. Milo's robot searchers, who were methodically moving across the ice shelf and letting off seismic charges to determine what lay beneath, were still a long way away from the habitat's location. Again she had asked what the programs planned to do when Milo finally succeeded in finding Shangri La and as usual he told her, "Don't worry. Everything will be all right."

"I don't trust him," she said aloud. "I don't trust any of them."

Robin, who had been about to make a foolish move with one of his knights, looked at her. "Who?"

"Who else but Davin and the other programs? They're up to something and whatever it is I don't think it bodes well for us."

He frowned. "I don't understand. The programs wouldn't do us any harm. They're here to look after us."

"They're here to look after the Eloi, and, in theory, you. I'm just a guest here on sufferance, and probably expendable now that they've picked my brains clean of information. And I'm not sure of your rating with them either."

He looked even more perplexed. "What are you saying, Jan? I may not be an Eloi but the programs have always looked after me. The Ethical Program insists on it."

She gave a sniff of disdain. "Yes, the so-called Ethical Program. I distrust that most of all. Okay, it let you live and grow as a non-Eloi, a throwback, but don't ask me why. I don't believe the official explanation. That the Program is still governed by the ancient United Nations' rules regarding embryo research. Hah!"

Robin now looked worried. "But what other explanation could there be?"

"I don't know," Jan said, then, seeing that she had upset him, gave him a reassuring smile and touched his hand. "Oh, don't mind me. Maybe I'm just being paranoid. I'm sure everything will turn out for the best." She realised, with disgust, that she was treating him as Davin had treated her.

Her empty words had the desired effect. His worried frown vanished and he smiled. *Poor Robin*, she said to herself. She still loved him, in spite of his major personality change, but sometimes it was difficult to remember the *passion* they had shared. Now she often thought, unkindly she knew, that he had more in common with the Eloi than the vigorous young man she had originally encountered.

She reached across the chess board with both her hands and held his face. "Robin, how do you feel about me now?" she asked him gently.

His puzzled expression returned. "Feel? About you? How do you mean?"

"Do you still love me?"

"I . . . I think so."

112

"The way you used to? Do you remember how it was between us?"

He lowered his eyes. "Yes," he said reluctantly. "But . . ."

"But what?"

"It's different now. You know why."

"But Davin says the changes they've made to your body to compensate for the loss of . . . they should restore your normal feelings. It's not working, is it? You feel no *desire* for me, do you?"

He was staring at the chess board. "Not the way I used to," he said slowly, "but I still do . . . love you, Jan. Really."

"Yeah, sure you do," she said, with sadness. She let go of him. "Come on, let's finish the game."

The game ended predictably, then Robin announced he was tired and was going to his room for a nap. Jan went to hers as well, but not to sleep. As she masturbated she remembered the time when she and Robin first made love. After she had climaxed she discovered that her eyes were full of tears. Mother God, she said to herself, perhaps Davin, and Milo, were right. Perhaps the human mind was nothing more than the end result of an interplay between different hormones, all genetically controlled. Robin certainly seemed to prove the point. Alter his hormonal output and he was no longer the same man. And look at the Eloi if you wanted further proof. . . .

She lay there and reflected on her latest philosophical tussle with Davin. It had been this morning, after she had fruitlessly questioned him about Milo. He had been about to leave when she said, "Wait, Davin. You remember that conversation we had? About the evolution of the human mind? That you said it was just an evolutionary tool, no more significant than the flexible nose on an extinct animal?"

"Those weren't my exact words but, yes, I remember the conversation."

113

"I still say the human mind is unique. That human consciousness far transcends the consciousness of any animal."

"That is your prerogative," he said, with a smile.

"But you don't agree with me?"

"I'm afraid not."

"Well, then, how do you explain the human sense of humour?" she asked, triumphantly. "It's unique to human beings and clearly doesn't have any survival value so it couldn't have evolved for any particular reason. Doesn't that prove that human consciousness exists outside your purely mechanistic world view? That it is something special and unique?"

"On the contrary," he replied, "it evolved as a specific survival tool. And it is not unique to human beings. Didn't your worker chimps back in Minerva laugh at all?"

"Yes," she admitted, "but they were enhanced chimps."

"Natural chimpanzees also had the ability to laugh, in chimpanzee fashion, of course. The human sense of humour, and that of a chimps, is simply a more sophisticated, more highly evolved, version of the 'playfulness' characteristic that is common in all higher mammals."

"Playfulness?"

"Yes, you must have observed it in your pets, if you had any. But let us return to the example I used before—the species of big cats known as lions. A lion cub will 'play' with its fellow cubs, and its mother. It is a form of mock combat. The cub learns how to fight but without inflicting any real damage on his opponent and without sustaining any damage himself, unless by accident. It is also a safe way of letting off the cub's natural aggression."

"There seems to me to be a vast difference between lion cubs playing with each other and a human being's sense of humour," Jan said.

"It's only a matter of degree. The higher primates have much more complex social structures than, say, a pride of lions. Therefore the apes' 'playfulness' characteristic had to become, by necessity, much more sophisticated. And as human beings are the most sophisticated of the higher primates, so is their 'sense of humour'. But it is still only a means of mock combat. It allows aggression to be channelled into safe forms; a means of letting off emotional steam without inflicting physical damage. Without it the early families and tribes of the higher apes would have self-destructed as internal pressures built to bursting point. The human race would never even have evolved without this particular survival tool. But in reality humour is just another form of aggression. And almost always cruel."

Jan was getting that out-gunned feeling again. She still didn't agree with Davin but for the moment she couldn't think of an effective counter-argument. Annoyed, she said, "And what about you? Do you have a sense of humour?"

"No."

"But you make jokes. Sly ones."

"We can *simulate* a sense of humour, that's all. Why would an artificial intelligence need a sense of humour? We are not social animals. We have no need for one."

"How about cruelty. Are you capable of that?"

"To be cruel one requires emotions."

"You can simulate a sense of humour so maybe you can simulate cruelty too."

"Why would we want to?"

"Good question," Jan had muttered.

As Jan lay there on the bed she wondered if she was doomed to remain in the habitat for the rest of her life, provided that the programs let her continue to live. And if she did ever manage to escape what was there for her in the outside world? Nothing but blight and Sky Lords, several of them controlled by crazy Ashley programs. Oh, and there was Milo too. Milo, who had cannibalised the body of her dear son, Simon, to resurrect himself. She hoped the programs would destroy both him and Ashley when they located

115

the habitat, as they inevitably would. The programs had the Toy and she knew from experience that the Toy was impervious to laser fire.

She had lost so much; so many people who had been dear to her. Her mother, Alsa, Ceri . . . Simon. There was only Robin left now, and she was losing him too. A long life in the habitat might be easier to bear if he returned to his old self but as it was now spending year after endless year in this place was a grim prospect.

Perhaps eventually she would beg the programs to transform her into an Eloi. Boredom was something the Eloi certainly never suffered from. Intrigued by the thought, Jan got up from the bed and went over to the large mirror that hung on one wall. There was no shortage of mirrors in Shangri La. The Eloi liked staring at themselves and could spend hours doing so. As she stared at herself Jan wondered what it would be like to be an Eloi. A sexless being. No genitals, not even an anus. The Eloi didn't possess a conventional excretory system. What few by-products did remain after their transformed digestive systems had processed their carefully balanced nutrients were eliminated through their sweat glands.

And as their bodies had been transformed so too had their minds. The Eloi existed in a permanent state of mental bliss, their brains constantly flooded with a wide range of natural, pleasure-inducing neuro-transmitters such as encephalins which are analogous to opium. The Eloi never worried, never felt sad or distressed, never felt fear. Never felt much of anything at all, in fact, except incredibly, marvellously bloody *happy*. And what was wrong with that, Jan asked herself. Wasn't the pursuit of happiness the central aim of humanity?

But no, the Eloi happiness was the wrong kind of happiness. Some vestige of her abandoned religion told her that the Eloi were morally corrupt. And as she stared at herself in the mirror she knew she could never let herself be turned into an Eloi, even if it was possible. They were not human. And she liked being a human being—a human woman—and everything good and bad that came with that. Even the shitting.

Chapter Fifteen:

The Karaganga space habitat orbited at a point called Lagrange 5, while Belvedere was positioned at Lagrange 4. These two points were on the orbit of the moon and had the advantage of being the most stable positions within the constant gravitational tussle between the Earth and the moon. There were three other Lagrange points but they weren't as stable and the habitats located in them had to make periodic manoeuvres to maintain their positions. Belvedere and Karaganga, being the first two habitats to be built, were naturally the ones to gain the prime locations.

Milo was enjoying his stay on Karaganga. Like the Belvederians, the Karagangans were Christians but being Russian in origin their Christianity was based on the old Russian Orthodox Church. They had little in common with the puritans of Belvedere. For one thing there was no segregation of the sexes and they also indulged in such pleasures as alcohol. Milo had hugely enjoyed witnessing the look of horror on Father Shaw's face when, during the first official meeting with the Karagangans' ruling clique, he had accepted a glass of vodka.

"Brother James! What do you think you are doing?" Father Shaw had spluttered in a hoarse whisper.

"I don't want to be impolite to our hosts," he had whispered back, his face expressionless.

"You are putting your immortal soul in danger! I am going to report you for this as soon as we get back!"

"Of course, Father," said Milo as he put the glass to his lips. He took a large swallow. The liquor burnt his throat. It tasted wonderful. Raw, yes, but definitely vodka. How long since he had had a drink? Not since his early days on Belvedere, before the moral clamp-down. A long time ago.

The Karagangans, seated around the table, also looked surprised. They knew only too well the strait-laced customs of the Belvederians. This was a new departure and they eyed Milo curiously. "Interesting," Milo had said as he put the empty glass back onto the table. Father Shaw looked as if he would expire from extreme high blood pressure. Only the presence of the Karagangans prevented him from running verbally amuck.

The meeting had been held to acquaint the two Belvederians with the details of the planned expedition to Earth. Apart from the members of the ruling clique, the man who would head the expedition, Captain Ilya Vyushkov, was also present. Like the others, he had broad, Slavic features but looked still to be in his late twenties. He certainly displayed an enthusiasm and vitality that his superiors lacked. Milo wasn't surprised to learn later that Ilya had volunteered for the mission, as had all his crew. Milo thought he would be able to put Ilya to good use, eventually.

"The final modifications are still to be carried out on the ship," the Karagangan President, Sasha Iakinfovich, had told them at the start of the meeting. "They have taken longer than we expected but we hope that you will be underway within seven days. In the meantime we hope you will enjoy our hospitality here in Karaganga."

"We will do our best," Milo had replied, and that was when he accepted the vodka. Life on the Karagangan habitat no doubt had its restrictions but the Belvederian atmosphere of austerity was absent here. This conference room, Milo observed, was comfortably furnished and there were prints hanging on the walls. They were of a religious nature, true, but it made a change from the starkly bare walls of Belvedere. "So you intend to set up a trading agreement with the Earth people?" he asked the President.

119

This question provoked amusement among the Karagan-gans. The President replied, "Hardly. That is what we have told the Earth people, of course, but we will simply conquer them."

"Of course," Milo murmured. "But surely there will be resistance?"

"No doubt. They have told us themselves they have guns, even artillery, but they have no lasers or other beam weapons. Overcoming their resistance should present no real problem to Captain Vyushkov and his men."

Captain Vyushkov smiled and nodded at these words. Milo gave him another appraising glance then said to the President, "Well, Father Shaw and I are only concerned with determining whether the souls of the Earth people are worth saving. By subduing them as you plan you will make our task all the easier." He reached out and raised his empty glass. "I will have some more of your fine vodka, please, and then we will drink a toast to the success of our combined missions." As the glass was refilled he could hear Father Shaw spluttering beside him.

When they were finally alone in their cabin, Father Shaw was at last able to vent his spleen. At first all he could do was make incoherent noises while pointing an accusing finger at Milo. Milo sat down on his bunk, folded his arms and watched him calmly. This seemed to infuriate Father Shaw even more.

Words began to emerge. "You . . . you . . . it's . . . it's . . . you . . . it's intolerable . . . your behaviour . . . intolerable . . . you will suffer . . . I will see to it!"

"Being once again under the influence of gravity has, I see, brought the colour back into your cheeks," Milo told him.

"More insolence!" stammered the Father. "Brother James, when we get back to Belvedere you . . . you will be stripped of your rank in the Church. I will see that you are so severely disciplined that you will wish the good Lord would claim you before your allotted span has run its course!"

"Oh shut up, you fool," said Milo. It was time to take off the mask. "If you don't start behaving yourself you will never see Belvedere again."

Father Shaw flinched. He clearly could not believe what he was hearing. "Brother James . . ." he whispered, in astonishment, "you act as if you were possessed."

Milo nodded. "A good enough analogy. I am possessed. By *me*. Milo Haze. Brother James was just a façade. But a very useful one. It has kept me alive all the long and dreary years I was obliged to dwell in your ghastly society. But I'm free now and will not keep up the pretence a moment longer. Certainly not to merely humour *you*, you fat, ridiculous prig."

Father Shaw took a step away from him. There was now fear in his eyes. "You *are* possessed! It must be this godless place! I will pray for you. . . ."

Milo sprang up from his bunk, grabbed the Father around the neck with both his hands and lifted him easily from the floor. For the second time in an hour Father Shaw's face went puce, but this time for an entirely different reason. "Pray for yourself," Milo told him coldly as the Father struggled to breathe. "Unless you do as I say I will kill you. Understand?"

Father Shaw tried to nod. Milo released him and he fell to his knees, gasping and wheezing. Milo went and sat back down on his bunk. The Father stayed on his knees, regarding Milo fearfully as he rubbed his bruised neck. "What are you? What manner of demon?"

"I told you. My name is Milo Haze. I was once head of the Haze Genegineering Corporation on Earth. It was one of the major Gene Corporations before the Gene Wars. I fled the planet under an assumed name after the Wars, for obvious reasons. I've been hiding out on Belvedere ever since. Until now."

The expression on Father Shaw's face clearly showed that he thought Milo, or whatever entity it was that possessed him, was raving mad. "But you were *born* on Belvedere," he protested.

Milo told him the manner of his birth and explained how his original self had escaped to Mars. When he had finished he could tell from Father Shaw's expression that he no longer knew what to believe. "I'd appreciate it if you keep all this to yourself. Not that anyone would believe you if you did repeat it. And anyway, I'd say it was all the result of your space sickness. I'm the doctor, remember. Now all you have to do is to swear to obey me completely. The alternative for you will be, I assure you, extremely gruesome. So . . .?"

After a time, Father Shaw slowly nodded. "I swear it."

"Good," said Milo. "You can get up off your knees now. As gods go, I'm not really into ritual worship from my subjects. An attitude of genuine obsequiousness will suffice."

Milo was playing with Tyra when he was rudely interrupted.

"Milo!" The voice was so loud it hurt his ears and made Tyra flinch violently. But then, thought Milo, flinching violently was a speciality of hers. He rolled off the girl and sat up on the bed. "You really do pick the most appropriate moments, Ashley, to come and chat. What is it now?" As he spoke Tyra took the opportunity to spring from the bed and make a dash for the bathroom.

"I'm getting fed up, Milo!" boomed Ashley at the same painful volume. "When are you going to deliver me some *results*?"

"Be patient. It is only a matter of time. There are thousands of square miles of ice shelf to cover and only a limited number of spider-mechs to carry out the job. Perhaps if you would release your reserves . . .?"

"Don't be ridiculous!" she snapped. "Without them I would be helpless."

"You still don't trust me? I thought we were partners again."

"Hah!" The short, derisive laugh said it all.

"Seriously, the mechs have covered over half the shelf. We could strike pay dirt any day now."

"I'll give you one more week."

"Or . . .?" he asked.

"I'll put you down on the ice. And dressed as you are now."

"Ashley, be reasonable. I can't guarantee we'll find the habitat within one week. Ashley. . .?" But instinctively he knew her 'presence' had gone. He sat on the bed frowning for a time then got up and headed for the bathroom.

"We have established contact with Belvedere, sir," said the radio operator, and rose from his chair. Father Shaw took his place. He nervously wiped sweat from his forehead. "You may leave now," he told the operator, as he tried to keep the instructions for using the equipment clearly in his mind.

He waited until he heard the hiss of the door sliding shut behind the operator then leaned close to the microphone and pressed the send button. "This is Father Shaw calling from the Karaganga habitat. Who am I speaking to?"

There was no answer and he realised he was still pushing down on the send button. He released it and immediately heard a voice say, "I repeat, I am Brother Robert, Communications Officer Second Class. Over."

"Now listen carefully," said Father Shaw urgently. "I want you to ask CenCom for any available information on a man called Victor Parrish. Er, over."

There was a delay before the voice, now sounding puzzled, said, "You want this information now, Father Shaw? Over. . . ."

"Of course I want it now, you stu---" He stopped and forced himself to keep calm. "It's very important. Please hurry. Over."

"Yes, Father Shaw," said Brother Robert stonily. "It will take a few moments. Please wait."

Of course I'll wait, you fool, Father Shaw thought angrily, *what else could I possibly do*? But he waited with increasing impatience. And fear. He knew he was safe. Brother James was being given an inspection tour of the nearly-ready craft that would take them to Earth. Father Shaw was to have gone too but he cancelled at the last minute, saying that he was unwell. But the thought of Brother James, or whoever he was, finding out what he was doing made his stomach queasy and filled his chest with a growing cloud of panic. He resisted a nervous urge to look over his shoulder.

"Are you there, Father Shaw? Over."

"Yes, yes!" he snapped. "What have you learnt?" There was no reply, then he realised he wasn't pushing the send button. He did so. "I'm here," he said more calmly. "What have you learnt? Over."

"This man, Victor Parrish; according to CenCom there was somebody of that name but it was a long time ago. Over one hundred and sixty years ago, in fact. Surely that can't be the one you're interested in? Over."

His mouth dry, Father Shaw said, "What happened to him? Over."

"He died in tragic circumstances, Father. On an expedition to Mars in 2298. All but one of the crew were killed in a decompression accident. Over."

Father Shaw had started to tremble. Brother James *had* been telling the truth. . . .

He pressed the send button. "Now this is very important, Brother Robert. Listen carefully. I want you to call Father Massie right away. I have an important message for him. . . ." Father Shaw's heart gave a violent kick when a hand appeared out of nowhere, closed around his wrist and lifted it away from the send button. He twisted round. Brother James was smiling down at him. *It wasn't possible!* He hadn't heard him come in. "How . . .? How. . .?"

"I've been here all the time," said Milo. "I came in as the operator left."

"Hello? Father Shaw? Are you still there? Over."

"But . . . you were inspecting the ship. . . ." stammered Father Shaw, becoming aware that his wrist felt like it was being crushed. Brother James continued to smile down at him.

"I opted out as well. I told them I was concerned about your state of health. The trip here has been quite an ordeal for you and it was possible you might take a . . . turn . . . for the worse."

In a moment of chilling clarity Father Shaw realised Brother James's intention. "You're going . . . to kill me."

"No, of course not. Not as long as you do as I say."

"Father Shaw? Come in, Father Shaw! Over."

"You will," continued Brother James, "tell our colleague on Belvedere that your message for Father Massie is as follows: The mission so far, with God's help, has been successful and you have every reason to believe that the remainder will be equally successful. You look forward to carrying out God's work on Earth. Over and out." He let go of Father Shaw's wrist. "Do it."

Father Shaw depressed the send button and repeated the words. Again his wrist was gripped and his hand pulled away from the button. "Now," said Brother James, "I think we should return to our quarters. You look tired. You must rest."

Chapter Sixteen:

Jean-Paul knew it was going to be a long time, if ever, before he began *enjoying* underwater swimming. Down here below the waves Ayla was clearly in her element. The way she moved communicated her joy for this medium but for him it was still alien. Until he had fallen out of the crashing *Lord Montcalm* he had never been in the sea before. That had been bad enough but to go beneath the surface was even worse. On the first occasion it had been quite unnerving and he had to fight against panicking.

One problem was the feeling of claustrophobia. The breathing piece was the main cause of this; the device that forced air into his lungs at the same pressure as the surrounding water. To know that his every breath—his very life—depended on this small piece of equipment made him very uncomfortable. The other problem was the lack of visibility. Even here, close to the shore, where the water was exceptionally clear, Jean-Paul didn't like the way his field of vision rapidly faded away to a hazy barrier. He kept seeing shadowy movements in the fringe of that barrier and, having been told by Ayla that very occasionally small sharks managed to penetrate the metal grids in the sea walls, he found it impossible to relax.

Ayla swam in front of him and signalled that they should swim back. Jean-Paul felt relieved. As he swam beside her he felt secure enough to enjoy observing the graceful way Ayla's body moved underwater. He knew now, without a doubt, that he was fiercely in love with this woman. He was intoxicated by her. How absurd to think that only a short time ago he would have been shocked at the idea that he could ever make love to a ground dweller—earthworm—much less fall in *love* with one. How quickly the prejudices of a lifetime could wither away. . . .

They entered shallow waters where it was possible to stand. Jean-Paul was happy to be able to remove his breathing piece and restrictive face mask. Then he pulled off his flippers and slung them over his shoulders. He grinned at Ayla. "Well, what is the verdict?"

She made a face. "You still move like a drunk turtle. But you're getting better."

"Does that mean I can come with you on your jaunt tomorrow beyond the sea walls?"

"I'd prefer it if you had more practice but, yeah, I guess so."

They began to wade towards the shore. The sea people were still conspicuous by their absence but Ayla and her friends continued to go to the designated meeting point regularly in the hope they would eventually reappear. Ayla's plan to take the submersible all the way out to the underwater habitat had been predictably vetoed by her father when he had learned of it.

"Uh oh." Ayla had come to a stop and was peering towards the beach with her free hand held above her eyes to shield them from the bright sunlight. Jean-Paul looked. He saw Kell waiting for them on the beach. And standing some distance from him a group of three people he didn't recognise.

"What's up?" he asked her as she started moving forward again.

"The Banks brats. Jelker Banks's little brood. Just what I need."

There were two males and one female. One of the males and the female appeared to be in their early twenties, while the other male had reached his optimum age and therefore could be any age from thirty-five onwards. It was the latter who spoke first as Ayla and Jean-Paul walked up onto the beach. In a sneering tone, he said, "So it's true. Ayla Haddon is going with a Sky Man. The daughter of one of our ruling sextet has taken one of our enemies as a lover."

Ayla looked angry but said nothing. Kell, who had come over to help her out of her diving harness, looked even angrier, though Jean-Paul wasn't sure at just whom his anger was being directed. Jean-Paul decided he had better remain silent too while he waited to see what developed. He unbuckled his harness and dropped the heavy air bottles to the sand with relief.

"It's a disgrace, and an insult to your people." This came from the girl. "You daring to share your bed with someone who wanted to conquer Palmyra."

Ayla couldn't hold back this time. She faced the girl and said angrily, "Don't let your filthy tongue go any further, Joy! You know perfectly well that the council voted for amnesty towards the Sky People!"

"Not *all* the council, Ayla. Our father didn't, for one." It was the older man again.

Ayla turned to him now. "Well, he wouldn't, would he, Bron? Anything my father is for, your father is automatically against, no matter what it is."

"Our father isn't a traitor," said Joy.

"Are you saying that my father is?" asked Ayla coldly.

"Yeah," said the younger man. "He's selling us out to the spacers."

"That's nonsense and you know it!" cried Ayla, looking furious now. "The spacers are coming to help us!"

"Help us back to the stone age, you mean," sneered Bron.

"Why don't you just shut up," said Kell, finally joining in the argument.

"Like to try and make us?" said Bron, taking a step forward.

"Sure I would," Kell said, also moving forward.

"Don't, Kell," said Ayla, with a sigh. "It's not worth it.

It's just what they want. Stirring things up for the sake of it is something they learned from their father. It's his only pleasure. Come on, let's go."

She began to move off along the beach, carrying her equipment. After a few moments' hesitation, Kell reluctantly followed. Jean-Paul picked up his own equipment and, after giving the Banks group a polite nod, did likewise.

"Bye, Sky Man," Bron called out. "We'll be seeing you later." The implied menace was clear.

"God, I hate them," muttered Ayla when Jean-Paul had caught up with her and Kell. "How dare they say that about my father!"

"You should have let me thump Bron," said Kell, casting a glowering look back over his shoulder.

"No, it's like I said. Starting a fight is what they want. Damn that Jelker and his stirring. He's getting new followers every day. All saying that we're wrong to trust the spacers."

"Well, you don't have long to wait to prove them wrong," Jean-Paul pointed out. "The spacers will be here in a week."

"Yeah," nodded Ayla. "And then a whole load of people are going to have to apologise to Dad."

After helping Ayla and Kell to store the diving equipment, Jean-Paul left them and headed for the hospital. As usual Ayla asked if he wanted her to accompany him and as usual he thanked her and said no. It was his responsibility alone, and also he didn't want to inflict the sight of the burns victims upon her. He knew how such things affected her.

As he approached the hospital he saw that there was a knot of people in front of it. They turned in his direction when one of their number pointed him out and he realised they were waiting for him. They were all survivors from the *Lord Montcalm*. "Jean-Paul, we want to talk to you," said a man as Jean-Paul neared them. He counted eight. Five men and three women.

"Obviously," replied Jean-Paul. "What about?" He was

trying to put names to faces. He had only come to know these people since the crash. All his close friends and acquaintances had died in the disaster.

"About your plans. For us," said another man.

Mystified, Jean-Paul said, "What plans?"

"You're our leader. It's your responsibility to do something about our situation," cried a woman. Jean-Paul thought, but wasn't sure, that her name was Charlotte.

"Our situation," he repeated, still mystified. "And what is that exactly?"

Some of them exchanged worried glances. The man who had first spoken to him, whom he now recognised as Phillippe, said, "Being trapped down here with these damn earthworms. How long must we endure these humiliations? You must do something!"

Jean-Paul's first reaction was to laugh. After stifling that response he began to feel angry. These people—*his* people—were no better than the Banks trio he'd encountered earlier. "What do you expect me to do?" he asked sarcastically. "Knit a new Sky Lord out of thin air?"

"What we want you to do," said Phillippe, "is come up with a plan that will allow us to get the upper hand over the earthworms. As our leader it's your duty."

Jean-Paul was feeling angrier. Slowly he said, "It is not, because for one thing I am no longer your leader. And for another I think we owe these . . . *earthworms*, as you call them, our gratitude."

"Our gratitude!" cried Phillippe. "They shot us down! They killed most of our people!"

"We were about to bomb them into submission so that we could steal their food and all their other resources. They had every right to defend themselves. And after that they have offered us their hospitality and given us food and shelter. We have our freedom too. The best course of action would be to blend into their community; become a part of them."

"But we're *Sky People*!" protested a man called Raphael.

"We *were* Sky People," Jean-Paul said gently. "It's rather difficult to be Sky People without an airship. Therefore we are earthworms."

"No, never! Never!" cried several of them.

"Well, I'm prepared to call myself an earthworm," Jean-Paul said defiantly. "And I advise you to do the same."

There was silence as they stared at him with outright hostility. Then a woman, whose name he couldn't remember, said, "They say you've taken up with an earthworm whore. I can believe that now."

Her words electrified him. He trembled with fury but fought the urge to wade into the group with his fists flying. When he had regained control he said as calmly as he could, "I don't care what you think of me personally but you must believe me when I tell you that you must adapt or perish. And now if you'll excuse me I have business in the hospital." He pushed through them, using a little more force than was needed, and started up the wooden steps to the front door. As he reached it he heard one of the men call out, "Traitor."

"Poor Jean-Paul," said Ayla as she stroked his forehead. "They really upset you."

"They made me angry more than anything. My own people. How stupid can you get? What the hell do they think they can do? Form an underground army and take over Palmyra by force?"

"There's so few of them."

"I know." He sighed. "Even though there's enough of them to cause trouble. I had better speak to your father about it. He should arrange to have them watched."

"They are already. All you Sky People are being kept under observation."

He raised his eyebrows. "Oh yes? Who's watching me then?"

"Me," she said and kissed him hard, her tongue darting deep into his mouth.

Later he said, "You take your duties very seriously. Very commendable."

"Do you think I'd be here in your bed if it wasn't for my highly developed sense of civic duty?" she asked playfully.

"No, of course not. This isn't sex as far as you're concerned, it's purely a matter of good citizenship."

She laughed. "So they call me your earthworm whore, do they?"

"Yes," he said, unamused.

"I've never been called a whore before. I rather like it. The idea of being Jean-Paul's whore. . . ."

He turned his head and gave her a scowling look. She stuck her tongue out at him. "You are being ridiculous," he told her sternly.

"Oh, is that what you call it?" she said. Then she sat up and leaned over his groin. He felt her lips envelop him, felt the wetness of her mouth.

"Don't. . . ." he said, without conviction. "It's time we got some sleep."

To his relief she didn't stop. He was rapidly becoming erect again. When he was fully erect she sat up again. "We don't want to wake your father. . . ." he protested, even more feebly.

"We won't," she said as she swung one leg across him and then, with teasing slowness, lowered herself onto him. "He came home exhausted from the spacers' landing site. Nothing is going to wake him tonight."

Jean-Paul was no longer thinking about Ayla's father. He gave a low moan. Ayla looked down on him, smiling mischievously. "Am I still being ridiculous?"

He couldn't answer. She stuck her tongue out at him again and then slowly arched her back. He groaned with pleasure. And as he looked at her, consuming her body with his eyes and filled with a burning mixture of love and lust, he suddenly knew with a profound certainty that it was moments like this that swung the balance in life's favour. In

132

spite of all the blood and pain and death, *this* made it all worthwhile. He reached up and seized her breasts. "God, I love you, Ayla . . . I love you so much."

"Ayla, can you please keep your elbow out of my face," he said with annoyance.

"Sorry," she muttered and shifted her position. There was little free space in the spherical, forward pressure hull of the submersible. He and Ayla were cramped together directly behind Kell who was piloting. With Jean-Paul on board there had been no room for Juli who had been obliged, unhappily, to remain ashore.

"I must say I'm impressed by this vessel. It was constructed here in Palmyra?" he asked.

"Well, not exactly. Our two subs come from the habitat. We got them section by section and put them together ourselves. And a lot of the fittings were manufactured by us. But all our electronics come from the habitat. That's why it's important not to lose the link with the sea people."

"Is it much further?"

Ayla peered over Kell's shoulder and down through one of the lower viewing ports. "No," she told him. "We'll be there in about five minutes. Right, Kell?"

"Yeah." Kell sounded sullen. He was not the only one to be unhappy about Jean-Paul's presence in the submersible.

Jean-Paul tried again, unsuccessfully, to shift into a remotely comfortable position. Then he said, "The air seems to be getting stale, or is it my imagination?"

"No," Ayla told him. "The carbon dioxide is building up faster than the CO_2 scrubber can handle it. . . ." She pointed to a box-shaped device attached to the wall of the hull. "I'll bleed some fresh oxygen into the air mix."

For her to reach the oxygen cylinder, which was by his side, involved a great deal of intimate physical manoeuvring. When they were practically face-to-face he smiled at her and said, "I think I had a religious experience last night, thanks to you."

"Is that what you call it?" she said lightly, but at the same time indicated her disapproval with a flick of her eyes. He realised she didn't want him to say such things in front of Kell. He immediately understood and nodded. She succeeded in turning the valve on the oxygen bottle and the gas hissed out. Jean-Paul noticed the difference immediately.

"We're here," announced Kell, then pulled two levers. The submersible began to sink and Jean-Paul presumed that Kell had let water into the buoyancy tanks. Ayla began opening the hatch that led into the diving chamber. "Come on, let's suit up."

He followed her through into the chamber which was also spherical and they began to pull on their wet suits. Ayla had explained that the deeper water was also colder. There was a gentle bump, which told them that the vessel was now sitting on the bottom. Kell then joined them in the chamber and sealed the hatch behind him. When they were all suited up, and had made sure that all their breathing systems were functioning properly, Kell turned a handle on the side of the chamber and water began to flood in.

It rose rapidly and Jean-Paul felt very uneasy as it passed his face. The sensation of claustrophobia was intense. When the chamber was full Kell reached up and turned the handle of the upper hatch. The hatch opened and Kell, after picking up his spear gun, swam up through it. Ayla indicated that he was to go next. Jean-Paul picked up his weapon too then followed Kell.

When he emerged from the submersible he got his first view of his surroundings. The vessel was sitting on a clear stretch of sand surrounded by outcrops of coral and a wide variety of underwater vegetation. The light here wasn't as strong as it had been on his previous dives which meant that his field of vision was further reduced. That hazy barrier seemed much closer. . . .

He took a firmer grip on his weapon, in the hope that it would provide him with some much needed comfort. It was not a spear gun; Ayla had called it a stun-stick. It consisted of a wooden rod, two and a half feet long, with a grip on one end and a short metal cylinder on the other. The cylinder contained a rifle cartridge. All Jean-Paul had to do was jab it at whatever he was aiming to kill and the cartridge would automatically detonate. The resulting concussion, he had been assured by Ayla, was enough to destroy the nervous system of even the biggest shark. Jean-Paul didn't fancy the idea of being only two and a half feet away from even a small shark. The other drawback about the stun-stick was that it could be used only once.

Ayla had joined them now and she pointed in the direction from which they could expect company to arrive. Unlike them she was unarmed. Indicating that they should remain by the submersible she swam some ten to fifteen yards from them and then came to a halt, waiting.

Jean-Paul rather hoped that it was going to turn into a wasted journey. From Ayla's description of the sea people they didn't sound too appetising, despite her claim that they were now totally peaceful towards humans. He looked at his watch. They could wait for only forty-five minutes—that was as long as their air supplies would last.

After a time Jean-Paul grew bored with swimming in small circles and, by means of hand gestures, indicated to Kell that he was going off to explore one of the nearby outcrops of coral reef. Kell made gestures that Jean-Paul read to mean "be careful".

The reef rose from the seabed up to a height of about twenty feet. When he reached it, he looked back at the submersible and Kell, both of which appeared to be an uncomfortably long distance away. But he shrugged off his apprehension as he watched the small inhabitants of the reef swim or scurry away from him—brightly coloured fish, crabs . . . an octopus that kept changing colour as it moved across the coral to blend in with the differently coloured backgrounds.

By the time he reached the top of the reef all thought of potential danger had fled his mind. So he got a bad shock when he found himself face to face with a monster.

Chapter Seventeen:

The thing was about ten feet away from him, hovering just above the reef. Jean-Paul stared in frozen surprise. Whether the creature was also surprised to see him was impossible to tell; its facial features were unreadable. The thing was about seven feet in height, though the plume of spiky fins growing out of the top of its head made it seem taller. It was humanoid in shape and covered in thick, bony scales that were bluish-grey in colour. It had round, fish-like eyes, no nose and a very wide mouth. It had large webbed feet with long talons protruding from the toes. The large hands were webbed and taloned too, and there were wicked-looking spurs protruding from the outer side of each wrist, and from the elbows.

His initial reaction was to flee but he told himself that this thing had to be one of Ayla's missing sea people. One of her *peaceable* sea people. And he didn't want to wreck anything for Ayla by scaring the creature away, so he raised his free hand in what he hoped was a universal peace gesture. The round, expressionless eyes continued to regard him. The creature made no attempt to duplicate the gesture. Jean-Paul was wondering whether to move closer when he was suddenly, and violently, shoved aside. . . .

It was Kell. The young black man was moving through the water like a missile, finned feet kicking furiously, straight at the sea creature. As Jean-Paul watched in surprise, he saw Kell fire his spear gun. The spear struck the creature in the centre of its chest with considerable force. But it didn't penetrate the tough scales; instead it merely bounced harm-lessly off.

Kell was starting to turn now, clearly planning to give the creature a wide berth, but suddenly the creature erupted in a flurry of movement. It was so fast Jean-Paul didn't quite see what happened, but then he saw Kell floating limply in the water, his only movement a feeble kicking of his feet, a black cloud of threads spreading out from the front of his body. As Kell slowly rolled over in the water Jean-Paul saw what the threads were and where they were coming from. Kell had been ripped open. There was a jagged gash stretching from one side of his stomach to the other.

He had no time to be shocked. The creature was coming straight at him. Blindly, Jean-Paul stabbed out with the stun-stick. A shock-wave ran up his arm as he heard a muffled *thump*. Desperately, he kicked his legs and swam back-wards, trying to see through the cloud of tiny bubbles that obscured everything, knowing that at any moment he might feel the claws of the creature ripping through both his wet suit and his flesh. He had used up the single charge in his stun-stick but he still held it out protectively in front of him. He had a knife strapped to his left calf but he knew it would be useless against the scales of that thing. . . .

He tried to scream around his mouthpiece when a hand closed on his shoulder. It was Ayla. She was helping him to swim away. He followed her example and tried to keep his movements calm and coordinated and immediately made better progress. As he looked back at the cloud of bubbles, something was thrashing around in its centre, plainly out of control. The stun-stick had worked; the creature's nervous system was shattered.

The swim to the submersible seemed to Jean-Paul to be an awfully long way. He kept looking about nervously, expecting another of the creatures to loom out of the haze. But they reached the vessel without further incident. Ayla signalled that he should enter the hatch first. He didn't need

138

much persuasion. After a final glance towards the reef he lowered himself through the hatchway, banging his airbottles on the rim as he did so. Almost as soon as his feet touched the bottom of the chamber Ayla came in after him. She screwed shut the hatch then threw a lever. Instantly the water level began to drop.

By the time the water had dropped to his waist Jean-Paul was aware of an awful sensation in his ears and sinuses but all he could think about was what he had seen happen to Kell. As soon as Ayla had removed her mask and mouthpiece he seized her by the shoulders and cried, "What the hell went wrong out there?! Why did Kell attack it? I thought you said those things were safe!"

Ayla was trembling violently and tears were running down her face. She couldn't get any words out at first, then, between choking sounds, she said, "That . . . wasn't . . . one of *ours*. Too big . . . different markings. Our sea people . . . had striped bodies. Kell . . . he . . . saw . . ." She couldn't go on. She buried her face in her hands and wept. Jean-Paul held her to him, trying to comfort her. Realisation dawned. Kell had saved his life. And at the cost of his own. . . .

"Ayla, come on, let's get going before any more of these things turn up. Open the hatch to the forward cabin."

She shook her head. "Can't . . ." she snuffled. "We have to depressurise . . . can't do it quickly otherwise we get the bends . . . have to wait until the air pressure drops to normal . . . to one atmosphere."

"How long will that be?" he asked.

"Fifteen to twenty minutes."

"Oh, marvellous," he muttered.

Suddenly there was a loud bang on the submersible's outer hull. Ayla looked up at Jean-Paul, wild hope in her eyes. "Kell! It's Kell! He's not dead, just injured! He wants to come in!"

"It can't be him," Jean-Paul told her firmly. He could still

139

see the hideous wound across Kell's abdomen, the pale intestines spilling out along with the black cloud of blood.

"Yes it is!" She pulled free of his grip and reached for her mouthpiece.

"What are you doing?" he demanded.

"I'm going back outside. Kell needs help! He's hurt!"

He grabbed her again and shook her. "Ayla, listen to me. That *can't* be Kell! He's dead!"

She tried to pull free. "No, he's not! Let me go! He needs me! You don't have to come. . . ."

There was another bang. Louder this time, and a crunching sound. The submersible actually rocked. Ayla stopped struggling and stared into his eyes. "That is definitely not Kell," he said. "It has to be that thing. Or another one like it."

She nodded and said, "Yes," in a small voice.

Another bang and more crunching sounds. "It sounds as if whatever it is out there is eating its way through the hull," said Jean-Paul, in a tone that was supposed to make light of the situation but failed. He was remembering the powerful jaws on the creature.

"It's just the outer hull fairing," she told him. "It's pretty fragile stuff. But there's no way it could get through the pressure hull."

More bangs. The vessel shuddered. Ayla stepped close and hugged him hard. "You don't seem too positive about that," he told her as he hugged her too.

"Oh, I am. We'll be all right in here, but it's all the damage it can do to the exposed parts of the sub that I'm worried about—the power cables, the thrusters, the planes— the sub could be completely disabled."

"I see," he said slowly. "So we'd either have to make a dash for it outside in our breathing gear or stay in the sub until we die from lack of air."

"It may not come to that. When we don't return on time

Juli will sound the alert and they'll bring the other sub out to look for us."

"And when will that be?"

"In about two hours at least." She peered at a pressure gauge on the chamber wall. "In another ten minutes we'll be able to open the hatch to the forward section. . . ."

It was a long ten minutes as they stood there holding onto each other while the submersible was rocked about with increasing violence accompanied by terrible sounds of destruction. Jean-Paul feared that by the time they finally got to the controls there would be nothing left of the sub but its two spherical pressure hulls.

Ayla finally announced that the air pressure in the chamber was back to one atmosphere. She opened the hatchway and they crawled through into the forward section. She sat in the pilot's seat and examined the instrument panel. "Well, we've still got power. That's something."

He knelt behind her and peered over her shoulder. "See anything out there?"

"Not yet." She threw a row of switches and Jean-Paul heard a whine as the thrusters started up. Ayla pushed the levers that controlled the buoyancy tanks. The submersible started to rise, but as it did so it began to list to one side. And at the same time there was another violent thump on the sub's outer hull, followed by the now familiar sound of tearing metal. "Temper, temper," muttered Jean-Paul.

"They've ripped open one of the port buoyancy tanks," Ayla told him. "The rear one. Lucky it's only one."

"So far." Jean-Paul stared out through one of the view ports. He couldn't see much; the straining thrusters were kicking up too much sand. But he saw something he didn't want to see—a face pressed up against the port. It was the face of a creature like the one he had seen earlier, but it was much closer to him. "Jesus!" he exclaimed.

Another thump on the side of the sub and Ayla said, "Uh oh, there's more than one of them. They must have been attracted by the vibrations given off by the one you got as it died." The creature, clinging to the nose of the sub, attempted to smash the glass in another of the ports with the spur on his wrist, all the time keeping his blank gaze fixed on the pair of them. Jean-Paul wondered how long it would be before the glass shattered.

Milo unlocked the door and slid it open. To his disappointment Shan didn't try anything; no attempts to hit him with a chair, no booby traps, nothing. Instead he was just lying on the bed, his hands behind his head. No sign of anger either. He even looked bored. A pose, no doubt, but it irritated Milo. And he hadn't been in a good mood all day.

"This is very unlike you, Minervan," he said sourly. "Given up already?"

Shan looked at him. "I've given up playing your games, Milo."

"Have you? No. . . ." Milo shook his head. "I'll decide when the games are over, not you."

"Whatever you say, Milo." Shan resumed gazing at the ceiling. Milo went to the bed and looked down at him.

"Perhaps I shall break one of your arms. Strictly for amusement, of course."

"You know I couldn't stop you."

"Yes. But it would be too boring. Perhaps breaking Tyra's arm would be more stimulating."

He knew that would get a reaction and it did. Shan abruptly turned his head towards him, eyes narrowed with anger. But he didn't speak.

"Aren't you curious about the state of her health?" Milo asked him. "After all, it's been three days since my last visit. Anything could have happened to her in that time. You know me."

Shan couldn't help himself. "How . . . how is she?"

Milo smiled. "Oh, the same as usual. A few fresh cuts and

bruises but nothing serious." He observed Shan's involuntary grimace with satisfaction. "And she's definitely getting better in bed. Coming up with all sorts of interesting tricks to divert me. By cooperating now instead of resisting she hopes I won't er, chastise her so frequently. I'm letting her think this ploy is working . . . for the time being."

Shan's expression was now one of total loathing. "Let her go, you filthy bastard!" he snarled. "Or I'll kill you! Somehow, someway, I promise I'll kill you."

"That's more like it," said Milo approvingly. "I was beginning to think you were becoming a bore."

Shan sprang up from the bed and grabbed Milo by the throat. Milo laughed, broke Shan's grip with ease and punched him in the mouth. Shan collapsed back onto the bed, blood streaming from his cut lips. "Is that any way for a Minervan man to behave?" he asked, mockingly. He was enjoying himself now and his previous bad mood was fading.

The cause of the mood had been that damned dream again. Of Miranda, the female clone of himself that he had created, and of their final night together back on his estate all those years ago. Milo had known that the mob was on its way and had told her to prepare for a quick getaway. He had been astounded when she refused to leave with him, but then it had all come out; her true feelings about him. ". . . You can't see what you've become. The human personality is the product of infinitely complicated and sophisticated biological processes and science has a long way to go before it unravels them. You can't chop great chunks out of the system—as your genegineers did with you—without destroying something vital. . . . Yes, yes, that's it. In a sense you've *killed* yourself. It's ironic, actually. All that money and effort to turn yourself into a superman, but by doing so you've committed a form of suicide. You're walking around thinking you're immortal but you're dead inside and the ants are already feeding on your soul."

The dream was remarkably vivid. Every detail was crystal

143

clear and the centuries that separated him from that night simply fell away. There was Miranda, dressed in a man's dinner jacket and trousers, standing in front of him, face contorted with anger and contempt. It was the contempt that got to him. The contempt in her final words when he'd asked her to change her mind and escape with him. "No, Milo. Because I just can't *stand* being in your presence any more. It's not just your altered personality, it's physical as well. Those 'enhancements' of yours again, they've screwed you up on some subtle level. I'm telling you the truth when I say that you physically revolt me. And I mean that with every one of *your* cells in *my* body."

Yes, those words had sealed her fate. He had sabotaged her flipper and then watched from a safe distance in his own flipper as the mob tore her to pieces on the landing pad.

He smiled down at the dazed Shan. Perhaps he *would* break his arm. . . .

"Milo . . ."

"Not now, Ashley, I'm busy."

"This is important. We've found Shangri La."

Chapter Eighteen:

Ayla retracted the articulated grappling arm as far as possible, turned it and closed its pincer round the creature just below the shoulder. The pincer dug deep and the creature reacted as hoped; it released its grip on the submersible and kicked itself away. It was powerful and almost managed to tear its arm loose from the metal pincer but failed. Ayla let the arm extend to its full length and then activated the other arm, which contained the arc-welding unit. It was all over very quickly. She released the dead creature and it slowly began to sink. At the same time, the sub began to rise, but the sound of tearing metal above them indicated that another of the things was still with them.

"Look," said Jean-Paul, pointing over her shoulder. "More of them!" He could see at least a dozen of the creatures coming across the reef. Ayla turned the submersible around and gave the thrusters full power. "What the hell are they?"

"I don't know . . . genetically created sea people like Tiger's people but a different breed, or design, genegineered by a different corporation. Or maybe they've mutated. That's what Tiger was trying to warn me about, where those scars he had came from. His territory was being invaded by these things. Maybe they came from deeper waters. That's why he wanted weapons . . . and I let him down."

"You weren't to know."

"But I knew *something* was very wrong. I should have tried harder to convince Dad and Lyle. And Kell would still be alive. . . ."

He was about to say that she shouldn't blame herself when

there was a cacophony from above. "Still got company up there," he muttered when the noise had died down. "What do you think? Are we going to make it?"

"Depends on how much more of the sub our passenger wrecks. We've still got power, but if he gets to work on the cables from the batteries then we are . . . sunk."

More sounds of angry destruction and Jean-Paul felt the sub lurch. Ayla glanced at the instrument panel. "Another buoyancy tank flooded. We can't maintain negative buoyancy. I'll have to switch over to the treads. . . ."

The submersible touched bottom again. A few moments later it began to move slowly forward as Ayla engaged the sub's caterpillar treads. "This is going to eat up our power but we have no choice."

"How far to the outer gate?" he asked.

She threw a switch. A loud *beeping* noise filled the cabin. "That's the gate's transponder signal, loud and strong. It's dead ahead. Less than a hundred yards."

"And what happens when we reach it?"

"What do you mean? We go through it, of course."

"Yeah, and what about our friend on top? And the ones following us? They're probably right behind us by now."

She turned and stared at him. "You're right. I'm just not thinking straight."

"Perfectly understandable. I'm not flying level myself right now. But what are we going to do?"

"Let me think."

"Be my guest."

The outer sea wall loomed up ahead of them. Ayla moved the sub right up to the gate and then switched off the power to the treads. There was a sound of something moving on top of the sub. Their unwelcome passenger was still up there. They both stared out through the ports at the massive gate made, like the sea wall, of heavy steel mesh and thick wood. He said, "Any brilliant ideas yet?"

"I wouldn't call it brilliant but it's better than nothing."

"I'm dying to hear it," he said and immediately regretted his choice of words.

She took a deep breath. "As you've seen earlier, the gate mechanism responds automatically when it receives a signal from the sub. I'll show you how to operate it. You'll raise the gate only a couple of feet. It will leave enough space for me to wriggle through but not those creatures. Of course, I won't be able to take any breathing equipment. What do you think?"

"I think you're right. It's not brilliant. Insane, in fact."

"Look, we don't have any alternative. And we don't have much time either."

He realised, with alarm, that she was serious about it. "Then I'll go," he heard himself saying, and instantly regretted his words.

"Don't be ridiculous. You're too big, too slow and you swim like a stone. You'd never make it back to shore."

"I guess not," he said, relieved. "But how do you think you're going to get by that thing out there? And his friends, who must be close by now?"

"There's another stun-stick in that locker," she said with a nod towards the locker.

"Just one?"

"It'll be enough. Element of surprise and all that." She got out of her seat and indicated that he should take her place at the controls. As they squeezed by each other in the confined space he took hold of her. She was shaking slightly. "Take a bloody deep breath and swim fast," he told her.

"I will," she said. "Now sit down and I'll show you how to operate the gate."

When she had finished he said, "One final question. What about me? Does your wider plan involve my possible survival?"

"Yes, dimwit. You just sit here safe and sound until I return with reinforcements. You've got plenty of air. Now I must go." She gave him a quick kiss and hurried into the

147

diving chamber. The hatch slammed shut, was secured and a short time later Jean-Paul heard the water rushing into the chamber. His stomach went unpleasantly loose at the thought of what she was about to do. He peered intently out of the port at the gate, finger over the 'raise' signal button. He had to do this exactly right. Lift the gate too far and he would be as good as killing her; not lift it far enough and it would amount to the same thing. He sat there waiting tensely for her signal that the chamber was full and she was about to open the hatch.

He heard her bang on the hull wall. He pressed the button. Nothing seemed to happen at first but then the huge gate shuddered and began to move, raised by a system of heavy counterweights on the opposite side as well as by a powerful electric motor. He heard a *thump* outside and the pressure hull rang like a bell. The stun-stick detonating? He hoped so. But where the hell was she? He stared at the slowly rising gate. How big was the gap now? A foot? Eighteen inches? It was hard to judge. . . .

Ayla flashed into view, swimming furiously. And she wasn't alone. One of the creatures was close behind. And *another*! Coming from the other side! Jesus! Swim! Swim! He realised the gate was still rising. He took his finger off the 'raise' button and pressed 'hold'. Ayla had reached the bottom of the gate and was starting to wriggle under it. Did she have enough space, he wondered frantically? Her body was under the gate now and only her legs, kicking furiously, were visible. But now the nearest of the creatures was almost upon her . . . a dark claw lashed out at one of her vulnerable legs . . . trying to seize her ankle. The creature failed, but left a long gash down her calf. Jean-Paul winced as blood blossomed from the wound. Then she was gone from view. She'd done it! But the first creature was also wriggling under the gate. . . . *Christ*, thought Jean-Paul, I've raised it too far!

He pressed the 'down' button. Again, nothing seemed to

happen at first and it looked as if the creature was going to get through. A second creature was starting to wriggle under it as well. Finally the gate came down, and trapped both of them. As the full weight of the massive gate settled on them they were crushed into the sand and a large cloud of black blood erupted into the water, obscuring them from Jean-Paul's relieved view.

He gave a deep sigh and leaned back in the seat, letting the tension—some of it, at least—seep out of him. He was still worried about Ayla. That had been a bad gash in her leg. She would be losing blood. Would she have the strength to make it all the way to shore? It was a long way to swim. . . .

Jan reacted with surprise when Davin materialised in front of her in her bedroom. She put down the book she'd been reading and said irritably, "That's all right, come right on in. Don't bother to knock."

"Forgive me. I didn't mean to startle you."

"Oh? Then what *did* you mean to do?"

He ignored the question. "I have some information that might be of interest to you."

"Yes?" she said suspiciously.

"The habitat has been located by your, and our, enemies."

Jan sat upright. "Milo . . . and Ashley?"

"If what you have said is correct, then yes. An airship sits directly above us. It is presumably theirs. Our sensors show that they are boring through the ice shelf with lasers. The lasers are being fired through an array of weighted optic fibres which is being gradually lowered through the melting ice. An ingenious system. And one which will be equally effective underwater. Once through the ice the array will be lowered until it makes contact with the hull of the habitat. The choice we will no doubt be given is to surrender or suffer destruction."

It was the calm way that Davin said all this that really

annoyed Jan. Bitterly, she said, "So what are you going to do about this *ingenious* system? Applaud it while it fries us?"

"It won't come to that."

"I'm relieved to hear it. So what are you going to do? Move the habitat to a new location?"

"No."

"Then you'll destroy the Sky Angel with the Toy? Or some other weapon?"

"No. We intend to negotiate with this Milo, and the Ashley program."

"Negotiate?" she cried in astonishment. "You can't *negotiate* with Milo. Nor with Ashley. I told you she's mad. And you'd be mad to try."

"Nevertheless, we intend to try. And we want you to be our representative. We want you to go up to the airship in the Toy and negotiate with Milo and Ashley on our behalf."

"Me?" she said, blankly.

"Yes. You."

It was nearly an hour and a half since Ayla had got through the gate. Surely she had reached the shore about an hour ago, even with the handicap of her injured leg. Help had to be on the way. The possibility that she had failed to get ashore he kept buried in the back of his mind.

He was also trying to ignore the creature who was doggedly banging at one of the viewing ports with a jagged chunk of coral. The glass was holding but was becoming scored with scratch marks. He had made ineffectual attempts at driving the creature away with the grappling arm but he lacked Ayla's skill. He kept the thing away with the arc-welding arm but it rapidly ran out of power. He was sitting in darkness now apart from the lights from the control panel, and what little light was coming in through the ports.

Elsewhere, the other creatures continued their assault on the submersible. From the sound of it, they too were using

150

pieces of coral, or rocks, to assist their efforts. The creatures had long since given up their attempts to raise the gate by sheer strength alone. Jean-Paul couldn't be sure just how many of the creatures were in the area but from the numbers he'd seen passing back and forth in front of the sub there were a lot of them. Maybe between twenty and thirty.

Something hit him in the face.

He blinked and looked. It was water.

Chapter Nineteen:

The Toy emerged from a hatchway in the side of the great metal sphere that was Shangri La and cut through the water with ever-increasing speed. Inside, Jan gave Robin a concerned glance. He looked uneasy. He hadn't wanted to come but she had insisted. She knew what they were doing was very risky but she didn't want to be separated from him again. She had been surprised when Davin had so readily agreed to her demand that Robin accompany her.

"Don't worry," she told him. "You'll stay in the Toy until I'm sure the situation is safe. If it all goes wrong and I end up a prisoner, or worse, the Toy will take you back to Shangri La."

"No, I won't leave you," he said, but there wasn't much conviction in his voice. Still, she appreciated the gesture.

She had the distinct feeling that she was being used. But Davin, and that other program, Phebus, had been very convincing. And if everything did go as planned it would be a way of getting out of Shangri La indefinitely. If . . . if . . .

She had initially refused when Davin had asked her to go and negotiate with Milo and Ashley. But then Davin explained that the so-called negotiations would be a cover for an entirely different plan of action. "We want you to take something on board the Sky Angel," Davin told her.

"Don't tell me . . . it's a bomb," she said, and remembered with embarrassment the last time she had been required to smuggle a bomb on board a Sky Lord and exactly where she had been required to hide it.

"It's not a bomb," Davin told her. At that moment a

mech scuttled into the room and extended a mandible towards her. She saw it was holding what appeared to be a small gun. Idly, she wondered how long the mech had been outside the door, waiting for its cue. She took the small gun and looked at it. "I think I'd prefer a bomb," she said finally.

"That is much more powerful than any bomb."

"Really? What does it shoot?"

"Me." A woman had appeared in the room beside Davin. Another program, of course, but Jan had never seen two program projections at the same time before. And she had never seen this particular program before. This projection took the form of an austere young woman dressed in a long, metal-coloured grey robe. She had very sharp cheek bones and her hair was pulled back into a tight bun. She looked at Jan and said, "I am Phebus. I will be coming with you to the Sky Angel."

Jan looked at her and then again at the small gun she held. "In *this*?" she asked, wanting to laugh.

"In a sense."

"We intend to infiltrate the ship's computer system," said Davin to Jan.

Jan shook her head. "There's no way either Milo or Ashley would let me near the central computer in the control pod."

"You won't have to get near it," Davin said. "Just fire this weapon at any of the ship's mechs. That will be sufficient for Phebus."

"Shoot it at a mech?" Jan said wonderingly. She presumed they had created some kind of new, miniaturised software. "How many chances to fire the thing will I have?"

"Only the one."

She sighed. "I don't know. It sounds very risky to me. How can you be sure it will work?"

"Trust us," said Phebus.

She laughed dryly. "Oh sure. Look, it isn't just Ashley

153

you have to deal with in that system, there's Carl as well. I told you about him. He's like you—a pure program, and very smart."

"And as we told you, we have been constantly evolving. Carl represents a centuries-old technology. Phebus will be able to handle him."

Jan still wasn't convinced. "I don't know . . . wouldn't it be simpler just to use the Toy to destroy the laser system they're melting the ice with? And then just blow the control pod to pieces, along with Ashley?"

"No. We don't want to damage the Sky Angel. We need it."

"You need it?" she asked, surprised. "Why?"

"We have decided to do what you suggested."

"Me?"

Phebus said, "We are going to use the stored biological resources on board the Sky Angel to aid what remains of humanity. As you yourself attempted to do, in your small way. But we will also create new organisms that will destroy the blight in all its forms."

"You *will*?" she said, feeling a sudden surge of elation. But then suspicion replaced it. "But why? You've always refused to involve yourself with the world beyond the habitat. All you care about is the Eloi. You told me yourself enough times that their protection is your sole motivation. Why the change of—hah!—heart? Why this new-found sense of altruism?"

"Believe us, our planned actions fit in with our prime directives. It is nothing to do with altruism. You know we are incapable of such an emotion. It is just that the situation has changed. New factors have entered the picture," said Phebus coldly.

"I don't understand."

"Be patient. All will be explained to you later," said Phebus.

"So will you do it?" asked Davin.

154

"Yeah . . . yeah, why not?" She again looked at the tiny gun in her hand. "Rats," she muttered under her breath.

The Toy emerged from under the edge of the ice shelf and turned upwards. It exploded out of the water and increased in speed. It turned in a wide curve and then began to fly back over the ice shelf. The Toy soon reached its top speed and so it was only a matter of minutes before the Sky Angel showed up on the visual monitors. "Toy," she said, "establish radio contact with the airship. With Ashley or Carl. Tell them we represent the habitat. We are coming to discuss a truce. We will make a bargain to give them what they want if they call off their attack. We will land on their upper hull and wait. Understood?"

"Of course."

The white Sky Angel was almost hugging the surface of the ice shelf. Great clouds of water vapour were billowing out from beneath it as the lasers continued to bore their way through the ice. It gave her ambiguous feelings to see the Sky Angel again. She had enjoyed her happiest times on board that airship. First the years with her son, and then later there had been Robin's arrival. But also she had experienced some of her darkest moments. First Ceri's death, and then Simon's psychological death when Milo had taken over his body. . . .

As the Toy drew closer to the Sky Angel the monitors blanked out. The Toy shuddered and bucked.

"We are under laser attack," announced the Toy.

"What a surprise. Have you sent the message?"

"Yes, on all frequencies. There has been no response."

"Repeat it when we're clear of all this," she ordered, then turned and gave Robin a reassuring squeeze on his arm. "Don't worry. We're perfectly safe."

Looking pale, he gave a tight-lipped smile and said, "You forget, I've been through all this before. But the last time *you* were doing the shooting."

155

The Toy tipped backwards, pushing them into their seats. The monitors came back on. Jan saw they were speeding up the side of the huge airship, very close to the surface of its hull. The lasers were no longer firing. "This is fun, isn't it?" she asked Robin.

"Hmph."

The Toy followed the curve of the hull, turned and then came down with a slight bump near one of the top hatches. "Still no response," said the Toy.

"Keep transmitting. All we can do is wait. I'm sure someone, or something, will turn up soon." Jan undid her harness and pulled the small gun out of her pocket. It was tiny enough to conceal in her palm. "Why do I feel I'm about to make a fool of myself?"

He patted her on the hand. "I think you're being very brave."

"That's one way of describing it, I suppose," she said, and laughed.

It was exactly fifteen minutes later that the nearby hatch opened and a man climbed out. Milo. He was followed by two spider mechs. Jan thanked the Mother God under her breath. She didn't know what she would have done if Milo had come alone. She zoomed in on Milo. She was relieved to see that no discernible physical trace of her son remained. Milo, now fully grown, looked exactly as she remembered his original self.

He and the spiders came round to the side of the Toy and halted ten feet away. He was wearing a pair of black overalls that didn't seem to be sufficient protection against the cold. He looked unusually uneasy. She could see his mouth moving and realised he was yelling something. She told the Toy to relay his words. . . .

". . . here. So come and show yourself and we'll get down to some serious talking."

"Open the hatch," Jan told the Toy. The double hatch

156

began to slide open. Jan started to crawl through. She heard movement behind her and saw that Robin intended to follow her out. "You're staying in here," she said, annoyed. "On top of everything else you're not dressed for it."

He shook his head. "No way. I'm not an invalid. Come on, get moving."

Reluctantly, she climbed through and jumped down onto the airship's hull, the weapon concealed in her hand. Immediately she felt her heat suit react to the drop in temperature.

The look on Milo's face as he recognised her gave her a great deal of perverse pleasure.

"Jesus . . . *you!*" he exclaimed.

"It's Jan!" cried one of the mechs with Ashley's voice, pointing out the obvious.

"Hello, Milo," she said, keeping all emotion out of her voice.

Milo looked just as surprised to see Robin also emerge from the Toy behind her but in typical Milo fashion he quickly recovered and smiled his familiar smug smile. "Well, well, Robin of Sherwood as well. This is indeed just like old times. I'm happy to see you both alive and well, especially you, Jan. I was afraid I didn't give much for your chances after Ashley dumped you two on the ground."

"Still dishing out the same old bullshit, Milo," Jan said. The small gun seemed to be burning into the flesh of her palm.

"Yeah, Milo, how come they're still alive?" demanded Ashley through one of the mechs. "And how come they're *here*?"

"We got lucky," said Jan. She wanted this whole thing over with quickly. She could hear Robin shivering next to her.

Milo thoughtfully ran a hand over his bald head and nodded. "I think I've got it. When the Toy took off from here it was heading back to pick him up. And you. Some sort of homing device that I missed?"

"Yes, Milo, something like that. Now let's get down to business."

"Yeah," said Ashley eagerly. "About the terms of your surrender, and the surrender of those other creeps down below in the habitat."

Jan took a step closer to the spider that had spoken. Her hand holding the gun was slippery with sweat. "I wasn't under the impression we were surrendering. I'm here to represent the Eloi and their guardians and to work out a solution that will be of mutual agreement."

"They agree to give me a new body or they all die," said Ashley.

"What?" asked Jan, taken aback. She glanced at Milo who gave a slight shrug and said, "I've explained to Ashley that from what we have learned of the marvels contained within Shangri La the provision of a new body for Ashley would be well within the limits of the habitat's bio-technology. I'm correct, of course?"

Jan quickly caught on and nodded. "Of course you are. They can do anything down there."

"Really?" asked both mechs simultaneously, voices full of eagerness.

"Yes," said Jan, taking another step forward. "Their technology is truly marvellous. Just look at this for an example." She revealed the small gun, and fired. She was only three feet from the nearest spider. She couldn't miss.

There was a fizzing sound and then a bright flash on the spherical body of the spider. And then, nothing. . . . Apart from Milo moving faster than any human should and driving the heel of one hand into her side while knocking the weapon out of her grasp with his other hand. She went down in a red haze of pain and confusion. When she could focus her eyes again Milo was standing over her and examining the weapon with an expression of disdain. Behind him Robin was also in a prone position and groaning. Milo had knocked him down as well.

"Same old Jan," Milo told her wearily. "Always trying for the impossible with inadequate planning and inadequate equipment. What you hoped to achieve with this little toy I have no idea. It's only capable of firing once and the mech you shot isn't even damaged. It's a shame. When I first met you I had such high hopes. I thought you might be shaped into something that would be worthy of me."

"You're missing . . . something . . . Milo," groaned Robin. "The mechs . . . the mechs aren't moving."

"What!?" Milo whirled round. "Ashley! Ashley! What's wrong?"

"Milo . . . help . . ." answered Ashley in a faint voice that sounded far off.

Milo turned to the spider mech that Jan hadn't fired upon. He kicked it with his foot. "Ashley! What are you playing at?"

Again the faint, far-off voice, "Milo . . . feel strange . . . can't think properly . . . I'm losing it . . . something in here with me."

Milo turned on Jan who was climbing to her feet and biting her lips against the pain in her side. She was sure he'd fractured a couple of her ribs. Milo grabbed her and shook her. "What did you do, damn you? Tell me what you did!" he yelled, furiously.

"I don't know for sure. But whatever it was it's working."

He threw her down and turned again to the mechs. "Ashley!"

"Mom . . ." came the faint voice, "I don't want to die, Mom . . . help me. . . ."

"I'm not your damn *Mom*, Ashley!" he yelled savagely and again kicked the mech. "Carl! Are you there? Tell me what the hell is going on!"

When Carl finally answered his voice was faint too, but as impersonal as ever. "Alien program . . . has invaded system . . . very complex . . . unknown to me . . . can't combat it

159

. . . it is wiping all existing software . . . including me. . . ."
Carl said a few more words but they couldn't be discerned.

Milo stood there staring at the immobile mechs for a time, then he laughed and ran his hand over his head. "Well, let's look on the bright side. I've been trying to get rid of that bitch for ages. Pity about Carl, though. I needed him. I'll have to get down to the control pod and deactivate the central computer and clear out whatever junk you put into the system. When I've done that I'll be in charge again. And then, Jan, you, me and Robin Hood there are going to have a little talk about that habitat . . . *uh!*" He looked down at his leg where one of the spider mechs had fastened a tentacle around his ankle. "Ashley?" he asked hesitantly. "You still here?"

Through her pain Jan smiled up at Milo and said, "Sorry, Milo. I'm afraid the boot is now on the other foot. You've just been deposed. *We're* in charge now."

"Not exactly," said another voice.

Jan turned her head and was astonished to see Phebus standing beside her.

Chapter Twenty:

Whichever way he looked at his predicament, Jean-Paul could only arrive at one conclusion—he was in serious trouble. The leak around the seal of the viewing port hadn't got any worse but the water level in the cabin was now up to his waist. And rising. That was bad enough but the sets of breathing equipment were all in the diving chamber, and that was flooded. And even if he knew how to unflood it the sub had run out of power. Therefore there was no way to pump air into the chamber. So, sooner or later, he would be forced to open the hatch to the chamber and then grope around underwater until he had located one of the breathing sets and managed to get the mouthpiece in place. Presuming he achieved this unlikely feat before drowning, then what? He would still be trapped in the sub because of those damn creatures. They had given up on their assault on the submersible but he knew they were still out there. The last time he'd checked he saw that they were still trying to break open the sea gate.

Another reason he didn't want to open the hatch to the diving chamber was the fear that one of the creatures might be lurking in there, waiting for him. True, he doubted if any of them could fit through the outer hatch, and he hadn't actually *heard* anything, but he couldn't shake off the fear. But then, considering his position, he felt he was fully justified in having irrational fears. . . .

He was close to giving up hope that help would arrive in time. Even if Ayla had succeeded in swimming back to shore—and the alternative was unthinkable—by the time a rescue party equipped to deal with these fearsome monstrosities could be organised it would be too late to save him. He would have drowned. . . .

The water continued slowly to rise. Something started banging on the side of the sub. The damn things were back at it! At least he had brought his face mask into the cabin with him. He pulled it down over his eyes and nose, took a deep breath and ducked his head beneath the surface to see what was happening outside. He hoped the viewing port wouldn't be blocked by the face of one of the creatures peering in at him. He put the glass of his mask to the glass of the port and gazed out. The sea gate was still closed but there was no sign of the creatures. Had they given up and gone? Or were they waiting out of sight, hoping to lure him out?

Then he started in alarm. He could hear something entering the diving chamber. He put his head out of the water, listening intently. He flinched when he heard banging on the hatch. *It's Ayla*, he told himself, *it must be*. It couldn't possibly be one of those creatures. . . .

He made a quick decision, took a deep breath, grabbed hold of the wheel of the hatch and began to turn it. The hatch opened and immediately the water level in the forward cabin rose rapidly. As the trapped air increased in pressure he again felt an intense pain in his ears. Then the water was above his head and he was vaguely aware of something coming through the hatchway towards him. *It wasn't Ayla . . . it was one of those things*. He closed his eyes and waited for the end.

But a female hand grabbed his shoulder. He opened his eyes. Ayla was in front of him. She had removed her mouthpiece and was offering it to him. He took it gratefully and breathed in deeply. Then he gave it back to her. She beckoned he should follow her. In the diving chamber she helped him into his own discarded breathing equipment and they swam up out of the chamber.

As he emerged from the sub he looked about warily. Almost instantly he spotted one of the creatures drifting just above the seabed only yards away but he saw that it wasn't moving. It was dead. There were several divers in the vicinity. They were carrying stun-sticks with bundles of spares tied to their belts. One was carrying some kind of weapon that he didn't recognise.

Ayla pointed upwards, indicating that they should swim to the surface. After two pauses on the way, to decompress, they surfaced near the sea wall. Rope ladders had been lowered from the wall. Jean-Paul clambered up one with difficulty and was grateful for the helping hands when he was near to the top. He undid his harness and sat down, completely exhausted. Someone handed him a cup of hot soup. Ayla sat down beside him. "How are you feeling?"

"Dead, but grateful to be alive. Thanks. I was afraid you hadn't made it to shore. I saw that thing badly gash your leg. . . ."

"It looked bad—bled a lot at first—but it wasn't very deep and I didn't even need stitches, just a bandage." She touched the leg of her borrowed wet suit where there was a bulge around the calf. "It took me an hour to reach shore. Juli helped me round up all the best divers and we came back here in the fastest boats available." She gestured at the landward side of the wall. Jean-Paul turned and saw several boats moored below. "Thanks again. You have much trouble with those things?"

"Not too much. Came down behind them. Got them by surprise. Killed nine of them and the rest fled."

Other divers had surfaced and were climbing up onto the wall. Jean-Paul was surprised to see that Lon Haddon was among them. He was the one carrying the strange weapon. Jean-Paul stared at it curiously as Haddon wearily sat down next to them.

"I see you're still in one piece," Haddon said.

163

"Thanks to Ayla. And you. It seems I shall forever be in the debt of the Haddon family."

"Well, as far as I'm concerned, you can repay it in full by looking after Ayla when I'm—"

"Dad!" cried Ayla sharply.

Haddon didn't continue. To ease the tension Jean-Paul pointed at the strange device and asked what it was.

"It's what gave us an important advantage over those creatures," said Haddon. "It's a laser that can be fired underwater. Normally electromagnetic radiation—light waves, radio waves—can't travel very far through water but this is the exception. And the laser beam changes frequency, and colour, depending on the depth of the water. It's obviously related to the available natural light, or lack of it, in the water but don't ask me how it works."

Jean-Paul held out his hand and Haddon passed the weapon to him. It was heavy. Jean-Paul had never seen a portable laser before. "Does it work in the air?"

"No. Only underwater."

"Pity. I presume you didn't manufacture it yourselves."

Ayla answered, "No, it's Old Science. It came from the sea people. They got it from the habitat. It's funny really, Tiger was asking us for weapons and yet he himself gave us the ideal weapon to use against those creatures. He had no way of knowing, of course. And nor did we, at first. Our technical people racked their brains over it for ages before one of them finally had a bright idea about its function."

Jean-Paul handed the weapon back to Haddon. He said, "Do you know yet what those creatures are, or where they come from?"

Haddon shook his head. "We can only theorise that they once dwelled much further out in the ocean, like our sea people did. And similarly they were driven towards shore by deteriorating conditions out there."

"One thing is certain," said Ayla. "They wiped out our

164

sea people. Tiger and all the others. Gone for good." She gave a sigh. "Things are changing too fast. Much too fast."

That night Jean-Paul held her as she wept for Kell. His body had been recovered by the rescue party later that day. It had been partly eaten.

"Who the hell is she?" demanded Milo.

Jan got slowly to her feet, her eyes fixed on Phebus. It was impossible. She couldn't be here. "Her name is Phebus," Jan said. "She's a program from Shangri La, and she shouldn't be here."

"But as you can plainly see, I *am* here," said Phebus.

"You're a hologram," Jan said, accusingly. "And there's no holographic projection equipment here."

"Why do you assume I'm a hologram?" Phebus asked her.

"What else could you possibly be? Outside of a computer you have no real existence," Jan said.

"Come and touch me and then tell me what you think."

Jan walked towards her and tentatively reached out a hand. When her fingertips touched Phebus's shoulder and encountered solid flesh Jan jerked her hand away in fear. "I don't . . . I don't believe it! You're *real*!"

"No, I only seem real to you. In reality I'm a hallucination that you're all sharing. I'm being directly induced into the relevant centres of your brains from micro-second to micro-second."

"Oh," said Jan, relieved that there was a rational answer even if she couldn't understand it. "But where is this hallucination coming *from*?"

"From the ship. I *am* the ship now. I permeate the ship's entire system. And I am in the process of changing the system. Improving it."

"I don't care if you're re-arranging the furniture and painting polka dots on the walls of the latrines," said Milo angrily. "Get this thing to let go of me!"

165

Phebus turned to him. "I know all about you, Milo. You're dangerous and cannot be trusted. You will remain under constraint at all times." The tentacle released Milo's ankle but then wrapped itself around his neck. "Hey!" cried Milo. He tried to pull it away but couldn't. He looked angrily at Jan. "Have you been telling lies about me?"

"Oh, Milo," she said disgustedly and went to help Robin up. He was very pale and shivering. He held his hand to his stomach. "Are you all right?" she asked him worriedly.

"Yeah. Just a bit winded."

Jan said to Phebus, "Can we go below now? Robin is freezing."

"Yes. There is much to do. But first you will need to attend to the two other humans on board. Both are in a distressed condition . . . thanks to this one." Phebus indicated Milo.

"That's his speciality," said Jan.

"Who are you?" asked the girl fearfully. She was very thin and there were dark shadows under her large eyes. She was dressed in just a short, flimsy white shift. Jan saw that it was flecked with spots of dried blood. "I'm Jan. What's your name?"

The girl didn't answer. Jan slid the door shut and walked towards her. The girl backed away. "Where's Milo?"

"Don't worry. He's not going to bother you any more. Are you going to tell me your name?"

The girl continued to back fearfully away from her. "It's a trick. It's another of Milo's tricks. You're doing this for him."

Jan halted. "It's no trick. Milo is no friend of mine. On the contrary. You may find it hard to believe but I have even more cause to hate him than you do."

The girl was now backed up against a wall. "He *hurts* me. He *keeps* hurting me," she said, her voice breaking.

"I know," said Jan softly. "But he won't be hurting you

166

any more. Things have changed here. Ashley has, well, gone . . . and Milo is . . ."

"Dead?" asked the girl hopefully.

"Unfortunately, no. But he's locked up. And he's going to stay that way."

"I won't be safe until he's dead," said the girl. Tears were now running down her face.

"I know how you feel," said Jan, "but really, you *are* safe now. I promise you." She held out her arms to the girl. After only a short hesitation the girl ran to her. As Jan hugged her she burst into tears. It was some time before the girl's weeping subsided. "Are you going to tell me your name?" Jan asked gently.

"Tyra."

Jan undid the bolt, slid open the heavy metal door and stepped through. "Hello, Shan," she said.

Shan was lying on a filthy bed. He sat up quickly. "Mistress? I don't understand . . . they told me you were dead!"

"Not quite."

He got off the bed and approached her, a look of amazement on his face. "Jan . . . Mistress . . . it *is* you! But how . . .?"

"I'll tell you the details later. The important thing is that you're free now. Milo and Ashley are no longer in control."

At the mention of Milo's name his face changed drastically. Until then, despite the bruises and swollen lips, he still resembled the old Shan she had known for years, but now she was looking at a stranger. The hate in his eyes chilled her. It was hard to believe he was a Minervan male. "Where is Milo? I'm going to kill him."

"Calm down. There's a considerable queue ahead of you. Be assured he won't be doing any more harm from now on."

"Where's Tyra? What did he do to her?"

Jan turned to the doorway. "You can come in now," she called.

Tyra entered. She and Shan stared wordlessly at each other for several moments then rushed into each other's arms. Jan observed them with satisfaction then quietly left the room. In the corridor outside she said, "Phebus?"

The unsmiling 'young woman' appeared in front of her. "Yes?"

"Those two are all right for the time being, but there's a lot of emotional damage that's going to take a long time to heal, if ever."

"It will be taken care of."

Jan raised an eyebrow. "Really? How, exactly?"

"Don't concern yourself about it now. I want you to come down to the control pod."

"All right," Jan agreed. "But on the way I want to check in on Robin."

"You may."

"Thanks a lot."

They set up home in Jan's old quarters. Jan was relieved to see that Robin was looking better now. In fact he was looking better than he ever had in Shangri La. Getting him out of the habitat was obviously a good idea. She kissed him and said, "I can't stay long. The Ice Queen wants me down in the control pod. Don't ask me why."

He kissed her back, which took her by surprise. "It's great, isn't it? Everything went as planned and Phebus is in control."

"Yes, she sure is," said Jan, sourly.

He looked at her. "What's the matter?"

"I can't help it, but I still don't trust her."

Chapter Twenty-One:

Jan, fascinated, peered down at the ice field. "It's actually going to come up?"

Phebus, who was standing beside her in the control pod, said, "Yes, there are materials I need from it before we begin our mission. We need to construct many more mechs, and certain equipment, such as the Toy, needs to be adapted for what lies ahead."

Jan looked at her, marvelling at how real she seemed. She couldn't resist it; she reached out and poked Phebus's arm with her forefinger. Yes, still solid. Phebus turned her head and regarded her coldly. "Why did you do that?"

"I just find it hard to believe, that's all. Hard to believe that you're not real, that you're a contrived figment of my imagination. That you're just happening in my brain instead of the real world."

"Your perceptional 'real world' is a construct created within your brain. The way you perceive me isn't very different."

Jan thought about that. She supposed Phebus was right. Therefore, she would have to regard Phebus as 'real'. Then she felt her cheeks burn slightly. It was ridiculous but suddenly she realised she found Phebus vaguely erotic. What would happen if . . .? Mother God, she thought, I'm getting perverse in my old age! Entertaining sexual thoughts about a computer program!

"Here it comes," said Phebus.

Jan looked down again. They were directly above the hole in the ice that Ashley and Milo had dug with the lasers.

Vapour was still rising, concealing the base of the pit. Jan saw its sides start to shake and she heard a rumbling sound. Sections of the sides began to split and great shards of ice rose upwards before crashing backwards with a thunderous roar. Now the ice field all around the pit was cracking and buckling upwards. The ice shrieked and groaned in protest as it was pushed apart. Then Jan saw the top of the habitat emerge through the ice. As more of its dome-like top appeared, great chunks of ice shattered and slid down its sides. The habitat kept emerging until thousands of square feet of its grey metal surface were visible then it halted, looking like a dark boil on the pristine ice field. Jan knew that Shangri La was big but until now she hadn't realised just *how* big it was. What was visible was only a fraction of its vast spherical hull. She was impressed. And disturbed.

A hatch opened on the top of the habitat and she saw mechs come scuttling out. Already a cargo cradle was being lowered from the Sky Angel. Phebus said, "I estimate these preparations will take twelve hours. Then we will begin."

"Begin what?" asked Jan.

"We will need to collect tissue samples of all the flora and fauna that make up the blight in order to devise biological weapons against them. In this you will be of great assistance. You are familiar with all aspects of the blight. You will catalogue it for me. And you will also be of assistance if you use the Toy to collect samples on your own. Time is of the essence."

Jan shrugged. "Sure. I'll do all I can to help."

"Good. You may go now," she said, dismissively.

Jan stood there a while, wondering what would happen if she gave Phebus a good kick in the behind, but then decided it would be more useful to kick the computer. She left the control pod without doing either.

As she headed for the cargo section where Milo was being held she became aware of how *alive* the airship felt now. It had never felt this way when Ashley and Carl were running it. She could hear sounds all around her. Automatic machinery was becoming activated, as were the automatic labs and workshops. Thanks to Phebus's presence, the Sky Angel was turning into a giant, living organism.

Milo's new quarters consisted of a small, bare room containing a fold-out cot and a bucket. Milo, lying on the cot, gave her a sardonic smile when his spider-mech guard ushered her inside. "Well, come for some serious gloating, have you?"

Jan folded her arms, leaned against the door and regarded him warily. "I haven't come to gloat, Milo. I've come to talk to you. I want to see if I can make you see sense."

He put his hands behind his head and said, sneeringly, "I'm touched."

"I'm serious. You don't know what you're up against with these habitat programs. They're powerful, and Phebus seems to be the most powerful of all. You get up to your usual tricks and she'll . . . well, I don't know what she'll do. I'm surprised she hasn't disposed of you already. She knows what you are."

"Thanks to you, my little amazon."

"Don't call me that!" she snapped.

"Brings back memories, does it?" he asked, grinning. "Of the times on the *Lord Pangloth* when I was your protector? You know you owe me your life so I think it's time I called in a few favours. Use your influence with that frigid female and get me out of here."

"I admit, Milo, that you saved my life on more than one occasion but I don't owe you any favours. You raped me and left me pregnant with what turned out to be your clone. *You*, Milo. And you destroyed my son in the process."

"I told you, all that was unintentional."

"If that's supposed to make me feel better, it doesn't. And I remember you didn't put up much of a protest when Ashley dumped Robin and me onto blight land."

"Hey, what could I have done? Ashley was running the show. I had to watch my step."

Jan said, "And that's the situation here with me. I carry no weight with Phebus, and she's the one in charge."

"Oh well, no matter. I'll get out of this somehow. I always do. You know me, Jan. I can't be stopped."

"Really? I remember when you weren't only stopped but actually reduced to pulp under the feet of a mad cyberoid. . . ."

"Stop!" he said sharply. "I don't want to hear this."

"Your original self, Milo, who was even more powerful than you. But he made one small slip and the next moment it was all over. And so were you. All over the ground."

He half rose from the cot, his expression furious. "Shut up or I'll . . .!" He stopped when the spider-mech started towards him. Then he grinned and lay back on the bed. The mech returned to Jan's side.

"You were saying?" asked Jan.

"Nothing at all. But I won't forget this."

"Oh dear," she said and gave a mock shiver. "You're terrifying me. But here's something else you should remember. These habitat programs are something new. They've been evolving all these years. They're miles ahead of what Carl was. I don't understand them at all. I wouldn't underestimate them for a moment. And I'm advising you to treat them the same way. You do something stupid and you may be jeopardising Robin and me as well, not to mention Shan and Tyra."

He regarded her curiously. "You sound rather uneasy about your new-found allies."

"I am." She gave the spider-mech a glance. Phebus was probably listening in via the mech but what Jan had to say wouldn't be new to her. She had, after all, said the same things to Davin. "I just can't fathom their motives. Oh, sure, I understand that their basic directive is to protect and look after the Eloi, and all their actions spring from that programming core. But I can't understand how their destroying the blight fits in with that directive. I don't know *why* they're doing this and it makes me nervous."

Milo shrugged. "There was an old saying: Don't look a gift horse in the mouth. You're getting what you want. A cleaned-up planet."

"But why are they doing it *now*? They've spent centuries in that habitat, nursing the ghastly Eloi while the rest of the world went to hell. Outside their programmed sphere of concern, they told me. Nothing we can do. Sorry and all that. But now suddenly they're going to try to save the world. Something is not right with them." She glanced at the mech. "As I've told Robin, I simply don't trust them."

Milo said with a laugh, "What do you think they have in mind? Conquest of the world? That was an old sci-fi cliché."

"Sci-fi?"

He waved a dismissive hand. "A sub-branch of literature that consisted mainly of so-called 'scientific' extrapolations. Many of the stories were set in the then future . . . remember those 'Entertainments' you used to watch with Prince Caspar and his cronies on the *Lord Pangloth*? Well, it was stuff kind of like that. When I was a kid I was a real fan but in retrospect, of course, none of those damn sci-fi writers ever got anything right. Faster-than-light space drives, alien races, galactic empires . . . hah!" He shook his head.

"Anyway, a popular theme was that intelligent computers would want to try to take over the world." He chuckled. "I remember a classic movie on the subject. Pure hokum, but I enjoyed it at the time. And it made a fortune. Let's see. . . ." Milo closed his eyes. "It was called *A Bright and Shining Morning* . . . and it was about the world waking up one day to discover that all the different computer systems had linked up to form a super intelligence . . . yeah, and the hero won the day by inventing a computer virus that destroys the gestalt. Hell, fancy me remembering that! I must have seen the movie in 2010, when I was just thirteen. . . ."

"That's fascinating, Milo, but why are you so convinced that these programs wouldn't be tempted to take control of the Earth? I told you they're different. And very sophisticated."

"We're back to motives again. What would the *motive* of an intelligent computer program be for world conquest? It's a bodiless entity which exists only to fulfil its basic programming. It *is* its basic programming, just as we humans are defined by our entirely different biological drives. As humans we just want to breathe, eat, drink, survive and fuck, though not necessarily in that order. Our bodies define us."

"You've left out the urge to reproduce," Jan said. "Among others."

"No, reproduction is tied up in fucking and survival. What I'm saying is that we *are* our genetically programmed drives—all that humanity has done over thousands of years is a result of those basic biological programs. They shape our emotions. They shape our cultures, shape what we want. They shape *us*. But a computer program doesn't share any of these drives. It doesn't even have a survival urge so why would it want to conquer anything? Conquest is usually an act of self-preservation, whether it involves an individual or a society."

"But surely the urge to survive can be programmed into a computer?"

"Yes, you can instruct a computer program to protect itself but that's not the same as having a biological urge to survive, of *desperately wanting* to stay alive, of fearing death, fearing non-existence and so on. Sure, computer programs can be great at acting as if they had human emotions but it's just an act. We've made them in our image, but they're nothing like us at all in essence."

Jan said doubtfully, "Davin more or less told me the same

174

thing. But I don't know . . . I still can't see how helping ordinary humanity fits in with their prime directive of protecting the Eloi. Maybe it will all be clear eventually, but. . . ." She sighed, touched her side and winced with pain. She would have to have a spell in a med-machine. Her ribs still hurt where Milo had thumped her. "Well, I'm going," she told him. "Is there anything you need?"

"I need many things," he said, "but I presume you are referring to such mundane items as food and drink?"

"Yes," she said wearily. "I'll arrange to have something sent to you."

"You're so kind. By the way, on the subject of needs, how's my former playmate?"

"Tyra? Shan is looking after her."

"He must be very happy. The creep."

"He wants to kill you."

"I don't blame him."

"You certainly excelled yourself with Tyra. Why? Why did you treat her so cruelly?"

He shrugged. "Why? Well, we're back in the area of basic urges."

"I don't think I'd describe sadism as a basic urge," she said.

"Really? You'd be surprised."

"You never treated me that way, unless it was on your future agenda for me."

"You were never like Tyra, Jan. She's a natural victim. Her very docility excites the sadistic side of me. You were different. You were an ignorant savage but you had courage and strength. I actually admired you, right from the beginning."

"Oh, please spare me all that," she groaned and slid open the door.

"Bye, Mother," he said as she went out.

She froze, turned and looked at him.

He grinned. "Sorry. I just couldn't resist it."

175

Chapter Twenty-Two:

"Jean-Paul! Jean-Paul!" Jean-Paul groaned as he was pulled from a deep and satisfying sleep. Someone was gripping his shoulder and shaking him roughly. He opened his eyes and saw, in the pale dawn light, Lon Haddon leaning over him. At the same time he felt Ayla stir beside him and realised that there must be trouble. Otherwise Haddon wouldn't invade his daughter's privacy this way. . . .

He sat up quickly, rubbing his eyes. "What's wrong?"

"We have an emergency on our hands," said Haddon, his tone urgent. "Get dressed and come with me. . . ."

Ayla was awake now. "Dad, what is it?" she asked worriedly.

"Some of Jean-Paul's people have taken over the armoury. They have hostages and are threatening to kill them unless we give in to their demands."

"Shit!" said Jean-Paul and reached for his pants, hanging on a nearby chair.

"You'll have to try and talk to them, Jean-Paul, otherwise we're going to have a lot of bloodshed."

"Those damn fools!" cried Jean-Paul as he pulled on his pants.

"The truck's parked out front," said Haddon, and hurried from the room.

"I'm coming too," said Ayla and jumped out of bed. Jean-Paul looked at her as he put on his shirt. "I'd prefer it if you didn't."

"Too bad. I'm coming anyway."

*

The electric truck bounced its way through Palmyra. As he drove, Haddon told them what had happened. "They struck in the early hours of the morning. Must have overcome the two guards on duty. We don't know yet whether they're alive or dead. It was only when the relief guards turned up at 4 a.m. that the alert went out. The relief got fired on. Warning shots. Then they were told that the armoury was in the hands of the Sky Warriors of the *Lord Montcalm*, who had hostages, including women and children, and who intended to shoot the hostages at noon today unless we agree to hand over power to them."

"Power? You mean political power?"

"Nothing less."

Jean-Paul shook his head and said bitterly, "Jesus, those crazy idiots! They told me they wanted me to come up with a way of taking over Palmyra but I just didn't take them seriously enough. I was going to tell you about it but Ayla told me they were all being watched."

Ayla, perched on Jean-Paul's lap, said, "That's true, Dad. Jean-Paul told me all about it and I told him not to worry. It's my fault."

"Don't be ridiculous!" said Haddon. "I wouldn't have taken such talk too seriously either. And they *were* under surveillance."

"So what went wrong?" asked Jean-Paul.

"So far we've found the bodies of three of the people assigned to watch them at night. The rest must be among the hostages. The hostages mainly consist of the families who were providing accommodation for your people."

"Oh hell," muttered Jean-Paul. He felt wretched. And ashamed. Then, "How many of my people are involved?"

"We're not sure yet. At least a dozen. Their leader, or at least the one doing all the talking, is a man called Phillippe. Do you know him?"

"Yeah, I know him. He was among the group who wanted me to lead them."

"Do you think you can make him see reason?"

"I failed to before but I'm certainly willing to try again. It's the least I can do."

The armoury was located on the outskirts of the town and there were no other buildings nearby. It was a one-storey structure with a flat roof and no windows. There was a single door at the front. Palm trees had been planted around it to soften its utilitarian severity. Parked at a distance, to form a barricade, were a row of electric vehicles, cars and trucks. Men with rifles crouched behind them, keeping watch on the armoury. As Haddon halted his truck alongside the other vehicles he muttered a curse and said, "That's all we need. Jelker Banks."

Jean-Paul looked and saw a wide-shouldered man with red hair and beard advancing towards him. He was carrying a rifle. He was accompanied by two others who also carried rifles. Jean-Paul remembered them from the encounter on the sea front. The older one, he recalled, was called Bron.

"Ah, well done, Haddon!" boomed the red-bearded man. "You've captured their leader!"

"He is not their leader!" Haddon said loudly as he climbed out of the truck's cab. "And you know it, Jelker!"

Ayla climbed out the other side and Jean-Paul swiftly followed her. Haddon and Jelker Banks were standing face to face. "I know no such thing, Lon Haddon! He admits himself he was ruler of that Sky Lord!"

"That's all in the past! He's with us now!"

"Hah! He may have fooled you and your scatterbrained daughter but he doesn't fool us! And when we've flushed those murderous sky pirates out of there he'll be shot along with the rest of them!"

Clutching Jean-Paul's arm tightly, Ayla cried, "You try and shoot him and you'll have to shoot me as well!"

"Fine with me," laughed Bron.

"Look, I've come to help!" exclaimed Jean-Paul. "I'm going to try to talk them into giving themselves up."

Jelker Banks turned in his direction. He had very light blue eyes which seemed to bore into Jean-Paul. He said, "Is that so? My bet is that you've come to join them."

"Be reasonable, Jelker," pleaded Haddon. "If he was part of this plot he'd be in there with them *now*. We *need* him, Jelker! Unless he can convince them to surrender there's going to be a bloodbath. There's only one way into that armoury. We rush it and we're going to lose a lot of people."

Another man had joined the group. Jean-Paul recognised him as Lyle Weaver, the current head of the 'sextet' who ruled Palmyra. He too carried a rifle. He regarded Jean-Paul with something like relief and said to Haddon, "He's willing to do it?"

"Yes, he is," said Haddon, "but Jelker here is putting up objections."

Weaver glared at Jelker Banks. "Not any more, he isn't."

Jelker glared back, but after a time shrugged and said, "Very well, he can go and talk to them, but my gun will be on him the whole time. He tries to enter the armoury and join his friends he dies on the spot."

Weaver turned to Jean-Paul. "Try to ignore him. We all do. Think you will be able to persuade them to give up?"

"As I told Lon, I don't know. I don't know any of them very well. But I'll do my best."

"Good. I'll get someone to rustle you up a white flag." He turned to go but Jean-Paul said, "Wait. If I'm going to try and bargain with them I'll need something to bargain with. What will happen to them if they do surrender?"

"They'll be put up against a wall and shot," said Jelker Banks loudly.

"Shut up," said Weaver, distractedly. He rubbed the side of his face then said, "They've already killed people. And they've betrayed our hospitality. We can't let them back into our community. They'll have to take their chance in the outside—in the blight. They'll be given weapons and supplies and have to take their chance. But if they don't surrender, it's as Jelker says. They'll be executed."

Jean-Paul nodded. Weaver had no other choice. It was fair enough in the circumstances. In Weaver's position he would have said the same.

A few minutes later Jean-Paul, holding aloft the handle of a broom with a pillowcase tied to the end of it, stepped from behind the row of vehicles and walked towards the dark entrance of the armoury. He could still feel the impression of Ayla's lips on his from the hard and anxious kiss she had just given him. He could also feel a tingly sensation midway down his spine where he imagined Jelker Banks's rifle was aimed. And God knows how many rifles were being pointed at him from the gloomy interior of the armoury.

When he was about twenty yards from the entrance he halted, waved the pillowcase and called out, "Phillippe! It's me, Jean-Paul! I want to talk to you!"

There was silence. Through the open doors of the armoury he saw only darkness. He thought he could make out some sort of barricade some way inside but he wasn't sure. "Phillippe!" he called out again.

"What do you want, traitor?" came the reply, which caught Jean-Paul by surprise.

"Phillippe, is that you?"

"Yeah, it's me. I'm the new leader now, seeing as you turned traitor."

God, thought Jean-Paul. "Phillippe, this is madness! You can't get away with this! You've got to surrender before more people get killed."

"We won't surrender. Not all of us are like you, Jean-Paul."

"Look, if you surrender you'll at least have your lives. Palmyra's leader has agreed to let you go if you give up peaceably."

"Go where?"

Jean-Paul, his mouth getting very dry, swallowed and said, "Out of Palmyra."

Phillippe laughed. "That's the same as a death sentence."

"You'll be given weapons . . . supplies. You'll have a chance. You won't if you stay in there."

"No deal, Jean-Paul. Our ultimatum stands. Go tell their leader that. Come noon and we don't get what we want we start killing the hostages."

"Phillippe, be reasonable! They're not going to hand Palmyra over to you and the others, hostages or no hostages! You can't win! Stay in there and you'll be dead before the day is out."

"Then we'll take a lot of them with us. We've booby trapped the whole armoury. They rush us and the whole place goes up . . . and a fair chunk of Palmyra will go up too, considering the amount of high explosives they've got in here."

Jean-Paul was suddenly filled with frustrated anger. "God, you stupid, *stupid*, bastard. . .!" He started to walk closer to the entrance. "You had everything here and now you've thrown—" He didn't continue because someone had hit him very hard with what felt like a sledgehammer. He was thrown off his feet and sent whirling through the air. He came down on his back and found himself staring up at the pale, early morning sky that was just becoming tinged with pink. Then he was staring at nothing.

"You're the most peculiar priest I've ever met," Captain Ilya Vyushkov told Milo as he topped up his glass with vodka.

"As I said to you before, I am not a proper priest," said Milo, gratefully taking the glass.

"You can say that again," laughed Vyushkov as he refilled his own glass.

"No, what I mean is . . . is . . ." Milo was feeling

181

pleasantly drunk, ". . . is that I am just a member of our religious order but I haven't been ordained as a priest."

"You are certainly different to your companion."

"Ah, well, he *is* a priest. A proper one. A very proper one," Milo said, and giggled. *Uh oh, getting too drunk*, he told himself and adjusted his metabolism so that the excess alcohol would be removed from his system at a faster rate. Very soon he was sweating pure alcohol. Had to keep his wits about him tonight.

They were sitting at a table in Vyushkov's apartment. They had just finished consuming large amounts of a very agreeable borscht, a dish that Milo hadn't tasted for a considerable time. The quality of the food in Karaganga proved to Milo that the organics recycling units were still working properly, unlike their counterparts on Belvedere. The meal had been served by a smiling woman whom Milo first took to be Vyushkov's wife but was relieved to learn later was merely a servant. It would have been a nuisance if Vyushkov was married. Well, *happily* married, to be exact. The less attached the better.

Time to get down to business. Milo sipped his drink, eyed Vyushkov slyly, and said, "You realise you'll be in an enviable position once you have conquered the Earth community."

Vyushkov frowned at him. "What do you mean?"

"You'll be the virtual ruler of the place. All its natural riches will be yours . . . riches badly needed by Karaganga and the other habitats. And you'll also be in possession of the only ship capable of travelling between earth and a habitat. For a time at least. And it's also the best armed vessel in the system. I saw that from my inspection."

"Yeah, we've stripped virtually every beam weapon from the other ships, and the habitat itself, and put them on the *Christina*. . . ." He took another drink and said, "But I don't understand what you're getting at."

"What I'm getting at is that you will be in a unique

182

position. A position where you'll be able to call the shots. . . ."

Vyushkov's frown deepened. "Are you suggesting what I think you are suggesting?"

"Possibly."

Vyushkov slammed his glass down on the table. "I am a loyal Karagangan!" he said angrily.

"Of course you are. And, of course, you wouldn't deprive your habitat of what it wants from Earth, but there would be a price."

Vyushkov shook his head. "No. Out of the question."

Milo gave a sigh. "I admire you, Captain Ilya Vyushkov. You have the chance to become a sovereign power in your own right, not to mention very rich, but you won't be deflected from your loyalty and sense of duty. Such men are rare." He raised his glass. "I drink to you."

Milo returned to his cabin an hour later. He had left Vyushkov very drunk. And, he was confident, he had also left him with a certain seed taking root within him. *You'll soon be mine*, thought Milo with satisfaction.

Chapter Twenty-Three:

Ayla snapped out of her fitful doze when she heard Jean-Paul moan. She leaned forward anxiously, hoping that he had regained consciousness. "Jean-Paul! Can you hear me? It's Ayla." His eyelids fluttered but remained closed. She saw, with disappointment, that he was still unconscious. She sighed, touched his hot forehead with the back of her hand then settled back in the chair. She felt terribly tired and her head ached. She had been at Jean-Paul's bedside since he had come out of the operating room. That had been at 3 p.m., and it was now past midnight. But she wasn't going to leave him.

After the operation the surgeon, Steven Aldane, who was a close friend of her father's and whom she had known all her life, told her the grim news that she had been half expecting. "I'm sorry, Ayla," he said, "I've done all I can but his chances are slim. And even if he survives he's going to be paralysed for the rest of his life. The bullet shattered his spine."

"He's *not* going to die," she told him passionately, eyes streaming tears. "I won't let him, Steven. I *won't*."

Later her father had come in and stood next to her, his arm around her shoulder. "I'm so sorry, Ayla."

"He's not going to die," she said dully.

"I hope not, but I've spoken to Steven. His chances are not good, darling. Not good at all. And . . . and considering the extent of his injuries maybe he'd be better off if. . . ."

She turned to him and said fiercely, "No! He wouldn't! Don't say that!"

184

"I'm sorry," he said quickly and gave her shoulder a squeeze to show that he understood. Then, after a pause, he said, "Look, maybe the spacers will be able to help him when they arrive. They're sure to be much more medically advanced than we are. We've lost so much knowledge down here. . . ."

"You and your damn spacers! You think they're going to solve everything! I'm sick of hearing about them!" And as soon as these words had rushed out of her she was sorry. She turned and looked into her father's face, saw the pain there. "I'm. . . ."

"You don't have to apologise. I know I've become a bore on the subject. But I meant what I said about them. They really might be able to help Jean-Paul."

"Yes, I suppose so," she said doubtfully, but the thought fanned a flicker of hope that began to grow. Her father left shortly after that. Apart from periodic checks on Jean-Paul by both Steven and one of the nurses she had been alone ever since.

She kept reliving the horror of that morning. When Jelker Banks's gun suddenly boomed and Jean-Paul was knocked off his feet in front of the armoury she, at first, couldn't see the connection between the two events. She stared uncomprehendingly at Jean-Paul's twitching body. Lyle Weaver was shouting at Jelker Banks. She dimly heard Banks say, "The bastard was going to join them. Just like I knew he would." Then she was screaming Jean-Paul's name and running out from between two of the parked trucks. Her father tried to stop her but she easily shook off his gripping hands and kept on running.

Then she was kneeling beside Jean-Paul, lifting his head, kissing his face. His eyes were open but they weren't focused. "Jean-Paul!" she cried but he made no sound. She gently lowered his head back onto the grass and felt his throat. To her relief she could feel a pulse.

"We didn't do it!" cried a voice. "It wasn't one of us who

shot him!" She looked up, surprised. The voice had come from the entrance of the armoury. She had forgotten all about the sky rebels. "I know it wasn't you," she called back. "I know who did it." There was a sound behind her. She turned. Her father was approaching, hands in the air. His face was white. He knelt on the other side of Jean-Paul, keeping his hands held high. "How is he?" he asked, glancing nervously at the dark armoury entrance.

"I think it's bad," she said in a shaky voice. "Very bad." Blood was now staining the grass around Jean-Paul. "I'm going to kill Jelker Banks."

"Lyle has put him under arrest. His sons too."

"I'm still going to kill him." Then she looked imploringly at her father and wailed, "Oh Dad, what am I going to *do*?"

"Well, first we must get him to the hospital right away." He rose slowly to his feet and, facing the armoury entrance, called out, "We're going to carry this man away from here! Any objections?"

Ayla could hear the muttering of voices within the armoury and then someone called back, "No objections. Take him. But no tricks!"

Ayla's father bent down and took hold of Jean-Paul under his upper arms. "Take his feet," he told Ayla. "Think you can manage it?"

"Of course." Ayla took his ankles and they lifted him. Jean-Paul made a gurgling sound deep in his throat but that was his only reaction. He was heavy but Ayla would have managed if he was twice the weight. The amount of blood left behind on the grass beneath him made her want to scream.

They carried him to the line of vehicles—he dripped blood all the way—and laid him on some empty sacking in the back of their truck. Someone produced a blanket and Ayla covered him with it. She stayed with him in the back while her father drove as fast as he could to the hospital. She pressed her body against his, trying to lessen the amount of jolting he was getting. They finally reached the hospital and Steven and his staff took over. The sacking was soaked with blood when they lifted him from it. . . .

She found out later that, ironically, the mutineers had released the hostages and surrendered just an hour later. She didn't know whether the shooting of Jean-Paul right in front of them had been a contributing factor in their change of mind. She thought it might have been but really she didn't care that much either way.

The Toy screamed out of the sky and plunged into the Hazzini swarm that rose from a great nest to meet it. The swarm was so thick and the Toy so fast that continuous collisions between the Toy and the Hazzini were inevitable. Soon hundreds of the creatures were dropping from the sky with shattered bodies or shredded wings. Some screeched their anger as they fell, most were already dead.

Inside the Toy there was only the slightest shudder every time the vehicle struck a Hazzini.

"You're enjoying this, aren't you?"

"What?" Jan's attention was fixed on the monitor screens.

"I said, you're enjoying this. You should see the expression on your face. This is a side of you I've never seen before."

She glanced at Robin. He was regarding her with interest. "Yes, I am enjoying it," she admitted. "I hate the things. And I once told you the reason why. I wouldn't waste any sympathy on the Hazzini. They're just genegineered killing machines with little intelligence to speak of, though they are cunning."

"Oh, I'm not criticising you. I used to do a similar thing myself, with the squids around Shangri La. I enjoyed the actual killing sprees but afterwards I always felt . . . well, sort of unclean."

"Well, if that happens to me you can give me a good soaping in the shower when we get back to the Angel." She flashed him a quick grin then told the Toy to make another circuit through the swarm.

After scything through the massed Hazzini four times the Toy then flew down to the base of the nest, which, like all Hazzini nests, resembled a surreal version of the Leaning Tower of Pisa (which had finally fallen over in the year 2000). The Toy fired a series of rockets into the nest. They exploded with great force, sending huge sections of the nest walls flying through the air. Then the whole edifice began to collapse. The Toy retreated to a safe distance as the vast nest collapsed in upon itself, one level at a time. Jan watched avidly until a cloud of dust obscured the view. She nodded with satisfaction. "Yes, I really did enjoy that."

"I'm glad you're having so much fun, but isn't all this a waste of time?" Robin asked her. "Our job is just to collect the biological samples and get them back to the Sky Angel. Once Phebus does her work all the Hazzini will be doomed anyway."

"I know, I know . . . but just indulge my little whim, okay?" She reached over and patted his thigh.

Hazzini were still hurling themselves at the hovering Toy, trying to tear open the hull with their long cutting claws. Jan saw a close-up of a head on a monitor and shivered. She remembered all too clearly her near-fatal encounter with a Hazzini on the *Lord Pangloth*. This one was identical—the same desiccated horse-head with the mosquito-like antennae and proboscis. She said a few quick words to the Toy and instantly the Hazzini was seized by grappling arms that shot out from the bow. A spear-shaped probe plunged deep through the hard carapace of the creature's chest. "Bio-sample acquired," said the Toy as the probe retreated back into the hull. The Hazzini continued to beat its long, diaphanous wings, not realising that it was dead. The grappling arms, part of the new features built into the Toy, released it and the creature flew crazily about for a few moments, then began to drop from the sky. "I enjoyed that too," Jan told Robin.

"I could tell. Now what?"

"Oh, I guess we collect some more samples of blight fungi and then head back to the Angel." Then Jan asked the Toy, "Where exactly are we?"

"In the mid-west of the North American continent," replied the Toy.

"Can you be more precise, please?"

"My records are out of date. I can tell you what the area was *once* called."

"Then do so."

"When the United States of America existed it was known as the state of Iowa. After the break-up of the Federation in 2071 it became part of the feminist superstate known as Minerva."

This gave Jan a jolt. "Minerva? It can't be!" She peered hard at the monitor screens. The landscape over which they were speeding did not look familiar to her. "It can't be," she murmured.

"It was Minerva according to my records," insisted the Toy.

Jan was about to protest again when she recalled that the Minerva she had grown up in was only a fragment of what Minerva had originally been. Excitedly, she said to the Toy, "Criss-cross the entire area."

"Very well," replied the Toy.

Robin said, "What are you trying to do?"

"I'm trying to find my home."

"Do we have the time for all this?" he asked. "We're already behind schedule."

"I don't care," she said firmly and kept staring intently at the screens.

During the next half hour they passed over three small settlements—one completely besieged by blight—and each time the inhabitants poured out from their ramshackle

189

buildings to gape upwards in amazement at a flying machine that wasn't a Sky Lord but Jan paid them no heed. Then finally she cried out, "Slow down!" and the Toy obeyed.

Yes, that range of low hills . . . even from this angle she recognised them. "What direction are we travelling in now?" she asked urgently.

"Due east," replied the Toy.

"Then it should be twenty miles or so to the east of that range of hills. . . ."

The Toy cruised slowly over the hills, dropping in altitude as it went. "Mother God, this is it, all right . . . but where's the town? Where's Minerva?"

"You told me the place got bombed by the Sky Lord," said Robin.

"Yeah, but there were still some buildings left standing. Quite a few of the smaller ones." She frowned. "Though there were fires burning when I left. Maybe the rest burnt down." She stared at the screens and shook her head. "What we're flying over now used to be where the remains of our farmlands were . . . now it's all blight."

"There's something up ahead," said Robin.

Jan saw that he was right. Large shapes covered by the fungus of the blight. Minerva. Her throat constricted. All their efforts over hundreds of years had been in vain. The blight had won in the end. The Toy was passing over the fungus-draped town now. Jan told it to stop and land. To Robin she said, "We're above what used to be the town square." The Toy settled gently on the ground. Jan took the small beam guns that Phebus had provided them with, handed one to Robin and put the other in her belt. Then she asked the Toy to open the hatches. As they did so Jan said to Robin, "Be very careful out there. You've never been in blight land before . . . well, you *have* but you don't remember anything about it—it can be very dangerous."

"When are you going to quit treating me like a baby?" he asked.

190

There was an answer to that, Jan thought, but she was not going be so cruel as to give it to him. She led the way out of the Toy. The familiar stink of the fungi hit her as she emerged. And it was uncomfortably warm too. She glanced up. The sun was high in a clear sky. She figured it was just about noon in this part of the continent. She looked around, trying to orientate herself. It was hard because of the fungi draped over the few standing buildings that lined the square.

"So this is Minerva," said Robin.

"You're not exactly seeing it in its prime," she said sharply.

"I know that. I wasn't trying to be funny."

"Sorry," she muttered and began to walk across the square to the nearest row of buildings. The square itself was relatively clear apart from clusters of six foot tall toadstools and a few giant puffballs. There was also a large tree growing in one corner that vaguely puzzled her. She didn't remember any such tree there before and she doubted a new tree could grow to that size in the years since she'd last been here. Another odd thing about it was that the fungus had left it alone. Then she became aware that Robin had changed course and was walking towards the tree. "Where are you going?" she called.

"I'm going to take a leak," he called back. "Now aren't you glad you asked?"

"Very," she said, irritated, and was about to continue when something started to nag her. Something she should remember about certain trees . . . *Mother God*! She whirled round, pulling the weapon from her belt. "*Robin!!*" she screamed with all her lung power. But she could see it was already too late.

Chapter Twenty-Four:

"Off we go into the wild blue y-o-n-d-e-r!" sang Milo very loudly as he entered the cabin. Father Shaw was sitting at the small table where he had been reading his dog-eared bible—he had been reading it a lot of late—and looked up at Milo's boisterous entrance with anxiety-filled eyes. He wasn't looking too healthy these days. He had lost several pounds in weight and his face was haggard. He hadn't been sleeping well at all, being afraid that Milo would kill him in his sleep. Milo had actually considered doing just that but had decided to postpone the happy event.

Milo threw himself onto his bunk and said jovially, "All packed and ready for the big adventure? In just a few hours we'll be on our way."

Father Shaw licked his dry lips and said, "When are you going to do it?"

Feigning ignorance, Milo asked, "Do what, dear Father?"

Father Shaw licked his lips again. "Murder me."

Milo raised his eyebrows. "Murder you? Goodness me, you're not back on that stale old subject, are you? You're still alive and well, aren't you? You really are getting paranoid."

The priest stared at him silently for a time. Then he said, "You won't get away with this. God will punish you."

"You really think that? That this God you worship, creator of the entire universe, gives a stuff about *you?* That's one of the reasons I so detest you pious prats, you're all so damn egotistical! The way you talk you make it sound as if God and you were once room-mates at college."

192

"Blasphemy will only make things worse for you," Father Shaw told him through quivering lips.

"I'll take my chances. Meanwhile you should be preparing yourself for the great adventure on the mother planet. Just think of all those grubby little souls down there waiting for you to harvest them up for God and salvation."

"The Earth people are beyond redemption. Like you."

"Well, that's not a very positive attitude for a priest to take. The whole point of you coming on this expedition was to assess spiritually the Earth people."

"The reason I'm here is you!" said Father Shaw, his voice beginning to rise. "I see that now. You planned it that way. You were the one who suggested to Father Massie that we send a representative to Earth, but it was all simply to provide a means for *you* to get to Earth. There is no need for me to be here! None at all!"

Milo rose from the bed, went over and patted Father Shaw lightly on the top of his head. Father Shaw flinched. "On the contrary, you're very important to me. For the time being."

Father Shaw looked up at him. "Please let me stay here," he pleaded in a whisper. "I don't want to go to Earth. I don't want to go with you. Let me go back to Belvedere. I promise I won't tell anyone about you. I swear on my soul I won't."

Milo frowned his disapproval. "Careful," he warned. "Don't risk your soul on a promise you won't be able to keep."

"But I *do* swear it!" cried Father Shaw. "I won't say anything to anyone. Only please let me go!"

"Oh, all right."

Father Shaw's mouth dropped open. Milo could see that his lower teeth were badly discoloured. His personal hygiene had gone by the board too. "Do you mean it?" whispered Father Shaw.

"Of course I mean it. You can go back to Belvedere. You've served your purpose."

Father Shaw grabbed his hand and, to Milo's surprise, kissed it repeatedly. Then he cried, "Thank you! Thank you! Thank you! . . . ." This would probably have gone on indefinitely but Milo tapped him on the shoulder. "Father Shaw."

The priest looked up at him again, his eyes brimming with grateful tears. "Yes?"

"I was just kidding," Milo said, and gave him a wink. "I wouldn't think of sending you back to dreary old Belvedere; you're coming to Earth with me. We're going to have a hell of a time."

Milo watched with interest and great amusement as Father Shaw's face appeared to crumple from within. Then the priest covered his face with his hands, lowered his head onto the table and burst into tears. Milo returned to his bunk. Singing. "*Off we go into the wild blue y-o-n-d-e-r!*"

It was the way she screamed his name that saved him. Her scream would have stopped a giant reptile in its tracks. Robin froze just at the moment the tree sent its tentacle whipping out towards him at blurring speed. The end of the tentacle snapped through the empty air where Robin should have been, the tip missing him by inches. He didn't see it, he had turned his head towards Jan, but he felt its passage through the air and he jerked his head back towards the tree in time to see the tentacle retracting. Jan, as she pulled her beam gun from her belt, screamed again: "*Back! Back!*"

He took a faltering step backwards. Jan aimed and fired at the trunk. The beam cut deep and the tree shuddered. Two tentacles whipped out at Robin this time but he was even further out of range now, continuing to back away. And at last he was drawing his own gun. . . . He fired. The tree's shuddering grew more violent. Its tentacles were whipping about frenziedly. "Keep firing!" Jan yelled to Robin as she drew closer to him. Then she saw the ground around the tree begin to churn. Dark soil erupted around its base and then the trunk began to move. Upwards. *Mother God!* she thought in shock as she realised what was happening, *the tree is trying to uproot itself!*

Smoke was pouring out of the trunk as Jan and Robin continued to keep their twin beams moving back and forth over it. The great curving thorns, on which it impaled its victims, emerged from the blackened trunk. Jan could see its roots now in the churning soil. But they weren't roots . . . more like huge, sinewy limbs that ended in a kind of hand or foot consisting of three large claws. One of these, then another, extended from the trunk and dug itself into the soil. The thing was trying to drag itself away. Jan turned her gun onto these 'roots', raking them with the beam. The tree shook in protest, its leaves rustling. The tentacles continued to flay the air. Suddenly there was a loud crunching sound and the tree began to topple towards them. "Run!" she screamed but this time Robin didn't need her warning. He had seen the danger and was sprinting away like a maniac. She ran too.

The air filled with a shrill whistling sound and the ground shook as the tree came down. Jan stopped and turned. The top of the tree lay between her and Robin. He'd stopped too. The leaves still rustled and the tentacles continued to twitch as well, though with fading strength. "Keep shooting at it," she called to Robin and fired her gun into the leaves.

When the charred tree was completely still Robin warily came round to Jan's side. "What the hell was it?" he asked, wrinkling his nose as an acrid smell swept over them both.

Jan coughed and said, "Whip tree. But I've never seen one so big before. And I've never seen one uproot itself and try to walk away."

"A whip tree? What's that?"

"Just another leftover toy from before the Gene Wars. It's a mixture of animal and vegetable. Probably *more* animal than vegetable. It mimics different species of tree.

When an animal, or a person, gets close it grabs them with a tentacle, impales them on its thorns and then slowly absorbs their body fluids until there's nothing left but an empty husk. This it tosses far away so as not to alert the next victim. You were lucky you didn't experience the whole process first-hand."

"I know," he said as he wiped soot-blackened sweat from his forehead. "If you hadn't screamed out when you did. . . ."

"I saw a movement. Until then it just never occurred to me it might have been a whip tree. As I said, I've never seen one that big before."

"A new breed? A mutation?"

"I suppose so. There were plenty of whip trees around Minerva but I never heard anyone say that they saw the bloody things *walking*." She put the gun back in her belt. "We should take a sample of it before we go, but let's wait a bit. I want to make sure it's well and truly dead before we go near it."

"Fine with me."

They walked to the edge of the square and Jan looked around, frowning. Then her face cleared. "I think I've got my bearings now," she told Robin. "We're on the north side of the square." She turned and pointed at the fungus-covered ruins of a large building behind them. "This would have been the Town Hall. I remember seeing it take a direct hit." She turned to face the square again. "And there . . ." she pointed at one of many large depressions in the ground, "that was where the dais was . . . where the Head Women, my mother among them, waited to pay official respect to the *Lord Pangloth* when it came to pick up its tribute. That got a direct hit too. That day. I never saw my mother again. . . ." Her voice faltered. Robin put his arms around her. "Don't think about it if it hurts you so much."

She leaned against him. "No, I need to. I owe it to the

memory of my mother. And to others. Alsa, Helen, Simon
. . . even Martha."

"Martha?"

Jan smiled slightly. "Martha was a chimp."

"A close friend or a member of the family?"

She laughed in spite of herself. "More like an employee,
actually," she said, remembering a little guiltily how she was
often irritated with Martha. "Mother God, it all seems so
long ago. . . ." She pulled away from him and again surveyed the square. She pointed to the opposite side. "That's
the inn, what's left of it. I was on the roof the day . . . it all
happened. After we fired our futile rockets at the *Lord
Pangloth* the bombs started to fall. I saw a bomb actually hit
the roof of the inn, and then I fell *through* it. . . ." She
pointed in another direction. "The big gap over there . . .
that's where the Temple to the Mother God stood. It was
made entirely of wood . . . sacred wood . . . so it must have
completely burnt down." She sighed, then, taking Robin by
the hand, led him into a street. It was ghostly quiet, the
fungus that covered the still-standing remains of the shattered town muffled their footsteps. There were no birds and
no insects.

"Where are we going?" he asked.

"I'm just making a short pilgrimage, then we'll collect our
samples and leave."

To her surprise her house was still standing and seemingly
intact under its fungi shroud, whereas most of the others in
the vicinity had been razed. She used her gun to burn away
the covering on the front door, both of them holding their
noses against the stench of burning fungus. The exposed
wood was rotten and fell to pieces at her first kick. Jan
entered warily. Following her, Robin said, "Be careful, this
whole place could come down on our heads."

"I know," she said. "Why don't you wait outside? I won't
be long."

"No, I'm staying with you," he told her.

"Thanks," she said, pleased. Slowly, she went from room to room. The living room, her mother's room, her own room . . . the kitchen.

On the morning of the *Lord Pangloth*'s final visit, she had argued with Melissa, her mother, after Melissa had given her the small bomb and told her she wanted her to give herself up to the Sky Warriors if the attack on the Sky Lord should fail. "You are not my mother," she had finally said and Melissa had slapped her in return. Those were practically the last words they ever exchanged. Jan never had the chance to apologise. Now, in this dank room with its fungus-encrusted furniture, she said softly, "Melissa . . . Mother . . . I'm sorry. . . ."

Jan climbed into the Toy to get the sample kit. She was puzzled when she heard Robin coming in behind her. She turned to him as he came through the inner hatch. "What are you doing? I said I'd get the kit."

He joined her on the pilot's couch. Though the cabin had been enlarged to accommodate the two of them it was still pretty cramped. "Forget the kit for the time being. There's something more important we have to attend to first."

"There is? What?"

"This," he said, and he took hold of her and kissed her with what seemed to be authentic passion. She was caught totally off-guard but after her initial surprise began quickly to respond. And as they clung fiercely to each other on the couch she received another welcome surprise. She pulled back from him. "Robin! You . . . you have . . .!"

He grinned at her and nodded. "Yeah. I don't know for how long though, so let's not waste it."

With difficulty, in the confined space, they got out of their clothes and made frantic love. Even after climaxing Robin rapidly regained his erection. They made love again, much more slowly. Jan thought it was the best love-making she had ever had. With a man. "Welcome back," she whispered later as they lay limp and entangled on the couch.

Afterwards they took the kit outside and began collecting samples from as many different species of fungi as they could find. They left the whip tree until last. Jan approached it cautiously, after first burning off all its visible tentacles, while Robin stood back, ready to fire at the slightest movement. But when she drove the sample borer into its charred trunk there was not even the slightest twitch of a dying reflex action. It was definitely dead.

Jan felt relief when the Toy finally rose up from the square. She also felt a kind of release; as if something that had been weighing down on her for years had gone at last. "Goodbye," she said as Minerva fell rapidly behind them.

The Toy sped southwards towards the Sky Angel which was somewhere in South America. They had only been travelling for a matter of minutes when the Toy said, "I have a radar contact. A large flying object eighty-three miles south east. An airship."

Jan glanced at Robin. "A Sky Lord," she said.

"But you cleared all the Sky Lords out of North America."

"Yes. That means it's an Ashley. I suppose we'd better take a look."

"Permission to enter the bridge, Captain Vyushkov?"

Vyushkov turned in his seat and nodded, "Of course, Brother James."

Milo pulled himself through the hatchway and into the bridge which was lined with glowing read-out screens. Men, and one lone woman, sat hunched over them. By means of the netting on the ceiling, Milo made his way along the bridge until he was behind the Captain and his co-pilot. "Everything on schedule?" he asked.

"Perfectly," replied Vyushkov. "The flight program we're using may be ancient but is just as applicable now as when trips to Earth from Karaganga were routine."

Milo gazed out through the viewing port. The Earth almost filled it. *I'm going home*, thought Milo, *after all these years I'm going home*.

"How's Father Shaw?" asked Vyushkov.

"No better, I'm afraid," replied Milo. "I'm trying to persuade him to take a sedative but he refuses."

"I've never seen a man look so scared."

"It's being in free-fall. He can't adapt to it. He was the same on the trip from Belvedere. Perhaps once we reach Earth he will be all right."

"It's odd, I know," said Vyushkov, "but I got the impression he was also scared of *you*."

"An amusing idea," laughed Milo, "but one without foundation. He doesn't approve of me, true, but he has no reason to fear me."

Vyushkov turned and looked at him. "Hasn't he?"

Milo smiled at him. Then he said, "Have you been thinking over what I said?"

"Let's not discuss it now," Vyushkov said quickly, nodding his head towards his co-pilot.

Milo leaned forward and indicated the looming Earth with his hand. He put his lips to Vyushkov's ear and whispered, "One day all that could be yours, my son."

Chapter Twenty-Five:

The dot on the monitor swiftly grew into a Sky Lord. Jan had no trouble recognising it. "The *Perfumed Breeze*," she said sourly. It conjured up black memories. Of the Warlord Horado. And of her beloved Ceri's imprisonment on that Japanese airship. Ceri had never really recovered from her ordeal. She said to the Toy, "Establish radio contact, if you can. In the meantime, circle the airship."

"Do you think there are any people on board?" Robin asked.

"It's doubtful. All the Ashleys dumped their human cargoes. With the exception, I think, of the *Lord Montcalm*. But we'd better make sure before we take any action against it."

The Toy said, "I have a voice contact, Jan. I will patch it in."

A familiar voice came over the speaker. "Hello, hello? Who is that? Who are you? Why are you circling me? Answer me or I'll shoot you down. I can, you know!"

Jan sighed. The chilling reproduction of the voice of an adolescent girl who had died centuries ago. "Hello, Ashley. How are you?"

There was a short silence. Then, "Who is that? I know your voice."

"It's Jan, Ashley. Do you remember me?"

"Jan!" exclaimed the voice. "Of course I remember you! Hey, this is great. You've come to visit me!"

Jan glanced at Robin. Ashley was actually glad to hear from her. She had to remind herself that this wasn't the same Ashley who had abandoned her and Robin in the blight lands. "Yes, I've come to visit you. Er, how have you been?" The question sounded absurd to her own ears as soon as she'd spoken it.

"Oh, fine, I guess. But I'm kind of bored. And lonely. I can't talk to the other me's on the radio any more. I don't know why. So there's only Carl and me in here, and you know how much fun *he* is."

"You don't have any people on board?" *Real* people, she almost said.

"No, I jettisoned them all ages ago. They were boring, and a nuisance to look after."

Jan said, "Toy, cut the mike, please." She looked at Robin. "I suppose we'd better destroy her. She sounds okay at the moment but that's probably just a temporary condition. We can't leave her in charge of all that firepower. . . ." He nodded his agreement.

"Jan? Jan? Are you still there?" Ashley asked.

Jan told the Toy to activate the mike and said, "Yes, I'm still here. I'm coming to visit you."

"Hey, that's great!"

The Toy stopped circling and began to approach the *Perfumed Breeze*. "Aim for the control pod," Jan instructed the Toy. "Get as close as you can before you fire so she won't have time to use her lasers."

The Toy increased speed.

"Hey, Jan? What are you doing? Aren't you going to land up top?"

Jan didn't answer. The Toy streaked towards the control pod, a tiny, transparent blister beneath the huge bow of the airship. The blister grew bigger. Then the Toy fired its missile.

"Jan! What are you. . .?"

The missile hit its target and exploded. The control pod, and a large section of the hull surrounding it, was instantly vaporised. Ashley ceased to speak.

202

The *Perfumed Breeze*, no longer under any form of control, began to lose height. It also began to turn sharply to starboard. "Might as well finish the job," Jan murmured.

The Toy made another pass at the Sky Lord, firing several rockets into the hull. The great airship shook as the series of explosions tore through it. Then a gas cell containing hydrogen spectacularly ignited. As Jan watched the fire spread quickly throughout the *Perfumed Breeze* she realised she had just carried out her second act of expiation that day.

Jean-Paul sucked at the straw until the cup was empty. He sighed and closed his eyes. Ayla regarded him worriedly. His face was even more haggard and drained of colour. "The pain still bad?" she asked him.

He opened his eyes. "No, not too bad now," he said weakly. "That last injection is working. Worst thing right now is the itch under the cast." The cast went from his neck to his hips. "At least I can only feel it from here up." He touched his breastbone. He was paralysed from there down to his feet. "Other good thing is that I can't feel that damned catheter." He gave her a strained smile. Her smile back at him was equally strained. It was killing her seeing him like this.

She said, "It won't be long before the spacers land. I'm sure Dad is right—they'll know more about medicine than we do. They'll be able to help you."

"Yeah, sure."

"I mean it."

He took hold of her hand. "I know you do, darling. But, in spite of what the doctor, you and Lon have said, I have a pretty good idea how badly injured I am. This is no 'temporary' paralysis, and it's still touch and go that I'm even going to make it. I can see it in the doctor's eyes . . . and Lon's. Those spacers will have to be miracle-workers to be of any use to me."

"Can you see it in my eyes—what you see in Dad and Steven's eyes?"

"No. Only hope and love. You love me too much to see reality."

"And I have *faith*, Jean-Paul. You're going to make it, and the spacers are going to be able to help you."

"I hope so. But I've got to be honest with you, Ayla. If they can't fix me up I don't think I want to go on . . . like this."

"Don't talk like that!" she said hotly. "That's what a . . . a *coward* would say!"

"A coward?" he said, smiling faintly. "Yeah, well, I guess I am if I'd rather die than spend years like this—helpless and useless. And the thought of never being able to make love to you again, Ayla . . . I just can't take it, so yeah, I guess I am a coward."

Her eyes burned with salty tears. "Stop it, please."

"I'm sorry. Come on, let's talk about something else. *Anything* else. Like what's the situation with our deep-sea friends? They shown up again?"

Wiping her eyes with the back of her hand she said, "Yeah. Last night. A group got through the outer walls and raided the fish pens. They did a lot of damage, as well as eating a lot of fish. It was only discovered this morning. A party of hunters, led by Juli, went off after them. I don't know yet if they had any luck. I don't even know if they've returned."

"Sounds bad," he said. She noticed his voice was getting weaker.

"Yeah, it is. Let's hope the spacers can help us out there as well."

"You're pinning a great deal on these spacers."

"I know. I'm starting to sound like Dad and Lyle. But we do need help. Too much is going wrong too quickly. Palmyra isn't going to survive for even another decade unless we get outside help."

He closed his eyes and she thought he'd fallen asleep but then, without opening his eyes, he said, "What about . . . what about *my* people? Have they been banished yet?"

"Yes," she told him. "At dawn this morning. They were escorted to the boundary. There they were given supplies, water and a few rifles, told where they could dig up the ammunition, and then put out through the gate. There are a few untouched places up the coast—they have a chance of making it to one of them."

"Sure they do," said Jean-Paul, eyes still closed. He spoke in a 'if you believe that you'll believe anything' tone of voice.

"The trouble is . . ." said Ayla reluctantly, ". . . that they made *all* your people go. Not just the rebels, even the ones who didn't take part in it."

Jean-Paul opened his eyes. "All of them?"

"I'm afraid so. With the exception of the fire victims here in the hospital. And you, of course. Lyle didn't want to do it but there would have been a riot if he hadn't."

"Damn," he said.

Captain Vyushkov pulled himself into the corridor. He looked annoyed. "What is so important that you summon me here?" he demanded of Brother James. "We will be entering the Earth's atmosphere in twelve minutes and I should be on the bridge."

"Forgive me, Captain," said Brother James, "but it is important. And I thought you should be the first to know. . . ." Brother James opened the door of the head. Captain Vyushkov looked inside. Father Shaw was floating there. His face was blue. Vyushkov turned to Brother James. "He's dead."

"Yes, he is. About ten minutes ago he said he wasn't feeling well and came in here. As you know, I've been concerned about his health so I followed to make sure he was all right. I found him like this."

"What do you think was the cause of death?"

Brother James shrugged. "Until I can perform an autopsy I can't say for sure. But my guess is that it was a heart attack. He found the whole trip too stressful."

Vyushkov looked again at the corpse. The front of Father Shaw's suit was unsealed and there was the foul smell of excreta in the air. The priest clearly hadn't had the time to use the facilities before he died. From the colour of Father Shaw's face Vyushkov would have said he had died of asphyxiation. And from the expression on his face—one of stark terror—it couldn't have been a quick death either.

He wondered why Brother James had murdered him. He said, "We will have to leave him here for the time being. Strap him down. We don't want him bouncing around during the landing. I'll declare this facility off-limits."

"Yes, Captain. Ah, of course, you will send a message to Belvedere informing the other Fathers of Father Shaw's unfortunate demise."

"It will have to wait until we have landed." Vyushkov turned to go. Brother James said, "One last thing, Captain. While we are alone here . . . can I ask you again if you plan to follow my advice?"

Vyushkov frowned at him. "I am giving it serious consideration. It all depends on my appraisal of the situation on Earth." Then he turned and pulled himself quickly down the corridor.

Humming happily, Milo did as requested and strapped down Father Shaw's body onto the toilet apparatus. He patted the dead priest on the head then left, sliding the door shut behind him. He returned to the main cabin which was filled with a buzz of muted but excited conversations. Vyushkov's men were keyed up; a little apprehensive about what they would encounter on the mother planet which they had always been told, until recently, was a lost world of death, but mainly they were eager to carry out their training as soldiers. He knew how they felt. He went along the aisle until he reached his couch. He slipped into his harness and lay there, weightless and serene. He felt certain that Vyushkov would do as he wanted.

He amused himself by reliving Father Shaw's last moments . . . the look in his eyes when Milo opened the door of the head . . . and the way those eyes bulged as Milo squeezed Shaw's nostrils shut with one hand while clamping the other hand over his mouth. Shaw had struggled for over two minutes. Milo had held him for a further two minutes before releasing him, just to be sure. "Sweet dreams," Milo had whispered as he let him go.

A series of bumps began. Gentle to begin with, they rapidly became more pronounced. The *Christina* was skimming the outer fringes of the Earth's atmosphere. Milo grinned to himself in anticipation.

The squid thrashed about wildly in the implacable grip of the Toy's grappling arms. Black ink billowed out in the water around it but that made no difference to the Toy's sensors. Jan told the Toy to inject the sample corer. It did so. The squid thrashed about even more wildly. The grappling arms released it and it jetted rapidly away. It was about twenty feet long from tentacle tips to tail. Blood now mixed in with its ink. "Horrible things," said Jan.

"Yeah, I agree," said Robin. "That's why I used to enjoy exterminating them so much."

"Well, that's six different species of the mutated versions that we've collected. You're the squid expert—how many more are there?"

He shrugged. "I don't know. I was only familiar with the species that lived in the waters around Antarctica. It's different out here in the Pacific. There are obviously a lot more of them . . . hey!" The Toy was being violently shaken, and then all the monitors went dark. "Toy! What's happening?"

The Toy paused before answering, then said, "It appears that we have been consumed by some form of organism. A very *large* organism."

Chapter Twenty-Six:

Lon Haddon's soul soared at the sight. Or rather, as he didn't admit to having a soul, some essential part of his being swelled with pure joy as he watched the space craft approach the landing site. It wasn't as awesome a spectacle as seeing a Sky Lord looming over you at close range— compared to a Sky Lord the space craft was small in size— but it stirred Haddon so much because it symbolised hope for the future and was solid, flying proof of humankind's technological prowess.

As the silver, streamlined space ship came closer Haddon was aware of a tingling in his skin and the hair on his scalp rose. He realised that he was responding to a powerful electromagnetic field that surrounded the ship. There was a deep humming sound as well. He guessed both were created by the ship's drive system.

The ship hovered above the landing field, then slowly landed without any perceptible bump. Kissing Mother Earth like a long-lost lover, Haddon thought happily. The humming died away. Haddon raised his arms and a great cheer went up from all the people who lined the edges of the field. At the same time the Palmyra band, made up of a motley collection of instruments, not to mention players, began to play a specially composed piece of music to welcome the space travellers. The cheering continued.

Milo, on the bridge beside Captain Vyushkov, peered out through the port. "Interesting," he murmured. The olive-skinned, and attractive, people of Palmyra were a mixture of caucasian, asian, oriental and Pacific island races. "Well, they certainly appear to be a healthy lot, eh?"

"Yes, but they dress like savages," said Vyushkov, disapprovingly. "The men wear dresses, like the women. And look at how even the women leave their chests bare."

"I am," said Milo, feeling a slight regret that Father Shaw wasn't alive to witness such depravity. But he noticed that not all the people dressed in the same way. He had spotted several in the crowd wearing pants or shorts and a few wore t-shirts. . . .

Vyushkov raised his helmet over his head. "Well, let us go and meet our hosts while they are still in the position to be hosts." He lowered the helmet over his head and sealed it. "By this time tomorrow," he said via his helmet speaker, "they will be our subjects."

Their group consisted of just four, including Milo. None carried any weapons. As they emerged from the airlock the cheering from the surrounding crowd became even more intense. On Milo's over-loaded earpieces the cheering sounded like surf breaking on a beach. He noticed that they wanted to surge forward to meet the space travellers but were heeding the warning that the ship's hull would not be safe to approach unprotected for several hours.

Milo stopped and tilted his helmet back. Blue sky again! After all those centuries! He wished he could remove his helmet so that he could smell fresh air again but Vyushkov was insisting that they run a comprehensive series of tests on the environment before they risked exposing themselves. Milo agreed with his caution. The Palmyrians might have adopted a natural resistance to designer micro-organisms that would still prove fatal for the spacers. He continued after the others. He felt heavier than usual but that was to be expected. The habitat's gravity, generated by centrifugal force, was always slightly under one g. Vyushkov and his men, knowing that Earth gravity would be stronger than what they were used to, had undergone special training to compensate.

When he had caught up with the other three he saw that a delegation of six men had left the crowd and was coming to meet them. They all wore gold chains from which hung six-pointed gold stars, and Milo guessed that they represented Palmyra's ruling body. *Like everyone else they look so happy to see us*, thought Milo delightedly. *They look upon us as saviours. What a surprise they are going to receive tomorrow.*

Incredulously, Jan exclaimed, "You're saying we've been *swallowed* by something!"

"Yes," replied the Toy.

Jan looked at Robin and shrugged helplessly. "We've been swallowed," she said and started to giggle. It seemed so ridiculous. Robin smiled too and said, "What could possibly be big enough to swallow the Toy?"

"A giant whale maybe . . . but no, whales have been extinct for ages." Jan's giggling got worse and even when the Toy's bow suddenly tilted sharply upwards she couldn't stop laughing. Robin was laughing now as well.

"We're moving backwards, and also descending," the Toy informed them.

Between giggles, Jan gasped, "Maybe it's decided it doesn't like the taste of us and it's going to eliminate us. In one end . . . and out the other!"

"Going to be awfully painful for it, whatever it is. . . ." gasped Robin, which made Jan laugh all the more.

"Attention," said the Toy, "I am picking up a very weak signal from Phebus. I will have to get close to the surface in order to establish a proper radio link-up."

Still laughing, Jan said, "Tell Phebus we're otherwise engaged. Tell her something has decided that we make an ideal appetiser."

"I am about to take steps to remove myself from whatever

organism has consumed us. I suggest we take a bio-sample before I carry out such procedures."

Sobering up, Jan said, "Hey, who gives the orders around here?"

"Phebus does."

Robin's laughter died away as well. "You can't argue with that," he said.

Jan's amusement had quickly turned to irritation. "Oh, very well, take the sample and let's get out of here."

A few seconds later the Toy said, "The bio-sample has been secured. We are now leaving. . . ." The Toy began to move forward, slowly at first, then it picked up speed. Progress became increasingly bumpy. Jan and Robin were repeatedly thrown against the restraining straps of their couch harnesses. "Whatever swallowed us must be regretting it now," said Robin.

The Toy slowed, then stopped, even though Jan could hear the Toy's underwater thrusters still running at full power. All of a sudden it struck her that they might actually be in danger. Their situation no longer seemed an inconsequential distraction. She had been taking the Toy's seeming infallibility and limitless power for granted but now it looked as if that might be a delusion. They could *die* in here, wherever 'here' was. . . .

"There's an obstruction," the Toy announced. "Don't be alarmed."

Easier said than done, thought Jan as the Toy seemed to stand on its tail and be violently flung back and forth. A plastic container of sandwiches and a thermos of coffee, which had been under Jan's couch, started flying about the cabin. She grabbed Robin's arm. The thing was trying to dislodge the Toy from its throat or whatever section of its anatomy it had become stuck in. "There will be a powerful explosion relatively close by," said the Toy in its maddeningly calm voice. "Don't be alarmed." The Toy was then shaken so violently that Jan's teeth were slammed together with a loud click and she tasted blood. She had sliced off the tip of her tongue. "Gah!" she cried and spat it out. Then came the explosion, so 'close by' that the Toy vibrated as if it had been struck by a huge hammer. Jan's ears rang painfully, making her temporarily forget the pain in her tongue.

The Toy shot forward. Whatever had been covering the sensors was gone because the monitors started displaying pictures again, though Jan couldn't make sense of what she was seeing—just swirling clouds of black and grey. "We're out," announced the Toy.

"Out of wha'?" cried Jan, with difficulty, because it hurt to speak. "Switch to a sonic display so we can see wha's happening!"

The Toy complied immediately and all monitors switched from visual to computer-enhanced sonic images. The Toy seemed to be ascending through scattered chunks of flesh. Jan watched as a large piece with a round, staring eye in it drifted past one of the sensors. "Look," said Robin, pointing at the monitor which showed a view from the stern of the Toy. A huge snake-like form was slowly twisting and turning below them as it sank. It was so big that its lower body was beyond the range of the sonic sensors and faded into a haze. Where its head should have been were strips of trailing flesh arranged like the petals of a flower. They slowly billowed back and forth as the creature went down. The Toy had blown off the head in order to free them.

"Mother Go', wha' is i'?" she gasped, oblivious of the blood trickling down her chin.

"A sea worm," Robin told her. "But I've never seen one *that* big before."

Jan remembered Ceri telling her that sea worms had been one of the major hazards to life on her old sea habitat. She had described them as large but . . . Jan watched with morbid fascination as the still writhing corpse sank into the deeps. Things were clearly getting out of control.

"Jesus! What happened to you?" cried Robin. She turned. He was staring at her with shocked concern. She touched her wet chin and looked at her fingers. They were covered in blood. "S'okay," she said, "I bi' the en' of my tongue . . . off. S'no' as ba' as i' looks."

"I *hope* not. You're bleeding like crazy."

"We're approaching the surface," interrupted the Toy. "I will soon be able to establish a clear radio link with Phebus."

Jan spat out blood onto an ersatz paper towel and said, "Surface completely. We're goin' to have to return to Sky Angel. I think I nee' medical attention."

The Toy continued to rise. Then they were passing through a thick layer of clotted, pink algae. Thick, ropey strands attached themselves to the Toy. The mutated algae now covered vast areas of the Pacific and Atlantic. Jan couldn't remember what the original purpose behind it had been; either a new form of cheap foodstuff that the Corporations planned to dump on the Third World or a deliberate spoiling action from one Corporation to sabotage another Corporation's sea farm. Whatever, there was a lot of it about these days. A bio-sample of it was already in the rapidly growing store.

The Toy broke free and hovered some twenty feet above the pink surface of the sea. Jan scanned the monitors. A massive storm front was approaching from the east. A thunderhead of dark clouds extended miles into the sky. Lightning flickered deep in its roiling interior. The Toy said, "Here is Phebus." Then they heard Phebus say, "You are to return to the Sky Angel at once. There has been a new development."

"We were plannin' to return now anyway," Jan replied. "I've ha' an acciden'. Nothing serious, just in case you're worried."

The program didn't answer. Jan said, "Wha' is this new developmen'?"

"I detected a space craft entering the atmosphere. I have

tracked it to its landing place on the north-east coast of Australia. We must go there."

In any other circumstances Ayla would have been delighted to see her father so happy but with Jean-Paul in the condition he was there was no way she could participate in her father's joy. She felt guilty because he had rushed straight from the spacers' landing field to the hospital but at the same time she was annoyed with him because she feared that all this excitement would be bad for Jean-Paul. But she couldn't bring herself to tell him that. Not yet. . . .

". . . And they are all I hoped for!" he said as he paced up and down the room. "Perhaps they are even *more* than I hoped for! They have promised to provide us with every possible assistance—scientific, technological . . ." he glanced at Jean-Paul, ". . . medical. Everything!"

"Have you spoken to them about Jean-Paul yet?" she asked.

"No, darling, not yet. I didn't have the opportunity. We didn't really discuss anything specific. Hopefully I will get the chance tonight at the welcoming banquet. I know they have two trained medics on board. One is a Karagangan and the other is one of the priests from Belvedere."

"How do you know they'll be attending the banquet? I thought you said they had imposed a quarantine upon themselves."

"Yes, but it's only a temporary one, dear. Just long enough for them to analyse our air, soil, various foodstuffs and the samples of our blood that we provided them with. I'm sure it will be just a formality. After all, look at us— we're all perfectly healthy." Then he realised what he'd said and winced. He stopped beside Jean-Paul's bed. "Oh, God . . . I'm sorry. . . ."

"Forget it, Lon," said Jean-Paul weakly. "I know what you mean."

Ayla stroked Jean-Paul's forehead and said to her father, "They're afraid of catching something off us?"

"Well, yes, but you can't blame them for that fear."

"What about us? Couldn't we catch something off them?"

He frowned at her. "I seriously doubt it, dear. They've been raised in relatively sterile environments."

"How many are there?" Jean-Paul asked.

"We met only four of them this afternoon but Captain Vyushkov, their leader, told me that the entire crew consisted of twenty-nine people. There had been thirty but, regrettably, one of the priests from Belvedere died during the trip. A heart attack, said Vyushkov."

Ayla's own heart sank at this news. It didn't say much for the quality of Belvederian medicine, particularly as the man's travelling companion had been a doctor. Perhaps the Karagangans were more medically sophisticated. She certainly hoped so.

Jean-Paul asked, "How big is their ship?"

"How big?" said her father, surprised. "Well, it's pretty big. Over three hundred feet long, I'd say. It's a ship they usually use for trips to the Martian colonies. Why do you ask?"

"Again, just curious." Jean-Paul closed his eyes.

"Dad, you're tiring him," she said accusingly.

"I'm sorry. I'd better go. I want to check on how things are coming along at the Great Hall for tonight's banquet." Ayla went with him to the door. "I'm glad it's all worked out as you hoped," she told him quietly.

"So am I, darling, so am I. Are you coming to the celebrations tonight?"

She looked over at Jean-Paul. "I don't like to leave him . . . but perhaps I'll look in later."

"I hope you will," he said. He kissed her on the cheek and left.

*

By the time Ayla did arrive at the Great Hall that night the official welcoming ceremonies and the banquet itself were over. People were milling about in small groups between the tables, drinks in their hands and talking animatedly. She saw that at the centre of each group of Palmyrians was someone who could only be a spacer, distinctive in the tight-fitting black and yellow uniform. She looked about, trying to spot her father in the throng, and finally saw him at the far end of the hall, standing by the top table and part of a large group. She made her way over to him. He was with Lyle Weaver and they were both talking to a heavily built spacer who, judging by his more opulent uniform, was their leader. When she reached the top table it took some effort to attract her father's attention. When at last she did he grinned broadly and emerged from the scrimmage. "Ayla, darling, I'm so glad you made it! You must come and meet Captain Vyushkov, who's in charge of the Karagangan expedition."

"Dad," she said urgently, "Jean-Paul is getting weaker. I must speak to the Karagangan doctor. I want him to look at Jean-Paul."

Her father's expression became concerned. "The Karagangan medic is back at their ship. But the Belvederian doctor is here. Come. . . ." He took her by the hand and pulled her into the crowd. They pushed through to the High Table. "Brother James, I'd like you to meet my daughter, Ayla. . . ."

The bald man, seated at the table, turned in his chair. He was not dressed like the other spacers but wore a white two-piece suit. There was a red cross over his left breast. Then she noticed his eyes. One was blue while the other one was green. *How strange*, she thought. The man rose from his chair and held out his hand to her. "I'm delighted to meet you, Ayla. *Extremely* delighted."

Chapter Twenty-Seven:

Milo could scarcely contain his amusement. It had been a very entertaining night and he was glad that Captain Vyushkov had included him in the official party. There were twelve of them this time, and, according to what they had told the Palmyrians that afternoon, that left only seventeen on board the *Christina*; in reality there were another one hundred and fifteen people still on board, most of them soldiers.

He had been relieved when the samples had received the all-clear from the analysis computer: a lot of unknown species of fungal spores in the air and soil but none of them presented any potential danger. Some spores turned up in the food but it was all pronounced safe to eat. And the water was safe to drink. "There might be some minor reactions to certain bacteria, mainly in the food, that aren't on Karaganga," the medic had said, "but I guarantee there will be nothing serious or life-threatening." That was fine with Milo; he was more than willing to risk a case of diarrhoea for the chance of breathing fresh air and enjoying the hospitality of the attractive Palmyrians.

And the hospitality had been fine indeed. The Palmyrians' so-called Great Hall, where the banquet was held, was decorated with long streamers made of palm leaves and they were welcomed with a display of dancing by a group of bare-breasted young women. As Milo watched the dance, which mainly involved an erotic gyration of the pelvis accompanied by a loud and frantic drumbeat, he recalled that he had seen such dancing before in the dim, distant past. Another Pacific island connotation but he couldn't remember which particular island it was.

Seated at the big table, mounted on a slightly raised platform at the end of the hall, with the six Palmyrian leaders, the spacers were served a lavish feast of fish, roast pork, roast potatoes, paw paws, raw tomatoes, pineapples and various other fruits, and hot bread, with coconut cakes, covered in thick cream, for dessert. Throughout the meal their cups were kept constantly filled with a very good cold beer (though the single glass of red wine that Milo sampled he found less than mediocre). Milo spent much of the time speculating on the prices these delicacies would fetch on the habitats—with the exception of Belvedere which no longer had a monetary system—and the Martian colonies. He was seated between Captain Vyushkov and a Palmyrian called Lon Haddon. The latter was an intelligent if overly earnest and fatally naive man. Milo learnt that Haddon had been instrumental in the campaign to try to re-establish radio contact with the habitats. Old computer records had given the orbital positions of all four habitats and so they had beamed their signals at each one in turn, hoping that there were still people alive up there. Milo also learnt why they had working radio equipment when most electronic equipment had been eaten away by designer bacteria and fungi during and after the Gene Wars. They had been getting preserved equipment from a sunken Japanese habitat out beyond the great reef for years now, thanks to an arrangement with some kind of underwater tribe, but this had recently ended. "That's why your arrival here couldn't have been better timed," Haddon said. Milo smiled and nodded but said nothing.

On Vyushkov's other side sat the actual leader of the Palmyrians, Lyle Weaver, and at one point in the meal Milo listened with interest as Weaver described to Vyushkov how they had defended themselves against one of the marauding airships they called Sky Lords. Vyushkov had displayed interest too; he was particularly interested in Palmyra's anti-aircraft installations.

When the meal was finally over Lyle Weaver asked Vyushkov if his people would mind mingling with the other Palmyrians and Vyushkov said not at all and, after warning Weaver that not all of his people were equally adept at speaking Americano, passed on the word. Before Milo had a chance to rise he was accosted by a young, round-faced priest, dressed in a black cassock with a white collar, who introduced himself as Father John Baxter. Though he knew that Brother James was of the protestant persuasion he was inviting him to take part in a special service of Thanksgiving at Palmyra's Roman Catholic church the following Sunday. Knowing that no Palmyrian would be in any mood for thanksgiving by then, Milo warmly thanked Father Baxter and assured him he would be happy to attend.

The priest, looking pleased, hurried away. Milo sat there trying to conceal his profound amusement. He hadn't had so much fun since killing Father Shaw. Then he heard Lon Haddon call his name. "Brother James, I'd like you to meet my daughter, Ayla." Milo turned and saw, standing beside Haddon, a girl of such intriguing beauty he was instantly captivated. With her the mix of races had produced a genetic gem as far as physical appeal was concerned. He was especially taken by her out-sized, oriental eyes but not to the extent that he could ignore her tanned and finely proportioned body. A pity, he thought, that unlike the rest of her young female contemporaries in the hall she was wearing a shirt. As he rose to his feet he told himself that he would possess this little gem, no matter what. He held out his hand and told her, truthfully, how delighted he was to meet her.

"Jean-Paul, are you awake?" she asked softly. She saw his eyelids flutter, then open. He turned his head towards her and his eyes narrowed when he saw the stranger beside her.

"Jean-Paul, this is Brother James. One of the spacers. He's come to help you."

"Can—can you help me?" asked Jean-Paul hesitantly.

"Yes, I think I can," Brother James told him gently.

Ayla saw hope flare up in Jean-Paul's eyes. "You can repair my spine . . . so that I can feel again? *Walk* again?"

"I can't make any promises. Let me tell you that right away. I don't want to raise your hopes only to dash them later. I've spoken to your doctor and looked at your records. But I need to make a more detailed examination of the extent of your injuries. We have scanning devices which provide much more internal information than the crude x-ray machine you have here. In the meantime, I can save your life."

"My life?"

"Forgive me for being blunt, but your doctor informs me that your kidney function is deteriorating rapidly. Your kidneys are not responding to the limited range of drugs that are available to him. But I have on board our ship a drug that will restore your kidneys to full health in a matter of hours. I shall return here tomorrow and administer it. Then we can start to think about dealing with your spinal injuries."

"You think there's a chance—even a small one, that I will walk again?"

"Until I have all the facts, as I told you, I can't say for sure, but yes, I can say there's a chance."

Ayla felt a pain in her chest when she saw tears form in Jean-Paul's eyes. He held out his hand to Brother James who gripped it firmly. "Thank you," whispered Jean-Paul. "Thank you."

As Ayla drove Brother James back to the Great Hall he explained to her the problems of dealing with severe spinal injuries. " . . . So while the peripheral nerves are capable of regeneration the nerves in the spinal cord are not. When they are severed scar tissue forms between the break, acting as a barrier. Even back in the late twentieth century doctors had some success in stimulating severed spinal nerves to grow around the scar tissue and connect up but the problem was that there was no guarantee that the right nerves would connect up with each other. The spinal cord contains a vast number of individual nerve fibres so it was a very complicated job to identify each one and connect them up to the right counterpart by microsurgery. Human surgeons only ever achieved partial success at this, but then machines were developed that carried out the surgical procedures automatically and they were a hundred percent successful. . . ."

"And you have such a machine?"

He shook his head. "I'm afraid not. I doubt if there's still a working med-machine anywhere among the habitats or the Martian colonies. They were infinitely sophisticated machines with delicate bio-mechanical components and we lost the technology to repair them."

"Then you can't help Jean-Paul?" she cried.

"Oh, I think I can help him all right. It will need a series of operations but I believe I can link up enough of the right spinal fibres to restore many of his major motor functions. He will be able to walk, for example. Not that well, I hasten to add, but he will walk again. He will also regain control over his bladder and bowels . . . and, if you'll forgive the intrusion into an even more indelicate area, his sexual prowess will also be restored."

Ayla gave an embarrassed laugh. She had forgotten this man was a priest, or something like that. And from Belvedere. From what little her father had told her about life on that habitat she knew it was a very puritanical society. It probably took a lot for Brother James even to mention such matters to a woman. He was a strange man. There was something about him that she instinctively disliked but so strong was her gratitude towards him for giving Jean-Paul back the will to live that she deliberately kept this feeling buried.

She stopped the car in front of the entrance to the Great Hall. "Thank you for everything, Brother James," she said, taking his hand and gripping it hard. Then, impulsively, she leaned over and kissed him on the cheek. To her amusement he jerked back as if stung, then hurried out of the car. "I'll see you tomorrow morning, Miss Haddon," he said and quickly went inside.

Milo lay on his couch with his eyes closed and his hands behind his head, a centre of stillness amid the surrounding activity. All about him the soldiers were preparing themselves, checking their suits, their equipment and their weapons. While they thought excitedly of the coming military action Milo thought excitedly of the fun he would have with the young and beautiful Ayla Haddon.

His erotic fantasies were interrupted by someone saying his name. He opened his eyes. Captain Vyushkov's aide stood in the aisle by his couch. "Yes, what is it?" Milo asked.

"Captain Vyushkov wishes you to come to his cabin."

"My pleasure," said Milo, swinging his legs off the couch. He had been expecting this summons. All night Vyushkov had been conferring with his officers, planning the final stages of the attack on Palmyra. The aide ushered Milo into Vyushkov's cabin. Vyushkov sat at a desk. On the desk was an aerial photograph of Palmyra. Several locations in the town had been marked with crude crosses. "Sit down, Brother James," said Vyushkov as the aide left. He poured Milo a glass of vodka and slid it over the photograph towards him. Milo took it, observing that Vyushkov's face was very flushed and he was probably a little drunk, if not more than a little. For all his seeming confidence Milo guessed that the Russian was nervous. He had probably never seen real military action before; there had been no trouble between the habitats for over a century, and he would have been a child when the last rebellion took place on Karaganga. His

223

only military experience would have been in the simulation tanks.

Milo took a large swallow of vodka, put the glass down on the map and smiled at Vyushkov. "Everything ready?"

"Yes, Brother James. We move at 04.00 hours, just before dawn. It should all be over in an hour. The ground attack troops will start to move out in half an hour so as to be in position around the town when we strike."

"Good," said Milo. "And then, when the smoke clears, you will announce annexation of Palmyra for the Space Republic of Karaganga, yes?"

Vyushkov nodded. "Yes, for the time being."

"For the time being?" asked Milo, knowingly.

"It will depend on how things develop. But this place is indeed a treasure trove."

Milo smiled. "Perhaps just the first of many. It can't be the last such community on Earth. Others may not be as technologically advanced as this one—the Palmyrians have been lucky—but that doesn't matter. Using this as a base you could conquer the entire planet. Not that it appears to be in very good shape but we should be able to devise the means of reversing much of this genetic pollution, now that we know the killer plagues have gone. Needless to say, I possess invaluable knowledge about genegineering."

Vyushkov threw back the remaining vodka in his glass, wiped his lips and stared at Milo. "Just who *are* you, Brother James?"

"All you need to know about me is that I am your friend and ally, Captain Vyushkov."

"I hope so, because I am appointing you my special advisor."

"Thank you. I appreciate the honour."

"But at the first hint I have that you are not behind me totally then you are a dead man."

"Have no fear on that score, Captain, I am, and will

224

always remain, your obedient servant." Milo raised his glass to him and smiled.

Lon Haddon woke from a wonderful sleep. He had dreamt about Glynis, Ayla's mother. He had walked with her along the sea front, between the palm trees. The sun was going down. She shared in his triumph; shared in his joy about the spacers and what they represented. A future for Palmyra. And Ayla. "I'm so proud of you, Lon," she told him. And he told her, "Thank you for coming back. It's marvellous seeing you again. I miss you so much, Glynis."

But his feeling of well-being quickly evaporated. He could hear gunfire . . . distant shouting. Screams. As he jumped from his bed his first thought was that the banished Sky People had somehow returned and were exacting revenge. Then he became aware that a deep humming sound filled the air and his skin tingled. *Oh no!* he thought with horror. Naked, he ran out onto the verandah and looked up. It was as he feared. . . .

Drifting low in the pre-dawn sky above the town was the spacers' ship, the *Christina*. As Haddon watched a beam flickered down from the ship. It wasn't a laser beam—it was much wider than that, and colourless . . . more a *shimmer* through the air. Haddon heard an explosion. Where the beam had struck, in the middle of the town, smoke rose. Then he noticed other columns of smoke rising in other parts of town. From the position of each column he knew exactly what the targets of the spacers had been. He put his hands over his face and sank to his knees on the wooden floor of the verandah. "No," he groaned, "no, no, no, no . . . *no!*"

Jean-Paul didn't know which was worse. The agony in his upper spine, neck and head, his feeling of utter helplessness, or his fear on behalf of Ayla. She must have been gone for more than an hour now. When they were both woken up by the sound of gunfire she sprang out of the camp bed that had been set up beside his and said that she would see what was going on and hurry right back. Something had obviously prevented her. So what the hell was *happening?!* He yelled himself hoarse but there was no sign of the doctor or his nurses. That was why he was in so much pain—no one had given him his dose of painkillers that morning.

At least it was quiet now. No more shooting. No more explosions. He heard the occasional far-off shout but that was all. That was enough. *What was going on?* If only he could move. . . .

Hurried footsteps outside, then the door opened. It was Ayla, and he was shocked at the way she looked. Her face was bleached white and her cheeks were covered in dried tears. When she saw him she started crying again. She came over and lay her head on his chest, her arms around his head. This increased the agony tenfold but he bit back a cry of pain and put his own arms around her. In an act of supreme patience and stoicism he waited for her crying to run its course and for her to tell him *what the hell was happening*.

At last she raised her head, looked at him, then collapsed backwards onto the chair beside the bed. "It's terrible, Jean-Paul, terrible," she said, her voice catching on a sob. "They've taken over Palmyra."

"The spacers?" he said at once.

She nodded. It was more of a convulsive forward shaking of the head than a nod. "There were a lot more of them in that ship than they said there were. Groups of them entered the town just before dawn. Everyone was taken by surprise. Those who tried to resist were killed. The spacers took over the power house, the armoury, the militia centre, the council building . . . and while they were doing that their space ship came over the town and blew up all our anti-aircraft gun sites. They used some kind of weapon no one here has ever seen before. They said that the ship would destroy the entire town section by section unless we surrendered completely. Lyle Weaver had no choice. He surrendered to them about half an hour ago . . . everyone has to go to the Big House and hand in all their firearms. If you don't and the spacers find you with one it will mean instant execution." She drew in a large breath of air and hiccupped. "We are now subjects of the Space Republic of Karaganga. . . . Oh *God*." She lowered her head.

Jean-Paul didn't know what to say but he realised he wasn't that surprised this had happened. Had he been suspicious of the spacers' motives all along? He must have been. But because Haddon and Ayla were so positive about the arrival he had kept his feelings suppressed. "Ayla," he sighed, feeling even more helpless.

"There's more, I'm afraid. . . ." she said, lifelessly.

"More?" What else could possibly have gone wrong?

"Dad. They arrested him. Well, threw him in prison. There was no formal arrest."

"The spacers arrested him?"

"No. Our people did. Jelker Banks's followers, that is . . . and most of the population of Palmyra falls into that category now. They let Banks and his sons out and threw Dad in. There's talk of hanging him. . . ." She twisted her hands in her lap. "Oh, Jean-Paul, I saw him in prison. He won't even talk to me . . . he's in a kind of trance. I don't think he even realises what's happening any more."

"The shock must—" Jean-Paul began but got no further because the door was flung open with a crash. Ayla spun round in fright. With a sickening feeling, Jean-Paul saw that it was the two Banks brothers. Bron and his younger brother, whose name Jean-Paul didn't know. Both were carrying knives.

227

Chapter Twenty-Eight:

The younger of the two Banks brothers shut the door. Bron advanced on Ayla who had risen from the chair. "I knew we'd find you here . . . here with your dying sky pirate," he said, waving his knife from side to side.

"Get out of here!" cried Ayla, backing towards Jean-Paul's bed. Jean-Paul's awful feeling of total helplessness grew even worse. He struggled to rise but his efforts only produced an explosion of pain in his neck and back.

"Oh, we'll leave," said Bron, with a sneer, "but only after we've fixed you and your friend." His brother was also advancing on Ayla now. Ayla snatched up the chair and held it in front of her, but she didn't move from beside the bed. Jean-Paul realised, sickly, that her aim was to protect him. "You won't get away with this," she told them. "You kill us and you'll be arrested for murder."

"Who's going to arrest us?" laughed the younger of the two. "The spacers? They won't care less. And *our* people will hail us as heroes. To kill any Haddon is now considered a public service. When your father and brother are hung alongside each other—which is going to be in an hour's time—there's going to be a hell of a cheering."

"My . . . brother?" said Ayla, sounding dismayed.

"Yeah," said Bron. "A party went out to his farm. They should be back with him soon."

"But Len has nothing to do with anything!" she protested.

"He's a Haddon, isn't he?" said Bron, and suddenly he lunged at her with his knife. Ayla thrust the chair out to block him and as she did so Bron's younger brother grabbed

228

one of the chair legs and pulled violently. Ayla was jerked off balance. She had no choice but to let go or fall. Laughing, the younger one threw the chair into a corner of the room. Ayla was now defenceless. "Get away from her!" cried Jean-Paul, again trying vainly to raise himself from the bed.

"Shut up, Sky Man," Bron told him. "Your turn will come real soon." He moved in on Ayla who still refused to shift from the side of the bed. . . .

Then the door opened. Brother James wore the same white suit but was now carrying a black satchel. He stood in the doorway and stared with mild surprise at the tableau in front of him. "Oh dear, I seem to have interrupted something," he said quietly.

The Banks brothers whirled round to face him. Bron said, "What are you doing here, spacer?"

"Making a professional visit," Brother James told him. "I'm a doctor."

"You alone?"

"Yes, why?"

The brothers exchanged a glance and then Bron said, "Get him."

The younger brother charged Brother James, knife extended. Jean-Paul was never sure what happened next. One second Brother James was standing in the doorway and the next he wasn't. The air blurred around the younger Banks and then Brother James was standing behind him. He was still holding his black satchel. The younger man's knife was no longer in his hand but buried to the hilt under his chin. From the look in his eyes he had no idea what had happened either. He turned towards his brother, perhaps hoping for an explanation. Bron could only stare back with a look of shocked disbelief. Then the younger brother's eyes rolled back in his head and his knees sagged. He fell to one side and his head hit the floor with a solid-sounding *thonk*.

Bron stared down at his dead brother for several seconds

then looked at Brother James. "You killed him," he said, in a high voice.

Brother James bent down and carefully placed his satchel on the floor. "I can't argue with you on that one." Bron, keeping his knife pointed at Brother James, began to edge towards the door. "Are you leaving?" Brother James asked him cheerfully.

"Stay away from me!" cried Bron, his voice going even higher.

"I'm afraid you can't leave. Any attack on one of us by one of you is punishable by death. Bit extreme, I know, but I don't make the rules." He started to move between Bron and the doorway.

"*Don't touch me!*"screamed Bron, and lunged at him. This time it was only Brother James's right arm and hand that momentarily vanished. When they reappeared the hand was around Bron's wrist. There was a wet *snap* and the knife fell. Then Brother James's other hand was gripping Bron's throat. Bron made a gagging sound, then came various ugly crunching noises. When Brother James released him he fell to the floor like a pile of empty clothing.

Brother James turned to Ayla and Jean-Paul and smiled broadly. "Well, that's the unpleasantness over with." He rubbed his hands together briskly. "Now, onto more pleasant matters." He came over to the bed. Jean-Paul had the impression that Ayla wanted to flee but she didn't move. "How did you do that?" she asked him in a shaky voice.

He stood close to her, still smiling broadly. "The secret is all in the breathing. Don't give it another thought. It's just a party trick. Now let's get down to business."

"Business?"

"Yes." He pointed at Jean-Paul but without taking his eyes off Ayla. "I have the drug with me that will cure his kidney condition, but before I use it we must discuss the price."

Jean-Paul, though relieved to have been saved from the

230

Banks brothers, had swiftly developed a very bad feeling about Brother James. "What do you mean a price?" he asked.

Brother James ignored him. He continued to stare intently at Ayla. "Do you really love this man?" he asked her.

"Yes, I do," said Ayla.

"Good. Very good." Brother James seemed genuinely pleased. "In that case there shouldn't be any problems."

"I don't understand," said Ayla.

"It's simple. The price you must pay to save his life is yourself. I want you."

"You want me?" Ayla said slowly. She plainly didn't yet understand what Brother James was talking about. But Jean-Paul did. "Get out of here and take your damn drug with you!" he yelled. Ayla turned and gave him a confused, and frightened, look. "Jean-Paul . . . what . . .?"

"Ayla, don't you see? He's trying to blackmail you!" Jean-Paul cried. "He's threatening to let me die unless you become his . . . his. . . ."

"Why not try 'sex slave'. It has a nice ring to it," said Brother James cheerfully.

Understanding dawned on Ayla's face. "You want to have sex with me," she accused him.

"How delightful. Intelligent as well as beautiful. Yes, my little gem, I do indeed. Quite often, in fact. So let's get this settled quickly. I have a meeting to go to."

"Ayla, tell him to go fuck himself," cried Jean-Paul. "I don't need his help."

Ayla stood there silently staring at Brother James for what seemed to Jean-Paul a very long time. Then he saw her back slowly stiffen. "But you do need his help," she said in a dead voice. "*We* need his help."

"Ayla, no. . .!"

"I'll do whatever you want, Brother James. Only please give Jean-Paul the drug now."

Brother James reached out his right hand and took hold

of her chin. He tilted her head back a little and his eyes bored into hers. "I'm taking you at your word, little gem. Any tricks or attempts to wriggle out of our bargain and I'll be very, very angry with you. Understand?"

"Yes, Brother James," she said meekly.

Yet again Jean-Paul made a futile effort to rise from the bed and again collapsed back as the pain overwhelmed him. "Ayla. . . ." he groaned.

Ayla gave no sign that she heard him. "Apart from your helping Jean-Paul, can I ask you for a further favour?"

He frowned at her. "And what would that be?"

"My father, whom you talked to last night, and my brother are going to be hanged shortly at the prison. By my people. It's really thanks to him that you are here. And also it was him who did the most to convince the majority of Palmyrians that your visit here would be of benefit to us. I think, therefore, that you owe him something."

Brother James laughed. "Yes, you are right. I am seeing Captain Vyushkov after I leave here. I will do my best to have him halt the executions."

"In that case," said Ayla, "everything is settled between us."

"Excellent. I shall only be requiring your company at nights. You may spend your days here with your unfortunate lover. I will collect you at 8 p.m. tonight. Be ready."

"Yes, Brother James."

"Oh, and stop calling me that. You may call me by my real name. Milo."

"Yes . . . Milo."

Milo? The name triggered a memory. "You're . . . Milo?" Jean-Paul asked, puzzled.

For the first time since entering the room the man paid attention to him. "Yes? Why? You speak as if my name means something to you."

"You were with the Sky Woman . . . Jan Dorvin."

Milo frowned down at him. "Jan Dorvin? I've never heard of her."

It's just a coincidence, thought Jean-Paul. It couldn't be the same man. This Milo has just arrived from a space habitat. "It doesn't matter," he said. "It must have been a different Milo." "A . . . different Milo," repeated Milo and for a few seconds Jean-Paul thought he saw something close to alarm in the man's eyes. Then Milo abruptly turned and went over to his satchel. From it he produced a small glass vial containing a number of blue capsules. He handed it to Ayla. "He is to take one every six hours."

Ayla said, "All that you told me last night—about being able to operate on him and restore feeling in his lower body—was that nothing but lies?"

"On the contrary, every word of it was true." He snapped the black satchel shut. "But whether or not I operate at all depends on you. If you please me then I will indeed carry out the surgery. If you don't . . . well. . . ."

"I'll please you."

"Good. Tonight at eight." He turned and, casually stepping over the body of Bron, was soon gone.

"Ayla, you can't do this!" cried Jean-Paul. Very slowly, and reluctantly, she turned at last to him. Her face was set in hard, determined lines but her eyes revealed her true feelings.

"What choice do I have?"

Captain Vyushkov had set up temporary base in the Big House, the building that had been the venue for the previous night's banquet. A portable beam projector was positioned on the roof and Karagangan soldiers surrounded it. Inside, Vyushkov sat at the High Table, flanked by his lieutenants. Before him stood five of the six members of the Palmyrian ex-ruling body. They had the look of survivors of some major catastrophe; shocked and still not comprehending what had happened. The decorations hanging from the

233

ceiling looked somewhat incongruous now. The floor of the hall was covered with weapons, mostly rifles and handguns but Milo also saw a long row of spear guns. A trickle of Palmyrians, supervised by spacer soldiers, continued to enter the building to deposit their weapons. Milo went up to the High Table. Vyushkov was talking to the Palmyrians. ". . . And you will make sure that all your people understand that if any firearms are found in their premises during the search they will immediately be executed."

The Palmyrians mumbled that they understood. Vyushkov continued: "It must also be made clear that any attack on any of us, no matter how slight, will again be punishable by death. You will each accompany one of the search parties. It will be your responsibility to ensure that your people don't make any fatal mistakes. Once I am satisfied that no weapons remain in the hands of your population we will discuss the future of Palmyra. Now go." Escorted by a couple of soldiers, the defeated Palmyrians filed silently out of the hall. Vyushkov nodded to Milo. Milo noticed he looked slightly worried. "Everything going as planned?" he asked.

Vyushkov rose from his seat and came down from the platform. He took Milo by his arm and led him towards the rear of the hall and out of earshot of his men. "As far as consolidating our position here is concerned, everything has gone exactly as planned. There is no more resistance. Palmyra is well and truly ours."

"Then what's the problem?"

"We naturally took over the Palmyrians' rather crude radar installation. One of my technicians was examining the equipment, more for amusement than anything else, when he spotted a hard blip on the screen. It lasted only for a few moments before it vanished. But my man said it appeared to be a solid object. A solid *flying* object. And it was travelling in from the ocean toward us . . . at a speed he estimated to be close to a thousand miles an hour."

234

Milo raised his eyebrows. "When was this?"

"About thirty minutes ago."

"So where is this mysterious object? If it existed it should have been here by now."

"I don't know. I ordered the *Christina* to take off and had those on board do a scan with the ship's own radar and other sensors but I just got a report from them that they couldn't find anything."

"Well then, that proves that whatever your technician saw was just some phantom image. A fault in the equipment. You said yourself that it was crude."

"That's what I'm telling myself, but at the same time I don't like it. The technician concerned is very reliable. I want to be one hundred percent certain that there is nothing to worry about."

Don't we all? thought Milo. He said, "From what we have learnt from the Palmyrians about the state of the world the only man-made things in the air are those clapped-out airships. There are no heavier-than-aircraft in existence anymore. The self-styled Sky Lords banned them all centuries ago. So what your tech saw wasn't a flying machine. It had to be something else, and my bet is it was just a glitch in the equipment."

"I pray that you are right," he sighed.

"I am. Now, have you been in contact with Karaganga yet?"

"Yes, I spoke to President Iakinfovich and told him the good news; that we have taken Palmyra in the name of the Republic, and without a single casualty on our side."

Lowering his voice, Milo said, "And when will you be delivering your ultimatum? Or rather, your declaration of independence?"

"I don't know yet. First I have to know for sure how many of my men will remain totally loyal to me. The ones who are doubtful will have to be neutralised before I make the announcement."

"Well, there's no rush. We have plenty of time. . . ." He suddenly snapped his fingers. "Which reminds me, I'm supposed to be stopping a lynching." He told Vyushkov about the imminent hanging of Lon Haddon and his son. Vyushkov looked puzzled. "Why is their fate any concern of yours?"

"Let's say it's a business arrangement I have with Haddon's delightful daughter."

Vyushkov smiled knowingly. "Oh, I see. Well, yes, go ahead and stop the execution. We can't have these people thinking they have any right to carry out their laws any longer. Take some men with you. Come, I'll give them their orders."

As he followed Vyushkov towards a group of his soldiers Milo said cheerfully, "I do hope I'm not going to be too late. That could be a little embarrassing for me."

Chapter Twenty-Nine:

"Just in the nick of time," murmured Milo, brushing flies from his face. A mob of shouting people had begun to pour out of the prison moments before Milo and his escort of four soldiers entered the small square in front. A makeshift gallows had already been set up which consisted of a thick log, its ends lashed to two palm trees. Two nooses were suspended from the beam and each one dangled above a waiting chair. A third chair stood behind them. From the crude look of the nooses Milo surmised that hangings were a rare event in Palmyra.

Lon Haddon and his son emerged. Both men, their hands tied behind their backs, were being roughly hustled along. They made an interesting contrast: Haddon's son was struggling fiercely while Haddon, his face blank, was not resisting at all. To Milo he appeared to be in a trance. They were taken to the chairs and lifted up onto them. Then a heavily built man, with a red beard, climbed up onto the third chair and placed the ropes around their necks. Milo guessed that in the clumsy grip of those nooses death would be a long time in coming. Pity he would have to interrupt the proceedings. . . .

The red-bearded man stood in front, his hands on his hips. "Lon Haddon, have you anything to say before we carry out the sentence?" he called out in a booming voice.

Haddon didn't answer. He just stood there on the chair, swaying slightly. His son answered for him. "This is murder, Jelker Banks! My father is innocent! And so am I, you bastard!"

"You know perfectly well why you and your father are being executed, Len Haddon!" boomed the red-bearded man. "You Haddons are traitors to Palmyra. You have sold us to our enemies. Now prepare to die! Both of you!" He stepped forward and was about to kick the chair out from under Lon Haddon. At this moment Milo raised the beam rifle he'd borrowed from one of his soldiers and fired. The beam went over the heads of the mob and of the two condemned men and blasted a small hole in the sandstone wall of the prison. Milo swung the beam sideways and cut through the ropes of the crude gallows. He stopped firing and handed the weapon back to its owner. "Thank you," he said.

The Palmyrians all turned in his direction. The soldiers levelled their weapons at them. "Sorry to spoil the fun, everyone!"called Milo, "but I'm afraid the executions have been cancelled! Please disperse and go to your homes!" He and his escort entered the crowd, which parted before them like the Red Sea had for Gregory Peck. *Or was it John Wayne?* Milo wondered idly. As he approached the man called Jelker Banks, whose face was now as red as his beard, he said, "You, help them off those chairs and untie their hands."

Jelker Banks pointed a finger at him and cried furiously, "This is none of your business, spacer. Stay out of it and leave us to deal with our own affairs!"

Milo came to a halt some five feet in front of him. He said mildly, "We are the law here now. This would-be execution is illegal. By order of the new Governor of Palmyra, Ilya Vyushkov, these men must be freed immediately."

"No!" cried Banks. "These traitors must die."

Milo turned to the soldier he'd borrowed the weapon from. "If he doesn't start to obey my orders within ten seconds—kill him."

"Yessir."

Jelker Banks looked into Milo's eyes, saw that he meant

238

what he said and began to lift Haddon down from the chair. "Thank you," called Len Haddon to Milo from the other chair. Milo smiled at him. "Don't thank me, thank your sister."

Len Haddon looked puzzled. "Ayla? What has she to do . . .?"

Milo held up a hand. "Let her be the one to explain to you the situation. Thanks to her the Haddon family is under my personal protection."

"Humph!" grunted Banks as he assisted Len Haddon down. "See? Proof from the mouth of the conqueror—as I said, the Haddons are traitors and collaborators."

The crowd muttered its angry agreement. Milo ran his gaze over them and the muttering stopped. "As they are under my personal protection I will be very upset if anything should happen to any Haddon. Those found guilty of any such act will not be so fortunate as to die by hanging. Now disperse and go to your homes!" *This is fun*, he told himself happily.

As the Palmyrians began to leave the square, Jelker Banks said, with satisfaction, "I fear, spacer, that you will be too late to protect Haddon's daughter. . . ."

Len Haddon, whose hands had just been untied, whirled round and cried angrily, "What are you talking about, Banks? Has something happened to Ayla?"

Jelker Banks shrugged and said slyly, "I only know that earlier I overheard talk of some men going to deal with her and her sky pirate lover at the hospital."

Haddon turned to Milo. "We must go there at once!"

"Calm yourself," Milo told him, "I was with her when her inept, would-be assassins arrived. She is quite safe. The two men, of course, are dead."

"What? *What?!*" Jelker Banks exclaimed, looking as if someone had just kicked him in the genitals. "Dead? Both of them?"

"That I can guarantee. I killed them myself."

Jelker Banks's face twisted with grief and anguish. "My sons!" he moaned. "You have murdered my sons!"

Milo stared at him and then nodded, saying, "Yes, now that you mention it I can see the family resemblance. Ironic, really, don't you agree?"

It was getting dark as Milo made his way towards the hospital. He was alone but felt that he was in no danger. He knew he was capable of defending himself if any Palmyrian should be so foolish as to attack him. Not that there were many locals in evidence in the streets; the few that were still about were hurrying home to avoid being caught out by the curfew that Vyushkov had imposed.

Milo hummed as he walked. He was humming along to a small headset he'd borrowed from one of the soldiers. That was something else he had missed on Belvedere—music was banned in the habitat, with the exception of a number of dirgy hymns which Milo didn't count.

He looked at his watch. He was early by fifteen minutes. It wouldn't do to turn up ahead of schedule; far better to turn up late so as to prolong her anxiety. Perhaps she would think he was not coming at all. He smiled at the thought and took a detour towards the sea front. A stroll along the beach would kill the extra time.

A patrol of six Karagangan soldiers passed him in the narrow street. He nodded at them and they all saluted as they went by. Word of his new status as Captain Vyushkov's 'special adviser' had certainly spread fast.

He had requisitioned a small house within the area of the town that Vyushkov had cleared of all Palmyrians for 'security reasons'. It was quite comfortable even though Milo would have preferred something on the sea front. Anyway, his new home was well stocked with food and drink and he was looking forward to taking Ayla back to it shortly. It was going to be a night of fun and games. God knows, he deserved it after being celibate for so long. . . .

The sea front appeared deserted. He took several deep breaths, savouring the smell of the sea that he remembered from centuries ago. Then he began to walk along the path beside the row of palm trees that lined the beach. He hadn't gone far when he saw a shadowy figure ahead peering round one of the trees. Whoever it was he, or she, was definitely acting furtively. Certain that he hadn't been seen yet, he too ducked behind a palm tree. Intrigued, Milo crept quietly down onto the beach to approach the figure from behind. As he got closer he saw it was a woman. Her feet were bare and, oddly, she was dressed in dark clothing—a black shirt and black pants. All the clothing he had seen so far in Palmyra was brightly coloured. She was clearly up to no good. . . .

He came up silently behind her. She was too busy scanning the buildings along the sea front to be aware of him until he tapped her on the shoulder. She jumped and spun round, looking shocked. Milo's first impression was that she resembled an older version of Ayla. The same close-cropped black hair, same high cheekbones . . . even the oriental-like eyes were similar. Then he noticed that her clothes, and her hair, were soaking wet. He was about to ask what she was doing when she preempted him. "What the hell are you doing here, Milo? How did you get away from Phebus?"

It was one of the rare occasions when Milo was caught completely off-guard. He gazed blankly at her. He knew for certain that he had never seen this woman before yet she plainly recognised him. "We've met before?" he asked her. "Where and when?"

"Don't play games, Milo, it's *me*, J—" She stopped, her expression suddenly becoming wary. He saw that she knew she had made a serious mistake. "No . . . no, now that I look more closely at you I see I was wrong. You're not who I thought you were."

"You called me Milo," Milo insisted. He already knew what this was all about. First that paralysed Frenchman had recognised his name and now this woman knew someone called Milo who resembled him. It meant only one thing— his original self had somehow come down to Earth ahead of him.

The woman said, "It's just a coincidence. Now I must go. I'm late. . . ." As she turned to leave Milo grabbed her arm, just above the elbow, hard. "You're coming with me, whoever you are. We need to talk."

When Jean-Paul woke from his pain-soaked sleep he saw that Ayla had returned. She looked worn out. "What's the time?" was the first thing he asked her.

"Five minutes to eight," she replied. "Time for your pain-killer." She put the pill in his mouth and gave him a drink of water. He sucked thankfully at the straw while she supported his head. "Thanks," he said when he'd drunk the lot. She eased his head back onto the pillow. He no longer had the room to himself. Four other patients had been squeezed in on camp beds, all casualties from the spacer attack. All were in a bad way and not expected, Jean-Paul had learned from Ayla, to survive the night. The small hospital was overflowing with wounded.

"How is it . . . at home?" he asked Ayla.

She shook her head. "Not good. Dad just sits there, not saying a word. Won't eat or drink anything. And Len . . . well, he's very angry. Angry with everything . . . with the spacers, with Jelker Banks, with Milo . . . and with me."

Jean-Paul didn't say anything. He agreed with the way Len felt and he hated himself for it. Oh, sure, he felt gratitude for the sacrifice she was going to make on his behalf, but at the same time he resented it strongly. Why? Because it hurt his bloody male pride. And that was a laugh. What did he have left to be proud about? He was just a head with a pair of arms attached. Certainly no longer a *man*.

There were sounds of a disturbance outside. A nurse was

242

saying loudly, ". . . I said you can't go in there!" Then the door opened. It was, as Jean-Paul feared, Milo, but he wasn't alone. And, to Jean-Paul's astonishment, he recognised the woman with him. It was Jan Dorvin. He had never met the Sky Woman but he had seen her on several occasions, a few times at quite close quarters, and he was certain that it was her.

Milo propelled the woman into the room and Jean-Paul saw that he was holding her by the arm. He looked annoyed. "Thank you so much for your assistance," he told a protesting nurse then slammed the door in her face.

Ayla had risen from her chair to face Milo but he seemed not to notice her. He let go of Jan Dorvin and pushed her violently into the centre of the room. She nearly fell over the end of one of the camp beds before regaining her balance. The severely injured man lying on the bed moaned softly. Milo pointed his finger at Jan Dorvin. "Now, you know me, but I don't know you. So first, who are you?"

Jan Dorvin glowered at him and rubbed her arm where he had been holding her. She said nothing. Why Jean-Paul spoke he had no idea. He just couldn't help it. "She's Jan Dorvin," he said softly. Both Milo and Jan Dorvin looked at him in surprise. "Jan Dorvin?" repeated Milo. "How do you know?"

Jean-Paul glanced at the woman. She was regarding him with a puzzled frown. She clearly didn't recognise him but that was understandable. He said to Milo, "She was the Sky Woman . . . the Sky Angel. She conquered our Sky Lord. Among others. She had a whole fleet of Sky Lords. But then she lost control of everything and disappeared. I never knew what happened to her."

Milo stared at him for a while then asked Jan Dorvin, "What's he babbling about?"

"I haven't a clue," she muttered.

"Is that your name? Jan Dorvin?"

"Of course not. My name is Anya. Anya Ivimey."

"So why does he think he knows you?"

"A case of mistaken identity. Just like me mistaking you for someone else."

Milo looked doubtful. "Too many coincidences," he said.

"That's why I knew your name," Jean-Paul said to Milo. "There was a man called Milo with Jan Dorvin."

"I knew it!" Milo began to advance on Jan Dorvin. "My original self is here on Earth! Admit it!"

Jan Dorvin edged around the camp bed. "I'll admit to nothing, Milo."

Milo blurred. Jan Dorvin shuddered and was flung backwards. Jean-Paul saw her slammed up against the wall beside the door. Milo came back into focus. He had her by the throat and began to shake her head back and forth. "Tell me where he is, damn you, or I'll tear your throat out!"

Jan Dorvin made choking sounds and nodded. He released her and she slumped a little down the wall. "He's dead. . . ." she gasped.

"He's *dead*?" Milo said in astonishment. "Impossible. He—I—designed myself to be the ultimate survivor. I can't die, and neither could he."

"Well, it's true. He's dead. Or rather, *you* are. You got careless, thanks to a bad case of hubris."

"Tell me exactly what happened to . . . *him*," he demanded.

As Jan Dorvin began to relate the circumstances of the other Milo's death Jean-Paul was shocked to see Ayla pick up her chair and walk softly towards Milo. Her intention was clear and he almost cried out to her not to do it but that would have achieved nothing. It was too late now. He could only watch helplessly as she crept up behind Milo, the chair held high. Surely Milo would hear her. But no, he was transfixed by Jan Dorvin's story of his other self's fate. Jan Dorvin, of course, could see what Ayla was doing but her expression gave nothing away.

Now Ayla was directly behind Milo. Jean-Paul could

hardly bear to watch. The wooden chair suddenly looked so insubstantial. . . . Ayla brought the chair down on the back of Milo's bald head. Her cry of exertion and the splintering of the wood mingled together. Milo staggered forward from the impact but didn't fall.

Then he turned. . . .

Chapter Thirty:

"Stupid bitch," said Milo to Ayla. She stood there, holding a single chair leg in her hand, and felt she agreed with him. *Now what?* she wondered. Try to hit him again? Yeah, sure. She had seen how fast he could move. *Face it, girl*, she told herself, *soon you're going to be dead . . . if you're lucky*. She let the chair leg fall from her fingers. At the precise moment it hit the floorboards Jan Dorvin, behind Milo, struck. She brought the edge of her right hand down hard on the back of Milo's neck. Milo grunted and started to turn, but his movements were now slow and shaky. Jan Dorvin had enough time to deliver another vicious rabbit punch. Milo grunted again and fell face-down onto the floor. He lay there groaning. Jan Dorvin knelt beside him and quickly hit him two more times. He stopped groaning.

Jan rose, massaging the side of her hand. She smiled at Ayla. "That was rather painful, but I did so enjoy it."

Ayla looked at her then at Milo's unmoving form. "You've killed him?"

"I would like to think so but I doubt it. Milos are hard to kill. I was very lucky, thanks to you—distracting him with that chair."

"I was trying to kill him."

"Yes, well, Milo usually has that effect on people. But at least you shook him up . . . and gave me my opportunity." She held out her hand to Ayla. "Anyway, I *am* Jan Dorvin. And you are. . .?"

Ayla took her hand and—gently—shook it. "Ayla Haddon."

246

"You're very beautiful, Ayla," she said and, to Ayla's surprise, leaned forward and kissed her on the mouth. Then she let go of her hand and went over to Jean-Paul's bedside. "And what Sky Lord do you hail from?"

"The *Lord Montcalm*," he told her.

"Ah yes, one of my earliest conquests. Is the ship in the area? And how did you get away from your Ashley program?"

Jean-Paul told her what had happened to the program . . . and to the *Lord Montcalm* itself. "I take it you were injured in the crash?" she asked.

Ayla answered for him. "No, he was shot in the back. Just a couple of days ago. The bullet paralysed him. Brother . . . Milo . . . *him* . . ." she pointed at Milo, " . . . said he could help him with surgery, providing I—I went with him. Tonight."

"Same old Milo," said Jan disgustedly. She went over and looked down at him. "Still breathing. We're going to have to figure out a way of restraining him. And it's going to have to be good and strong." She looked at Ayla. "You say he was coming here for you?"

Ayla nodded. "I don't know where he was going to take me."

"Somewhere private, most likely. Which means he probably won't be missed until tomorrow. We can hide him here in the hospital. Make him look like one of the patients. Can you get your hands on another of these portable beds?"

"Yes," said Ayla.

"Then go and get it, now."

As Ayla left, Jean-Paul said, "I want to know why *you're* here in Palmyra. We've already got one lot of conquerors, we don't need a second lot."

"The spacers?"

"Yeah, the damn spacers. When they first arrived they were very friendly. Then the next thing you know they'd annexed us."

"From the little I saw from the beach I guessed as much. Armed patrols, and no citizens in the streets. Anyway I'm out of the conquering business. I never was much good at it. At the moment I'm following the instructions of a very powerful computer program that has taken over the Sky Angel."

"Ashley?"

"No, nothing like Ashley." She went on to explain the nature, and origin, of the superprogram called Phebus. "She knew a space craft had landed here so she sent us on ahead to see what the situation was."

"Us?"

"I have a companion. He's waiting in the Toy, which is . . . well, let's call it a very versatile vehicle. At this moment it's parked underwater about a hundred yards from the shore."

"You mean you simply dropped out of the sky in this thing?" asked Jean-Paul. "But they have radar here, and so do the spacers. You would have been spotted."

"Well, we were briefly spotted when we were about thirty miles out to sea. Didn't have our screens up in time. Later, to avoid any visual contact, we submerged and came the rest of the way underwater."

Jean-Paul was surprised. "But if you're only a hundred yards offshore you're well within the inner sea wall."

"Well, I'm afraid we had to force our way through your sea wall. But don't worry, I'm sure the damage can easily be repaired."

"Yes, but. . . ." Jean-Paul froze as Milo moaned and moved his arm. Jan Dorvin promptly walked over to him and kicked him hard in the side of his head. Twice. Milo became still again. "I'm beginning to enjoy this too much," she told him ruefully.

"This superprogram of yours. Will she help Palmyra free itself from the spacers?"

"To be honest, I don't know what she'll do," Jan Dorvin

248

told him. "Her motives are completely opaque to me. But the arrival of the spacers on Earth has certainly caught her attention. And I don't think that bodes well for the spacers."

"Whereabouts is she?"

"Right now, about eight hours flying time from Palmyra. We'll fly back and rendezvous with the Sky Angel, I'll pass on what has happened here and we should return before dawn. What'll happen then I have no idea, but it's sure to be an improvement on the current situation." She paused as Ayla returned with a bed. "Now let's get Milo under suitable restraint. . . ."

Jan reached the sea front without any problem, though she did have to hide behind a wall on one occasion to avoid being seen by a spacer patrol. At the water's edge she took out a small direction finder and clipped it on her wrist. She knew roughly where the Toy was sitting; in front of the sea gate, midway between it and the shore, but the finder would enable her to pinpoint its position quickly when she drew near to it.

She walked out into the warmish sea and when the water reached her lower chest began to swim, using the distant sea gate as a marker.

"He certainly looks secure enough," said Jean-Paul.

"I hope so," said Ayla, frowning.

Milo resembled a metallic cocoon. Jan and Ayla had wrapped him, using heavy pliers, in thick wire. The cocoon extended from his neck to his feet, and was itself wired to the bed. It had taken them an hour to do the job, while at the same time trying to convince the doctors and nurses that there was a good reason for their apparent act of madness.

"Better cover him up."

Ayla draped a blanket over Milo, pulling it up so that it half concealed his heavily bandaged head and hid the gag in his mouth. "Oh God," she suddenly cried.

"What's the matter?" asked Jean-Paul, alarmed. He struggled to lift his head from the pillow. "What's he doing?"

Ayla turned to face him, wide-eyed and with her hand covering her mouth. "It's not him . . . I've just remembered. It was because of all the excitement . . . I forgot . . ."

"Forgot *what?*"

"To warn her. Jan Dorvin. You said her machine had forced its way through the sea walls. That means those creatures can get in again. They could be in the inner waters already!"

Jean-Paul, relieved, let his head fall back on the pillow. "Is that all?"

"What do you mean, *is that all?*" cried Ayla. "If those hideous things get her it will be my fault! I can't let her die like that!"

"Ayla, calm down and be reasonable. What can you possibly do to help her now?"

"The underwater laser. It's still in the house. I'll get it and go after her."

"Jesus, Ayla, it's too late! She left nearly fifteen minutes ago. She'll be in the water by now."

"I don't care. I've got to try!" And to his horror, she ran from the room.

"Ayla!" he yelled. "Come back!" When a startled nurse looked in he screamed, "Stop her! You've got to stop her!"

Jan stopped swimming and started treading water to get her bearings. She saw that she'd gone a little off course and was no longer heading directly towards the sea gate. She raised her arm out of the water and looked at the finder. Its dim green light pulsed slowly on and off. When she was directly above the Toy its glow would be constant. Close but no prize. She started swimming again. It was then that something clamped round the calf of her right leg. She was pulled under.

Choking on water, she kicked out with her left leg. Her

foot made contact with something solid. *Shark!* she thought as panic filled her. She was pulled deeper and then came a blaze of agony as something very sharp ripped deep into her stomach. She screamed, releasing the remaining air in her lungs in a gush of bubbles. At the same instant she was aware that her right arm had just been bitten off. She hoped she wouldn't stay conscious, or alive, for much longer. . . .

But as teeth and claws continued to rip into her flesh it seemed a very long time before welcome oblivion enveloped her.

Robin was half asleep. When the Toy spoke he was jerked immediately to full awareness. "There's a disturbance in the water," said the Toy.

"What kind of disturbance?" he demanded. "Where?"

"Nearby. About sixty feet to starboard. I'm picking up vibrations and sounds."

"Can't you *see* what's happening?"

"Jan instructed me not to use any of my intrusive sensor systems while we are this close to shore in case our presence is detected."

"Well, I'm overriding that instruction! It could be Jan and she could be in trouble. Use your sonic scanners."

"Yes, Robin."

"Well?" he asked, impatiently. "What do you see?"

"Three humanoid sea creatures. Much larger than the average man. They are fighting amongst themselves. Over the remains of another sea creature."

"Patch me in!" One of the dark monitor screens began to glow. Even with computer enhancement Robin couldn't make much out of the image displayed on the screen. He could see the three creatures described by the Toy but couldn't make out any details. They were attacking something with a terrible ferocity. Like sharks in a feeding frenzy. Human-shaped sharks. "Move towards them," he ordered. Immediately the Toy lifted, turned and began to head towards the battling creatures. He was now well and truly in the grip of a crushing sense of dread. The thought of Jan swimming about in these waters . . .!

The three creatures turned to face the Toy when they sensed its approach. They released the shredded remains of their victim as they prepared to attack. Robin still couldn't make out any details. "Switch to visual and turn on your lights!" he ordered.

"Is that wise?" asked the Toy.

"Do it!"

The Toy obeyed. The image on the screen changed. Robin was able to see everything clearly. Too clearly. The three charging humanoids were revealed in all their ugly detail. All teeth and claws. Death machines. And he could see the remains of their victim drifting down to the sea bed. The exposed and mangled rib cage, the chewed flesh that remained on the upper torso, the muscle fibres that trailed from a half-eaten arm . . . there was no stomach; Jan's body didn't exist below the rib cage. "*Oh Christ no!*" he cried. "Kill them! *Kill them!*"

Ayla, clutching the underwater laser, ran panting onto the beach. In her other hand she was holding the face mask and underwater light that she'd picked up during the fleeting visit to her house. At the water's edge she paused and scanned the dark water. No sign of Jan. Perhaps she had safely reached her underwater craft. But Ayla would have to make sure for her own peace of mind. She kicked off her sandals, pulled on her mask and was about to enter the water when she was suddenly bathed in a bright light and a man's voice cried out harshly, "Halt! Drop that weapon and raise your hands!"

She dropped the laser and torch onto the sand, raised her hands and turned. Four spacers were coming down the beach towards her. All wore their armoured space suits—

sans helmets—and all carried the strange guns that fired beams of heat. All were pointing at her.

"You know the penalty for being found in possession of a firearm, girl?" one of them asked as they neared her.

"It's not a weapon," she said quickly. "It's an underwater tool. You try it for yourself. It doesn't work out of water."

They surrounded her and looked her up and down. The one holding the flashlight said, "You're a pretty thing. Pity we're going to have to execute you."

"I told you it's not a weapon!" she cried.

He glanced down at the laser lying on the sand. "Looks like a weapon to me. And that's all that counts."

Just then one of the other men exclaimed, "Lieutenant! Look! Out there!" He was pointing out into the bay. They all looked, including Ayla. There was a white glow out there. And it was coming from under the water.

"What the hell is that?"

"Some kind of underwater light," answered the one referred to as Lieutenant. "And moving, too." He turned to Ayla. "You know what that is, girl?"

She shook her head. "No," she lied.

He stared at her and then at the laser. "Just what were you planning to do before we came along?"

"I was going to make some repairs to the sea wall. It's been damaged."

"At this time of night? By yourself? Don't make me laugh."

"It's the truth."

"It's moving again, Lieutenant!"

"I don't like any of this," he muttered. "I'm going to alert headquarters. Captain Vyushkov should know about this." He depressed his chin into the collar of his suit and a small mike sprang up. "Lieutenant Bruschki calling. I'm on the beach. My patrol and I have spotted moving underwater lights out in the bay. I suggest they be investigated at once."

*

253

Robin lay slumped back on the couch, staring sightlessly at the ceiling of the cabin. *Jan is dead. Jan is dead. It's all over. . . .*

"May I make a suggestion?" asked the Toy.

"No. Shut up."

"It involves Jan."

"Haven't you noticed? She's *dead!*" he cried savagely.

"Yes, but I want to draw your attention to her head. Apart from the severe facial lacerations it appears undamaged."

Oh Christ, he thought.

"That suggests to me that her brain is intact," continued the Toy in its usual blithe fashion, "and so there exists a strong possibility she can be revived if we can get her to a med-machine."

Robin sat up, suddenly filled with hope. But then he was instantly plunged into despair again. "There's no way we could get her back to the Sky Angel in time. She's already been dead for about two minutes. Irreversible brain cell deterioration would begin long before we reached the Sky Angel."

"You overlook an important factor," said the Toy. "My storage facility for the bio-samples. It possesses a freezing unit. I can instantly freeze her. And, considering how little actually remains of Jan, there is sufficient space to accommodate her in the facility."

It took several seconds for Robin to react. Then he shouted, "Well, stop wasting time and *do it*, damn you!"

Ayla stood with the four spacers as they waited impatiently for reinforcements to arrive. She felt nervous and anxious. Would they actually go ahead and execute her, she wondered? What could she do? Make a run for it before more spacers arrived? She didn't think she'd get very far before being shot down on the beach. But whatever happened she had to keep silent about Jan Dorvin and the approaching

Sky Angel. If the spacers knew the airship was due at dawn they would be ready for it. . . .

They were all taken by surprise when the water out in the bay suddenly erupted in a great spume and up through it rose a tear-shaped metal object travelling at great speed. Its speed increased as it climbed high into the night sky. Then it levelled off and disappeared out over the sea . . . and Ayla seized her chance to flee. She didn't get far.

Chapter Thirty-One:

Captain Ilya Vyushkov stared thoughtfully at the device that lay on his desk top before returning his attention to the girl. She stood between two of his soldiers. She looked anxious but also defiant. She was wearing dirty white shorts and yellow t-shirt. Her feet were bare. Lieutenant Bruschki was also present.

"You say this is not a weapon?" Vyushkov asked her.

"Yes," she replied firmly. "It's an underwater cutting tool. It only works underwater."

"She might be telling the truth on the last bit," said Lieutenant Bruschki. "I certainly couldn't get it to work."

"What's your name, girl?"

"Ayla Haddon."

Vyushkov frowned. "Haddon, you say? Then you are Lon Haddon's daughter?"

She nodded.

He scowled and scratched his chin. Lon Haddon was an ex-leader, and he was also one of the men that Brother James had saved from hanging earlier in the day. That meant this was the girl Brother James had been after. So why wasn't she with him tonight? "You know Brother James, don't you?"

He observed her hesitation before she nodded. "Have you seen him at all tonight?" he asked.

"No. We were to have met at the hospital, at eight, but he never showed."

Now Vyushkov was convinced something was wrong. He said to Lieutenant Bruschki, "I want a search mounted for

Brother James. Use even the off-duty men. I want him found quickly."

"Yessir," said Lieutenant Bruschki, who saluted and hurried from the room.

Vyushkov stared hard at the girl. "What do you know of the machine that emerged from the sea tonight?"

"Nothing," she said, and added, "sir."

"Tell me the truth."

"I am. I have never seen that machine before. And I don't know what it is."

"You are saying, then, that it was a sheer coincidence that you happened to be down on the beach shortly before the thing took off?"

"Yes, I guess so."

"And, as you told Lieutenant Bruschki, you planned to carry out repairs on the sea wall. Alone and at night . . . with this." He held up the device.

"Yes."

"A pretty feeble story, even for one devised in haste on the spur of the moment. What were you really about to do?"

She looked down at the floor. No answer.

He smashed his fist on the desk top and roared, "Enough of these lies! I want the truth!"

She flinched but shook her head defiantly. "I *am* telling the truth."

He sighed. Now he was going to have to resort to violence to extract the information from her. He didn't want to do that, not to a female, but he had no choice. He had to find out what that strange flying machine signified. It shouldn't exist but it did and its existence put his whole enterprise here on Earth in jeopardy. He had to know the truth, at any cost.

Milo lay there in a fury of frustration. He couldn't move, he couldn't see and he couldn't speak. He had given up trying to loosen his bonds. It was impossible. And it had been utterly infuriating to lie there helplessly listening to soldiers ask the Frenchman about Brother James. They were searching for him and had been standing right beside him but still they failed to find him. The idiots. Oh yes, one of them had lifted the blanket from his bandaged face and head, taken a cursory glance, then dropped the blanket back again. Idiot. *Idiot.* And it was vital that he get to Vyushkov with the information about that damned woman Dorvin. She meant bad news. Where the hell had she suddenly sprung from? Vyushkov had to be warned to expect trouble.

He still couldn't fully accept what she had told him about his original self—that he was dead. And he still didn't know how it had happened; the bitch of a girl had hit him with the chair before Dorvin had finished telling him. And then Dorvin herself hit him—much more succesfully than Ayla. He couldn't remember anything after that, damn her. The next time they met the outcome was going to be very different.

Hell, to make matters even worse, he desperately needed to take a piss.

Captain Vyushkov regarded Ayla Haddon with weary gloominess. She sat slumped in the chair in front of him and would have slid off it if one of the soldiers wasn't holding her by the shoulders. Her head lolled sideways and her eyes were only half open. Bruises and swellings covered her face, arms and legs and he doubted if any part of her body was not similarly marked. Using sawn-off broom handles as makeshift clubs his two men had submitted her to three severe beatings. He had watched in distaste as the two men rained vicious blows on the girl while she, on the floor, tried to curl herself into a foetal ball, arms wrapped around her head. He also felt distaste for the feeling of excitement that her screams produced within him. It was a dirty business but hopefully it would all soon be over. The girl had finally cracked during the third beating and started crying out a name. *Jan Dorvin*. It meant nothing to him but it was a start. Now he was waiting for her to become fully conscious again so that he could learn more.

"Ayla! Wake Up! Speak to me!" he commanded.

She stirred. Her eyes opened and she tried to focus on him. "I want . . . a . . . drink . . . of water." She mumbled through puffy lips.

"You will have water when you have told me what I want to know. Who is Jan Dorvin?"

"The Sky Woman . . . she came to the hospital . . . tonight. Brother James . . . Milo . . . brought her."

"Milo? Who's Milo?"

"Milo is Brother James . . . it's his real name, he . . . said."

"His real name?" said Vyushkov, feeling increasingly uneasy. "So where did he find this woman, this Jan Dorvin?"

"I don't know. But I think they're . . . old friends. Knew each other . . . long ago."

What? How could that be? It didn't make any sense. Brother James—Milo—came from Belvedere. Or did he? As Vyushkov had noted before, Brother James wasn't like any other Belvederian he had ever encountered. "So who exactly *is* this Jan Dorvin?" he demanded.

"Very powerful . . . woman. She's the Sky Woman . . . most powerful person on . . . Earth. Rules . . . huge fleet of Sky Lords . . . big army. . . ."

Vyushkov stared at the battered girl in alarm. Then he cried, "Where is she? Where is her base? Where can I find her?"

But this time the girl didn't answer. Vyushkov gestured to the soldier holding her. The man released his grip on her shoulders and she toppled slowly from the chair. "Is she dead?" asked Vyushkov. The soldier knelt and felt her neck. "No, sir."

Just then Lieutenant Bruschki returned. "No sign of Brother James anywhere, Captain."

259

More worrying news. Was Brother James—Milo—really in collusion with this Jan Dorvin woman? Had he flown off with her in that machine? It seemed the only likely answer. The man was a traitor. He was plotting against Vyushkov. God knows what he and the woman planned to do. He rose abruptly from his chair. "I am going back to the ship, Lieutenant. For reasons of security."

"Jan? Jan?"

"What is it?" she asked irritably. She had been having the most wonderful, perfect dream of her life and it wasn't fair of Phebus to interrupt it in this way.

"I won't disturb you for long. I just need to talk to you for a short time."

"Talk?" Now Jan was feeling slightly puzzled. All she could see was a soft, blue light. And she appeared to be floating; though she couldn't feel her body at all. "Phebus, where am I?"

"Somewhere safe. Relax."

And Jan *was* relaxed. Totally and utterly. She had never felt so at peace. "Listen to me," Phebus said, "you are going to relive, for me, the events of tonight's visit to the town. You will picture every moment in your mind's eye, except for the final moments after you entered the water. Do you understand?"

"Yes, Phebus."

"Then begin." And Jan experienced over again everything that had happened to her in Palmyra. But when she entered the water to swim back to the Toy she suddenly found herself back in the blue light. "Thank you," said Phebus, "you can go back to sleep now." And Jan did. The beautiful dream continued.

As Steven, the surgeon, came in looking exhausted, Jean Paul immediately cried, "Any news yet of Ayla?"

The doctor shook his head wearily. "No. I'm afraid not."

"But it's been hours! Something must have happened to her! She's lying hurt somewhere out there. You've got to find her!"

"I'm sorry but my duty is here with my patients. I'm not risking my life trying to dodge spacer patrols. Face the facts, Jean-Paul, Ayla has either been arrested or shot by them."

"No, I don't believe it! I *won't* believe it!" Jean-Paul protested.

"Well, there's nothing that can be done until morning . . . except for one thing." He went over to Milo's bed. "I'm going to set this unfortunate man free. He can't be left in this condition for much longer. He might die." The doctor took a pair of wire-cutters from his jacket pocket.

"No!" cried Jean-Paul, "You can't release him! Think of Ayla! She'll be in serious trouble!"

"I believe she's already in serious trouble," the doctor said as he pulled back the blanket from Milo's wire-bound body.

"Just leave him for a couple more hours!" pleaded Jean-Paul. "Something is going to happen just before dawn! Something that may change everything here in Palmyra!"

The doctor was removing the bandages from Milo's head. "I'm a doctor, Jean-Paul, I can't stand by and watch a man be submitted to such cruel conditions, even if he is a spacer." He removed the gag from Milo's mouth.

"Thank you, doctor," said Milo.

Captain Ilya Vyushkov was spending an uneasy night. He kept pacing up and down the bridge but invariably his attention went back to the radar screens. He was also in constant radio touch with the Palmyrian radar tower. So far the skies remained clear of any objects, but that didn't reassure Vyushkov. He was even considering abandoning the whole enterprise and ordering his crew to prepare for a take-off as soon as all his men could be recalled back to the ship. But he didn't really want to do that. The thought of returning to Karaganga in disgrace and as a failure was just too painful to contemplate. No, there was too much at stake. He would have to take the risk and stick it out. "I'm going to inspect the defences," he announced to his bridge crew.

Once again he made a circuit of the *Christina*, inspecting the four portable beam cannon positions and casting anxious glances up at the night sky. He was about to return inside when an aide hurried up carrying a radio. "Sir, a patrol has found Brother James. He says it is urgent that he speaks with you." The aide gave him the radio. "Brother James, or whatever your real name is, what the hell are you up to?" demanded Vyushkov. Brother James's reply was drowned out by a loud whistling sound. Vyushkov looked up, and the next second was blown off his feet by a massive explosion. Dazed, and with his ears ringing, he got to his hands and knees and saw that the nearby beam cannon unit that he had finished inspecting only moments before no longer existed. There were just smoking fragments of metal and ceramics scattered about. And fragments of men.

The whistling sound again. Then another explosion—on the other side of the ship. He got to his feet and, followed by his aide, ran for the main hatchway. There had been two more explosions by the time he reached the bridge. He realised all four outside cannon positions had been destroyed. There was confusion and panic on the bridge. "Why aren't we firing back?!!" bellowed Vyushkov over the din. "Why aren't we using the ship's beam cannon?!!"

"There's nothing to aim at!" shouted back an officer. "Nothing shows up on the radar, the infra-red scanner or any of the cannon's automatic target tracking systems!"

The ship rocked. It was now the target. Someone began to pray. Vyushkov barged his way to the forward control panel and snatched up a mike. "This is Captain Vyushkov to all personnel! The man known as Brother James is to be shot on sight! I repeat, shot on sight!" Then the ship rocked again and the lights went out.

*

262

Milo didn't know what was happening but he didn't like it, whatever it was. The members of the patrol he had approached on leaving the hospital just stood there looking confused as the sounds of explosion after explosion came rolling towards them. "Captain Vyushkov?" said Milo into the radio, but it was dead. He dropped the useless device and stared anxiously inland where flashes of red light were visible. "It's the ship all right," he said. "It's being attacked, but by what?"

He turned back to the soldiers—just in time to see one fire his beam rifle at him. The beam went through Milo's chest and exited from his back. He glanced down in bemusement at the large but cauterised hole that the beam had drilled into his flesh. "Bugger," he muttered. He looked at the soldier who'd shot him. "Now why the hell did you do that?"

The soldier, and his five companions, gaped incredulously at him. "An order from Captain Vyushkov . . . it was just relayed to us," the soldier said hesitantly, touching his earpiece.

Why would Vyushkov want him dead, Milo wondered as he started towards the patrol. It was his intention to kill them all but he found he couldn't pick up speed. His genegineered powers of regeneration and recuperation were extraordinary but even they couldn't cope with the amount of damage that the beam had wrought internally. To Milo's surprise the strength suddenly went from his legs and he collapsed to his knees. It dawned on him that he was dying. "Oh, shit!" he muttered. He slowly leaned forward until he was resting on his hands, head bowed. "This is so bloody *unfair*! All those years in stinking Belvedere and now *this*. . . ." Warily, the soldiers came closer. All kept their weapons trained on him. He raised his head and looked at them. "You want to know what is *really* unfair about this?"

They exchanged nervous glances but didn't answer.

"I didn't get to fuck the girl even once," he said, then died.

Chapter Thirty-Two:

In the grey light of dawn Captain Vyushkov was trying to look on the bright side. The only alternative was to wander off into the bush and shoot his brains out. So he took a deep breath, stood straighter in front of his assembled crew and soldiers beside the ship and said, sounding as authoritative as he could manage under the circumstances, "It's not as bad as it looks. The ship has sustained damage but it can be repaired. In less than a month, according to the estimate I've been given.

"And though we have suffered casualties it could have been a lot worse." Yes indeed, if the thing that attacked us had been aiming at anything other than beam weapons we would all be dead by now. The same thing had happened in town. All the beam cannon units had been destroyed but nothing else. Well, apart from the Palmyrian radar tower. And their own radar no longer functioned either. Only good bit of news was confirmation that Brother James had been shot dead. At least he didn't have to worry about him any more. "We still have our hand weapons and we still control Palmyra." *But for how long?* "And when that thing returns we'll be ready for it! Right men?!" They all stared at him, stony-faced.

A soldier raised his arm. "Pardon, Captain, but what do you think that thing was?"

Damn. "Er . . . some kind of crude flying machine that the Palmyrians have cobbled together. I intend having a number of Palmyrians interrogated today to learn where the machine is based. Then we will attack and destroy it while it's still on the ground."

He paused. There was silence. Flies buzzed annoyingly round his face and he swatted at them as he waited for a response. Finally a soldier said, in a dry tone that infuriated Vyushkov, "What if that thing comes back again and attacks us before we're ready, like today?"

"Then I'll expect you to shoot it down, man!" he barked. "You've got a weapon, and in daylight you'll be able to see it! That goes for all of you!"

"What if it's invisible?" asked someone else.

"Don't be stu—" He didn't go on. A *thrumming* sound could be heard carried on the stiff breeze blowing in from the sea. He turned and peered into the early morning mist that filled the sky. He could see a vague form up there, far out over the sea. Whatever it was it was *big*.

The thrumming sound grew louder. And the vague shape became firmer. "Christ. . . ." gasped Vyushkov.

"What *is* that?" asked someone behind him.

"A Sky Lord," answered Vyushkov weakly. For several long moments he watched the huge, ghostly white airship materialise out of the mist, hypnotised by its awesome presence. Then he pulled himself out of his trance. He turned to his men, who were similarly transfixed by the apparition, and cried, "Right, men! Take up defence positions! When it comes in range of your beam rifles open fire!" Some of the men began to stir but Vyushkov's attention was suddenly diverted by a bird fluttering to the ground in front of him. A parrot, it was flapping its wings feebly. Then it became completely still. Vyushkov stared down at it. The bird's fate seemed to have a terrible significance but Vyushkov couldn't yet work out why. . . .

Then his men began to collapse.

"My eyes . . . my eyes. . . ." groaned Jean-Paul.

"It's all right . . . you're safe now . . . everything's okay," said a soothing voice. Ayla's. He opened his eyes. He could see light. White light. He put his hands up in front of his face. He could see them. *He could see!* A convulsive shudder ran through him as he recalled what had happened to him. After Milo had been cut free by the surgeon he demanded that Jean-Paul tell him everything that Jan Dorvin had said while he was unconscious. When Jean-Paul refused he calmly dug his thumb into Jean-Paul's left eye and crushed it. His scream of agony brought a nurse running into the room. Jean-Paul didn't see what Milo did to her. Then Milo threatened to crush his other eyeball if he didn't speak. Crazy with pain and fear, Jean-Paul repeated what Jan Dorvin said . . . before Milo went ahead and blinded him anyway. Milo had left him lying there in the blackness, helpless and in utter agony. He screamed and screamed. He didn't know how much time passed before he heard voices and then a needle slid into his arm. After that, nothing.

Full of wonder and relief, he sat up. Ayla was standing next to the bed. She wore a full-length white cotton smock. He saw he had on a similar garment. She was smiling radiantly at him. He looked around. They were in some kind of huge white room that seemed to go on forever. There were lots of other beds, some occupied, and strange machines scattered among them. Then he realised what he had just done. *He had sat up!* God, he could feel his legs again! What did this mean . . .?

He gave Ayla a pleading look. "Please don't tell me this is all a hallucination! Some kind of wish-fulfilment delusion. Or have I died and gone to some place I never expected to go to?"

"None of those things," she said, with a laugh.

"Then where are we?"

"On the Sky Angel. Jan Dorvin's airship, though I haven't seen her yet."

"But I don't understand . . . I'm well again . . . and I can *see*."

"What happened to your eyes?"

"Milo," he said and grimaced. "I don't want to talk about it. Not yet. But who performed these miracles upon me?"

"There are machines in here . . ." said Ayla, and pointed at one nearby, which consisted mainly of a large, white plastic cylinder festooned with cables and tubes, " . . . that fix you up. I know, because I woke up just as I was coming out of one."

"Why were you . . .?"

"The spacers beat me up. Pretty badly too. I thought they were going to kill me. They wanted to know about Jan Dorvin's flying machine."

"You told them what you knew?"

"Only part of it. I made up some stuff to worry the head spacer. I think he swallowed it."

He felt a twinge of guilt. She hadn't talked but he had. Still, he would have said anything to avoid being blinded and that was the simple truth. He swung his legs over the side of the bed, put his feet gingerly on the floor and slowly stood. He felt a little weak but otherwise fine. He smiled at Ayla who put her arm around his waist and kissed him. "You have any idea of what's happened down there on the ground since this thing arrived?" he asked.

"No," she told him. "I've asked people in here but they don't remember anything. There are spacers here too, you know. And your people."

"My people?" he said, puzzled. "But they all got banished into the blight lands."

"These were the burn victims at the hospital. They've been completely cured, like you. No scars or anything." She pointed. "They're over there somewhere."

"I'll go talk to them later. First I want to find out what's going on. Let's see if we can track down Jan Dorvin."

She shook her head. "You can't leave here. A few have tried, and failed."

"What stopped them?"

Looking over his shoulder, Ayla said, "Those things do."

He looked round and almost screamed. Scuttling down the aisle towards them was a spider-mech. Then he pushed Ayla behind him and began frantically looking for anything he could use as a weapon. Behind him, Ayla laughed and touched his shoulder. "It's okay, it won't harm you. It's one of our nurses."

"A nurse? Are you crazy?!" he cried, his eyes fixed on the advancing spider-mech. "It's a spider-mech!"

The spider-mech stopped in front of him. "Good evening, Jean-Paul. I trust you are feeling better now. If you would like any kind of refreshment, be it food or drink, please state your preference." It spoke with a woman's voice, but thankfully it was nothing like Ashley's. Jean-Paul could only stare wordlessly at the thing that had so many terrible associations for him. Ayla nudged him in the ribs. "Go on, tell it what you want."

Jean-Paul swallowed and said, "Er, well, I'd love a cup of coffee. Black."

"Certainly. I shall return shortly," said the spider-mech and hurried away. Jean-Paul watched it go and then turned to Ayla. "Are you sure you told me the truth when you said I wasn't dead?"

Jan woke with a buzzing in her ears. At first she didn't know where she was but then she realised she was inside a med-machine. Why? Oh yes, she had bitten the end off her tongue. But hadn't she already had that damage repaired . . .?

The hatch of the machine unsealed itself and the cradle on which she was lying began to move. She emerged feet first into white light. She smiled when she saw Robin waiting, and was puzzled by his intense expression of relief as he scanned her body. She propped herself up on her elbows.

"What's the matter with you? Afraid the machine might have lopped off one of your favourite bits?"

He winced and said, "You don't remember?"

"Remember what?"

"It doesn't matter." He leaned over her and kissed her. "How do you feel?"

"Fine," she said, then added, "Well, come to think of it, I am feeling quite horny." She lay back and put her arms around his neck, trying to pull him down on her. But Robin gently disengaged her arms and straightened. "I'd love to but we don't have the time. And this is hardly the place. You haven't noticed yet but we're not alone."

Surprised, she sat up. He was speaking the truth. There *were* other people scattered about in the vast medical bay. "Who are they? Where did they come from?"

"From Palmyra. Mainly Palmyrians, some spacers and even a few survivors from a downed Sky Lord." He pointed at a bed adjacent to the med-machine. She saw some of her clothes, neatly folded, in a small pile on the bed. "Better get dressed. A lot has happened."

"Yes, master." She got up off the cradle and went to the bed. "Care to tell me what I was doing in that machine? The last thing I can remember is. . . ." She paused and stared at the undershift she was about to put on. ". . . Actually, the last thing I remember was setting out with you in the Toy for Palmyra. Everything else is blank. How long ago was that?"

"That was the night before last."

"Mother God!" She put her hand to her forehead. "I've lost two days. . . ."

"Most of your lost time was spent in that machine. You had a serious accident leaving Palmyra."

"How serious?"

"Very serious."

Jan gave him a suspicious glance, dropped the shift back on the bed and then looked down at her body. After staring hard at both her arms she put her right arm across her chest.

269

"Apart from this arm the rest of me is as pink as a newborn baby."

"Just get dressed, will you," he said with a sigh.

"Tell me the truth—what happened to me?"

He took a breath. "You got yourself killed, Jan."

"Oh," she said, and sat down on the bed. "*That* serious, huh?"

"If you don't mind, I'll spare you the gruesome details. Phebus has removed them from your memory. Unfortunately, she hasn't removed them from mine."

"See, it *is* Jan Dorvin! I told you it was!"

Jan turned to see a man and a young woman approaching. Both wore the standard issue white smocks. The girl was very beautiful and the man had lean and saturnine good looks. It was the girl who had spoken. She looked vaguely familiar. "Have we met before?" Jan asked, then, realising she was still naked she jumped up and began hurriedly to dress.

"Of course we have," said the girl. "In the hospital at Palmyra. You remember, don't you? You saved my life. Milo would have killed me."

Jan slipped her tunic on. "Milo? You said Milo? Has he escaped from the Sky Angel?"

"I don't know about the Sky Angel," said the man, "but he certainly escaped from the hospital after you left. But before he did the bastard . . . the bastard . . ." He couldn't go on.

Jan, mystified, looked at him. He was beginning to seem familiar too. And the mention of Milo jarred something loose in her mind. Yes, there was Milo . . . on that dark beach, but it wasn't her Milo. Then it all came slowly back. And yet, not everything. She remembered going into the water, swimming and then . . . nothing. She smiled at both of them. "I remember you now, and what happened." She glanced at Robin. "Not all of it, of course."

"I'm glad to see you're all right," Ayla said to her. "I was really worried about you. I'd forgotten to warn you about those sea creatures."

"What sea creatures?"

"That's enough," said Robin quickly. "No more talk of sea creatures, *please*," and he gave Ayla a warning look. Though puzzled she didn't continue.

Jean-Paul said, "Okay then, let's talk about us. What happens now? And what happened down in Palmyra? What happened to the spacers?"

Jan shrugged. "Don't ask me. I've just woken up. Robin, what do you know?"

"Not much. I do know that Palmyra is under Phebus's control. She used the Toy to knock out the spacers' beam cannons and disable their ship. Then she brought the Sky Angel into shore and used some kind of gas to put everyone to sleep. After that a whole lot of mechs were landed. They disarmed the sleeping spacers and are now supervising things. The spacers have all been rounded up and kept separate from the locals."

"What I'd like to know is what that other Milo is up to," said Jan. "I won't be happy until he's locked up the same as our version."

"I won't be happy until he's dead," said Jean-Paul, with feeling.

"I'm worried about my father," said Ayla. "When will we be allowed to go home?"

"I just don't know," Jan confessed, "but I can't see any reason why Phebus would want to keep you up here any longer."

"And you still don't know what she's got in store for Palmyra in the long term?" asked Jean-Paul.

"No idea at all," said Jan. "I suppose we could try asking her . . . Phebus, are you listening to us? Are you there?"

Phebus appeared in front of Jan, startling both Ayla and Jean-Paul. "Yes, Jan. You are, understandably, curious about your fate, and the fate of all the other humans on Earth. So I will tell you."

Chapter Thirty-Three:

Jan had a strong suspicion that she was not going to like what Phebus was about to tell them. And she was soon proved correct. "As Jan and Robin already know," Phebus began, "my intention is to make the Earth fully habitable again by removing all aspects of the blight. With the genetic samples I am accumulating I will create biological weapons designed to act specifically on each species. Many species of the blight will be killed outright or made infertile, some merely modified into a harmless form. The agents by which these bio-weapons will be delivered will be virus-like organisms containing sections of modified DNA. Again, each virus will be designed to affect only its particular target species. When the blight, in all its forms, has been eradicated I will start rebuilding the planet's eco-system until it is much like it was before the Industrial Age. The Sky Angel contains a comprehensive genetic bank which will enable me to recreate all manner of the plant and animal life that has disappeared from the Earth."

At this point Jan interrupted. "Don't think I'm not grateful but again I want to ask you *why* you're doing this. I don't see how it fits in with your prime directive, which is the protection of the Eloi."

"It does," said Phebus.

Exasperated, Jan said, "But *how?* And if it does, why didn't you do this centuries ago, before the blight got so bad?"

"Because the situation has changed."

"In what way?"

"We saw that humanity posed the greatest threat to the Eloi. In their habitat beneath the ice they were safe from every other threat but there was always the chance that one day humanity would locate the habitat."

"So why didn't you destroy what remained of the human race?" asked Robin.

"The Ethical Program forbids the direct destruction of any human being," answered Phebus.

"Yes," said Jan bitterly, "but it does allow you to sit twiddling your metaphorical thumbs while the human race conveniently dies away over the centuries in a one-sided battle with the blight."

"Attaching blame to us is useless; we were only doing what we were programmed to do. By *your* human ancestors. Who are now the Eloi."

"You say you can't kill people," said Robin, "but I know for a fact that several spacers were killed when you attacked the town and their ship with the Toy."

"I was not aiming to kill them, I was aiming at the beam weapons. Their unfortunate deaths were accidental."

"I'd be careful there, Phebus," Jan said. "That's a very human trait you're displaying: the ability to split hairs."

"Do you wish me to continue?"

"Yes, of course," said Jan sharply. "Tell us in what way the situation changed to bring you out of your shell."

"The arrival of this ship over Shangri La, and Milo's attempt to burn his way through the ice to the habitat. Those developments meant that we had to change tactics. To prevent such a thing ever occurring again."

"And eradicating the blight for the benefit of humanity is part of these new tactics?" asked Jan. "How?"

"We won't just be eradicating the blight, we will be modifying the human race as well."

Phebus's words hung in the air. Ominous and unwanted. *Here it is at last*, thought Jan, *the part I don't want to hear.*

273

It was Jean-Paul who finally asked the question. "What do you mean by *modifying*?"

"It will be necessary to change you to protect the Eloi. To remove all potential threat from humanity towards them. But there is no cause for alarm, you will not mind the changes that will occur in your personalities. And you will live much happier and more contented lives than you do today."

Jan's stomach started to churn. "Mother God, you're going to turn us all into Eloi!"

"What are these Eloi you keep talking about?" asked Ayla nervously.

"No, you will not become Eloi," said Phebus. "The changes in your DNA will be only minor ones."

"I don't care how minor they're going to be, I don't want them!" cried Jan.

"I'm afraid you have no choice," Phebus told her. "There is no way that we can leave humanity as it is and carry out our duty to the Eloi."

"Just what exactly will these changes consist of?" asked Robin.

"They will relate primarily to your innate instinct for aggression. They will solve the problem that has plagued your species for tens of thousands of years. You have intellectually recognised the problem and from your earliest societies have created religious laws and social rules to try to deal with it. These have usually been sufficient to establish, if inefficiently, a working code of conduct within a society but are useless in dealing with members of your species who are regarded as being *outside* that particular society or group. You pay lip service to the ideal of the sanctity of human life but only in an intellectual way. Your ape selves, which lie not far below the surface of your psyche, don't accept that ideal for a second when either you yourselves are threatened, or your family, your tribe, your race, your religion, your nation, your class, your caste or

274

even your sex. You then have the ability literally to 'dehumanise' your opponents, which removes the moral constraints imposed upon you and allows you to commit all manner of atrocities upon your fellow humans. You have always done this and you will continue to do so, unless we change you."

"You're saying we're still just apes, in spite of all we have achieved?" asked Jean-Paul angrily.

"What you have achieved, Jean-Paul," said Phebus, "is the near destruction of your species and planet. Left to continue as you are you will undoubtedly complete the task. Yes, you are still apes. You are almost genetically identical to chimpanzees. Small differences in your DNA are all that set you apart. Admittedly, these small changes are crucial. They enabled you to become a highly successful species. Your rapid growth in intellectual prowess and the development of language gave you a tremendous advantage. You could pass on sophisticated information learned by experience from one generation to the next. This enabled you quickly to adapt to changes—and new dangers—in the environment without having to rely on the slow process of natural selection. You were no longer subject to the laws of natural selection—you stopped evolving, except in minor physical ways, skin colour and the like, as you adapted to different climates when you spread across the world.

"And this is the key to your problem. The clever, highly aggressive ape, who was ideally suited for surviving in that prehistoric, pre-agricultural world, became an anachronism when the world became heavily populated by humans with increasingly complex societies and, later, increasingly complex technology. A new sort of human needed to evolve to fit this new world you had created, but as you were immune from evolutionary pressures, and were now controlling the environment, this was impossible."

"So you're going to do the job for us, eh?" said Jan. "Give us a little boost up the evolutionary tree?"

"The use of a tree as an analogy for evolution is a misleading one. But yes, I am going to change you. You are going to have a moral code *genetically* imprinted within you."

"A code drawn up by you, a computer program?" asked Jean-Paul, with a sneer.

"I think that would be far preferable, for all your sakes, to one drawn up by a human being," said Phebus. "I am nothing if not neutral."

"Mother God," moaned Jan as she pictured an endless list of inscribed, unbreakable Commandments. . . . *Commandment number three hundred and fifty-four: NEVER TALK WITH YOUR MOUTH FULL; Commandment number three hundred and fifty-five: ALWAYS EAT EVERYTHING THAT IS ON YOUR PLATE* . . . two particular non-favourites from her childhood. "Just how long is this list of rules going to be?"

"It is not a list. It will chiefly be in the form of a heightened sense of empathy for your fellow humans, as a result of which you will not be able to commit any act that will lead to the death or suffering of anyone else," said Phebus solemnly.

Jan frowned. "I can see plenty of problems if we are biologically enforced to carry that out to the letter. Surely in certain circumstances that will have the reverse of the desired effect. I mean, what if you are obliged to kill someone to put them out of their unendurable suffering? Or you have to perform an abortion to save a woman's life?"

"All such permutations have been accounted for. The action taken will be decided by the individual's, or group of individuals', concerned appraisal of the situation. You will not be mindless robots."

"Coming from you, I don't find that very reassuring," said Jan.

Jean-Paul, who had been raised a Catholic, said, "But you are removing our most fundamental right as human beings—

the right to choose between good and evil. Our God-given free will."

Phebus said, "There are no such things as fundamental rights, apart from the arbitrary and temporary ones created by human societies. Nor is there such a thing as free will as you understand it. Indeed, nor are there such things as good and evil as you . . ."

" . . . understand it. Yeah," said Jean-Paul bitterly.

"You are resentful. That is to be expected. But as I said, you will not mind these changes once they have taken place. For example, fear is a common trigger for aggression; from now on you will be far less fearful creatures."

"Fear is a necessary survival mechanism," Jan pointed out.

"I said, you will be far *less* fearful creatures. You will still have the capacity to fear genuine danger."

"I still don't like the sound of any of this," said Jan, shaking her head.

"We are only going a few steps further in tinkering with your DNA than you humans did in the mid-twenty-first century when you created the Standard Prime. You extended your life span, improved your immune system and even altered yourselves psychologically—you eradicated chronic depression and, by modifying your brains so that they were protected from the viral and genetic causes of schizophrenia, eradicated all varieties of that mental disease as well. . . . And then *your* ancestors, Jan Dorvin, went even further in the early years of Minerva. Minervan women became bigger physically and slightly more masculine in emotional outlook while Minervan men became smaller physically, less aggressive and non-competitive. A step in the right direction but you didn't go far enough."

"Mother God!" gasped Jan. "I gave you this idea, didn't I? All those questions from Davin about Minerva and Minervan men!"

"You did provide a useful contribution to the scheme,"

agreed Phebus. "Your mention of throwbacks led us to create a genetic fail-safe unit which will prevent future mutations in the rewired DNA. But we had always considered the possibility of changing the basic nature of the human race if they ever presented a danger to the Eloi. For that reason we created a number of pre-Prime Standard humans for study. We made them pre-Prime Standard because of their short life spans." Phebus turned to Robin. "You were the latest such creation, Ryn."

Robin looked shocked. "But you always told me I was the result of a mistake in the breeding lab. . .!"

"We never make mistakes, Ryn. You had been a useful subject for the final stages of our research, but you were close, before escaping in the Toy, to reaching the stage where you would have been kept permanently tranquillised, for the safety of the Eloi."

Robin sat down heavily on a bed. "I don't belive it! You mean I'm only going to live until I'm sixty or seventy . . . that I'm going to *age?*"

Phebus said, "We will convert you into a Standard Prime, if you so wish."

"Yes . . . yes," he said hurriedly. He glanced at Jan. "Please."

Jan went and sat beside him. She took his hand. "You okay?"

"Yes . . . it was just a hell of a surprise. All these years I thought . . ." He shook his head. "I was nothing more than a damn guinea-pig to them."

Jan said to him, "And one due to be kept 'permanently tranquillised'. That's why they didn't fix you up properly when I brought you back in the Toy. Funny how you suddenly regained your potency as soon as you left the habitat. . . ."

"Yes," admitted Phebus. "When we knew he would be leaving Shangri La and unlikely ever to return we discreetly restored his masculinity."

278

Jan glared at Phebus. "And you're the one who's going to provide *us* with an ingrained moral code. That's a laugh. And all this is being done just for the sake of those stinking elves under the ice shelf. It makes me sick."

"You'll feel better about everything . . . afterwards."

"Yeah, sure," said Jan suspiciously. "So apart from a heightened sense of empathy for our fellow humans and a decrease in fear, what other *minor* changes will there be?"

Phebus seemed to hesitate before answering. Jan didn't like that. "To achieve the required results in the area of increased empathy and decreased aggression it will be necessary to narrow your emotional range. To, let us say, reduce the extremes at each end of your emotional scale."

"Could you, let us say," said Jan sarcastically, "be more specific?"

"You won't feel things so intensely," replied Phebus. "You will no longer experience extremes of passion. Admittedly, this will affect the way you experience your positive emotions as well as the negatives ones."

"In other words, you're going to blunt our feelings," accused Robin.

"That is your interpretation, not mine," said Phebus.

"It's mine as well," said Jan. "So when does this rotten transformation take place?"

"It has already begun in your case, and all the others on board. You have been infected with the synthetic virus. The change will be gradual and take three months before it is complete."

Shaken, Jan said, "It's in us already? Oh Mother God. . . ." She tightened her grip on Robin's hand.

"The virus will soon be aerially released to infect those on the ground. The spacers, when their ship is repaired, will carry the virus to the space habitats and the Martian colonies. Deep-rooted hypnotic commands will ensure that they visit all the human-occupied areas of space, sooner or later. And I, in the Sky Angel, will travel all over the world, dispersing the virus to ensure that the rest of the population is infected."

Jan didn't know what effect it would have but she had to do it, futile gesture though it was. She stood up, walked up to Phebus and punched her very hard in the mouth. There was the satisfactory sound of knuckles hitting flesh and Phebus fell backwards to land on her bottom. It may have all been a computer-generated delusion in her brain but the sight of Phebus sitting on the floor, with a startled expression on her face and blood trickling from a split lip, made Jan feel very good. "I just had to do that while I still *felt* like doing it," Jan told her as she rubbed her stinging knuckles.

Epilogue:

Jan sat on the beach with Ayla's six-month-old baby on her lap. Ayla had named it Lon in memory of her late father. Lon Haddon senior had died shortly after the events of that fateful period of nearly eighteen months ago. So he had missed out on the 'change', as it was called . . .

I'm still the same, Jan told herself. She told herself that several times a day. She had been telling herself that ever since she had learnt that the virus was inside her. For months afterwards she would go to sleep wondering if she would wake up an entirely different personality. And when she did wake up she would lie there and slowly catalogue all her feelings trying to detect any changes in herself. She never could. But. . . .

"Hi, Jan!"

She turned. Milo was coming down the beach. He was wearing only a pair of shorts and his once pale body was darkly tanned. "Hello, Milo," she said. He sat down on the sand beside her, tickled one of Lon's feet, which made the baby squirm, and said, "Beautiful day, eh?"

"Isn't every day a beautiful day here?" she said sourly.

Milo laughed. "Still fighting it, aren't you?"

She didn't answer.

"You're going to face it one of these days. You underwent the 'change' like the rest of us. You're not the same any more."

"I am," she said.

"Look at me—I finally faced it. But then my 'change' was

the most radical of all. The gap between what I am now and what I used to be is too big to ignore."

"Yes, I admit you have definitely changed, Milo," she said wearily. "You are no longer a . . . a. . . ." She didn't continue.

"A monster?" he asked, and chuckled. "It's okay, I know what you mean. When I look back at how I used to think—and how I thought of other people—I shudder. Yet at the same time a small part of me still resents being 'changed'. I loathe what I used to be but I know that was the *real* me. The individual I am now is a result of that damn program's meddling about with my genes. Yet the resentment is fading fast and I know that soon I won't give a shit. It'll be the same with you. None of us will care in the long run." He shrugged his bronzed shoulders.

"I will. I always will," she said. She looked at him. "Can you honestly say you can detect any change at all in my personality?"

"Not on the surface," he admitted.

"Well then!" she said triumphantly.

"Oh come on, surely you must be aware of subtle differences in yourself?"

She shook her head. The baby passed wind and gurgled.

"How are things with Robin?" Milo asked.

"Fine," she said warily. "Why?"

"Just curious. So your relationship with him is the same?"

"Of course," she said, but there was a lack of conviction in her voice.

Milo picked up on it. "No, it isn't, is it? That's because you've both changed. The old passion isn't there any more. Oh, sure, you still like each other and you still make love but the fire is gone."

"The fire goes out of every sexual relationship eventually," Jan said.

"True, but that's not what I'm talking about. Do you still have orgasms?"

282

The question startled her. "Well . . . yes, I do, I suppose. . . ."

"You *suppose?*" he asked, smiling.

"Yes, I *do* have orgasms," she said, flustered. "It's just that. . . ."

"They're not the same, I know," he nodded. "There's a lack of intensity to them. I've experienced the same thing. That girl I've been hanging around with lately, Juli, Ayla's friend—well, we make love and it's fine. I enjoy it. But that's it. No intensity any more. Not like it used to be. . . ."

"For that, Juli should thank her lucky stars," said Jan dryly.

"Hey, come on, you know what I mean. Sex isn't the same. And you admit it, right? And it's not just sex."

She sighed. She had been blaming Robin but she guessed it was her as well. She just didn't desire him the way she used to. She still *did* desire him but something was missing, as Milo said. And it was as Phebus had said would happen— "You will no longer experience extremes of passion"— though Jan still couldn't bring herself to accept totally that horrible fact. "Our feelings have been blunted," she murmured, remembering Robin's accusation to Phebus.

"Yeah," said Milo. "They've taken away our edge. One of the essential things that made us human. Or the way Jean-Paul puts it, they've removed our Original Sin. But I wonder how that's going to affect the race in the long term. We may no longer be a danger to ourselves but if we ever come up against any real competition I doubt if we'll able to cut it as a species. We're going to lack the old get-up-and-go, we'll be a walk-over. Not that we'll give much of a damn when it happens. We'll go down with a bloody smile on all our faces. . . ." He stood up, brushed sand from the seat of his shorts and stretched. "Looks like your baby-sitting stint is over—here comes Ayla."

Jan looked and saw Ayla's fishing boat coming through the inner wall. All the gates were kept open now and soon work would begin on demolishing the walls. "How's your boat coming along?" she asked Milo. Milo had been building one for months. His intention was to sail down the coast and see what was happening, if anything, in the south of the country. He would be, he claimed, roving emissary for Palmyra.

"Slowly, very slowly," he told her, "like everything these days." He walked off down towards the water's edge to help Ayla and Juli berth their boat. As Jan watched him go she realised she would miss him if he did manage to finish his boat and set off on his expedition. She rather liked Milo now.

I'm still the same, she told herself again.

But her doubts were growing.

The School
T.M. WRIGHT

In smalltown America, The Hitchcocks, a normal couple, buy an old school to satisfy their longing for security and to escape from the memory of their dead son. But it is not long before the ghosts of childhoods long gone begin to enter their daily lives. 'As ominous as rumbling thunder' – *Library Journal*

0 575 05028 4   £3.99 net

The Fall of The Sky Lords
JOHN BROSNAN

The fast, furious and devastating conclusion to *The Sky Lords* trilogy.

0 575 04556 6   £3.99 net

The Flies of Memory
IAN WATSON

'Ian Watson's latest novel is brilliantly imagined . . . stunningly evoked . . . Watson remains a joy to read' – *Venue*. 'Intriguing . . . Ian Watson gift-wraps startling ideas with great entertainment' – *The Times*

0 575 05163 9   £3.99 net

Homegoing
FREDERIK POHL

A dazzling tale of alien encounter by the creator of the celebrated Heechee aliens.

0 575 05161 2   £3.99 net

Illusion
PAULA VOLSKY

An original and epic novel, ILLUSION is set in a fantasy world which has parallels to, and the feel of, revolutionary Eighteenth century France. It is the story of Eliste vo Derrivalle, a young girl cast adrift in a world about to be torn apart by bloody insurrection.

0 575 05138 8   £7.99 net
Also available in hardback

Blue Moon Rising
SIMON GREEN

A classic fantasy in the tradition of Piers Anthony involving witches, dragons, enchanted kingdoms and a beautiful princess, and told with a lightness of touch reminiscent of Gordon R. Dickson.

0 575 05136 1   £7.99 net
Also available in hardback

The Stochastic Man
ROBERT SILVERBERG

Stochastic prediction – a mixture of sophisticated analysis and informed guesswork is the closest later-twentieth century society has come to predicting the future. THE STOCHASTIC MAN is a thorough and satisfying exploration of the popular Sf concept.

0 575 05123 X   £3.99 net

Wulfsyarn
PHILLIP MANN

A brilliantly imagined tale of humans and aliens. 'A revelation that haunts the mind long after the book is finished. Here be tygers of the mind. Great.' – *The Times*

0 575 05162 0   £3.99 net

A Small Killing
ALAN MOORE & OSCAR ZARATE

A tale of murder and betrayal in the world of American advertising, full of irony and tension and superbly brought to life by the illustrative genius of Oscar Zarate.

0 575 05023 3   £8.99 net
Also available in hardback
Graphic novel

The Luck in The Head
M. JOHN HARRISON & IAN MILLER

Originally a short story from M. John Harrison's *Viriconium Nights*, THE LUCK IN THE HEAD is set in a decadent fantasy world and has been re-fashioned as a graphic novel by the inspired vision of Ian Miller to portray a nightmare society steeped in violence and ritual.

0 575 05037 3   £8.99 net
Also available in hardback
Graphic novel